THE BOOK OF DAHLIA

This Large Print Book carries the
Seal of Approval of N.A.V.H.

THE BOOK OF DAHLIA

ELISA ALBERT

THORNDIKE PRESS
A part of Gale, Cengage Learning

Detroit • New York • San Francisco • New Haven, Conn • Waterville, Maine • London

GALE
CENGAGE Learning™

Copyright © 2008 by Elisa Albert.
Thorndike Press, a part of Gale, Cengage Learning.

LIBRARY OF CONGRESS CATALOGING-IN-PUBLICATION DATA

Albert, Elisa, 1978–
    The book of Dahlia / by Elisa Albert.
      p. cm. — (Thorndike Press large print reviewers' choice)
    ISBN-13: 978-1-4104-0847-1 (hardcover : alk. paper)
    ISBN-10: 1-4104-0847-7 (hardcover : alk. paper)
    1. Young women — Fiction. 2. Venice (Los Angeles, Calif.) — Fiction. 3. Cerebrovascular disease — Fiction. 4. Jewish women — Fiction. 5. Domestic fiction. 6. Large type books. I. Title.
PS3601.L3344B66 2008b
813'.6—dc22   2008014357

Published in 2008 by arrangement with Free Press, a division of Simon & Schuster, Inc.

Printed in the United States of America
1 2 3 4 5 6 7 12 11 10 09 08

For David

'Tis easier to pity those when dead
That which pity previous
Would have saved —
A Tragedy enacted
Secures Applause
That Tragedy enacting
Too seldom does
— Emily Dickinson

Anger is more useful than despair.
— The Terminator,
Terminator 3

CONTENTS

1. Something Wrong 11
2. Understanding Your Diagnosis . . . 26
3. A Different Kind of Disease 52
4. The Bright Side. 66
5. Get a Second Opinion 87
6. You're the Boss 111
7. Trust Your Treatment 139
8. Choose Life. 167
9. Find a Support System 168
10. Evaluate Your Relationships . . . 199
11. Heal Yourself. 228
12. Live Now 254
13. Laugh 281
14. Reframe. 311
15. Be Grateful 337
16. Have Faith. 355
17. Forgive and Forget 381
18. Be Well 402

1. SOMETHING WRONG

Were there signs, willfully ignored? Did you know, on some level, that something was wrong? Did you avoid knowing? What were the signs? What did you know?

She had been having symptoms. Only recognizable as such in hindsight, but symptoms, nevertheless. A headache. Some sluggishness. Disinclination to do much of anything but hang around her house, take hot showers, slather herself with lavender moisturizer, watch movies on cable, smoke a bowl every few hours, make toaster pastries and consume them methodically, in quarters. Check her email, then check it again. But none of these things much distinguished themselves from Dahlia's normal state, so there had been zero cause for concern.

Well, concern, sure, but not *concern*. Just that her life was passing her by. That she might be, in point of fact, wasting her time, herself, utterly. That this might not be a phase. That, okay: What the fuck was she doing?

She'd figured she was due for a period. She always got those awful headaches, and/or the distended belly, bloat, and/or the general exhaustion. An impending period could explain away pretty much anything.

There was also the urinary tract infection for which she'd only just the week before completed a course of antibiotics. So there were all these things wrong with her. Not to mention everything, you know, *wrong* with her.

On the last day of her ignorance Dahlia Finger woke up shortly before noon, and ate a bowl of Cheerios in front of the television. *A League of Their Own* was on, for the eighteen-zillionth time, and yet again she found the thing totally irresistible, wound up watching all the way from Jon Lovitz's entree up through Tom Hanks's delivery of a tragic military telegram — pause for bong hit — and then straight on to the end, the disappearance of the young lovelies and appearance, in their stead, of riotous old ladies. By then it was almost two in the afternoon and Dahlia was weeping openly about the passage of time and the fact that Geena Davis and Hanks — so

12

clearly meant for each other — never got it on, and the sun was threatening to go away for yet another day and so she made herself a cup of tea and looked in the magnifying mirror for a while. Then she called Mara, who was busy at work in Boston and, as usual, could not, or would not, talk.

"Do you think the Tom character just died alone and drunk?"

"I don't know, dude. I'm working." Little bit of judgment there, sure. Mara had, as they say, a life. "I'll call you later."

Dahlia's mother, upon meeting Mara fifteen years earlier, had refused to understand why this girl's name was *"mar-ah,"* which translated, in Hebrew, to *bitter*. "Marah!" Margalit would squawk. "What kind of name is this for a girl?" Dahlia and Mara had come to appreciate this as funny and fitting. Dahlia always pronounced her friend's name with just that Hebraic lilt to it, because she liked to think Mara was just like her: a match, a true, bitter friend to the true, bitter end.

Dahlia had taken the GRE a few weeks earlier and was still resting on that semi-laurel: having (sort of) studied for and completed a standardized test so singularly uninteresting she might even have chalked up the headache to her brain trying to rid

13

itself of useless information. The fucking GRE. Barely touched study guides still lay piled in a corner, under some health insurance forms and credit card offers she occasionally considered considering.

Why the GRE? Possibly social work school. She could consort with drug addicts, or battered women. The broken, the fucked, the totally broken, the irretrievably fucked. This seemed doable. Maybe she had a calling. Maybe she would be happy, self-sufficient, fulfilled, of use to humankind. Make her dad proud. She had just about given up on making Margalit proud, or even holding her attention for too long, come right down to it.

Anyway, the time had come to do something with herself. "What is your battle plan?" Margalit would often demand. As though life were a long fight one had to orchestrate carefully.

Dahlia had also toyed, intermittently, with the idea of rabbinical school. A pulpit would allow her to cast Talmudic judgment on people who pissed her off, and work on herself a bit, too, have an answer for everything. She'd be a cool rabbi, a real human being, a pot-headed, pop-culture-expounding Universalist. Except, goddamn it all to hell: Danny was a rabbi. Her

14

douchebag brother, the rabbi! So the whole notion, over before it could begin, defeated her. Everyone already knew Danny, anyhow. They knew him as "Dan" or "Dan the man" or "Rabbi D," from his lifetime of camp counselor-ing and high school mentoring and University Hillel visiting and youth group shepherding: It was an insular, imbecilic universe, and Rabbi Dan, Dahlia's only sibling, was king of it. King Douchebag, Rabbi Dan.

Fine. So what sort of occupation wouldn't make her want to fucking kill herself every single godforsaken day? Law school sounded like a freaking curse; the words together (LAW-SCHOOL) like some sort of prison sentence handed down in a language she didn't speak, for a crime she didn't commit, by a totalitarian, undemocratic judge in a third world country. Too many rules, too much precision. *Laws,* for Christ's sake. Thank you, no.

She had no creative talent to speak of, though she had made a mean mix-tape in her day and certainly counted herself a reasonable connoisseur of culture (witness the umpteenth, slightly ironic *League of Their Own* screening, the bimonthly live music attendance, the requisite, half-read *McSweeney's* stacked on the floor by the

15

untouched GRE study guides and untouched health insurance forms, indie theater movie stubs littering the bottom of her bag). She had attempted a spec script or two when she'd moved back to L.A. (because how could she not? She of the ecstatic, repeated viewings of every cheesy movie on cable during any given month's cycle), but they were derivative, unimpressive. One was *Sex and the City.* The other: *Scrubs.* Which she had never watched. But Dahlia's mean streak amounted to narratively unaccountable jabs everywhere: at materialism, stupidity, douchebag rabbis, dating websites. "Some fun moments, but way too hostile for episodic television!" said the only TV lit agent she could get to read the thing, the son of an old friend of her father's. "Why would Carrie stop wearing Manolos and decry the shallowness of her own fashion obsession? *Sex and the City* isn't in production anymore, anyway. Also: *Scrubs* is a hospital comedy, so it'd be advisable to set the show at or around the hospital. Best of luck."

It was a pain in the ass, this figuring out what to do with your life. A matter, as the famous book intoned, of finding the shade of parachute that best complemented you. But really: With no parachute at all you'd

16

hit the pavement so hard it probably wouldn't even hurt, and you'd unleash a whole new color palate — bone, blood, muscle — in the process.

So screw the parachute, screw the battle plan. So weed and *A League of Their Own.* So napping in the breeze. So toaster pastries. So maybe social work school. Or journalism school (though there was the problem of facts with that one, namely a responsibility to them). So the GRE. Whatever. Things would "figure themselves out," as she told her mother. (*"Mah zeh,* figure themselves out? Nothing figures itself out! What is your *battle plan?"*)

She was living her life isometrically: action with no movement.

This was officially a new start, at any rate. She had what her father called "options"; she had nothing but the time and freedom to explore them. She was twenty-nine years old and dear old Daddy Bruce had wiped the slate clean for her. Life in New York, never sustainable in the first place, had become downright unlivable. Bruce, bless his uncomplicated, wealthy heart, had offered her this out: Come home.

And, indeed, Bruce welcomed his little girl back "home" with a lovely cottage in Venice. He acted like this was Dahlia's right,

17

as expected as hearing her Mirandas or voting. As inevitable as the bearing of arms. Of course she would have a house handed to her, a microscopic mortgage in place for her to pay (but only so she would "learn about money" and be "responsible" for it herself: he had a good deal of cash, but Bruce had "values" as well).

Dahlia adored the house, loved that it was hers (given, sure, but still). It was a haven, her very own airy bungalow box of clean ocean air. The Spanish tile, the stainless steel, the open kitchen, the recessed lighting, the beamed and soaring ceiling. To get to the front door you had to enter through a wooden gate and walk down a short stone path beset by night-blooming jasmine. She was going to go to Morocco and bring back colored lanterns to hang along this path. She was going to find a wind chime. She was going to get a hammock. She was going to paint the door blue. She felt safe, beyond the reach of all the shit that had dogged her in New York, in college, in high school, in childhood, in utero, and possibly even before that. She was anonymous in Venice; she knew almost nobody and almost nobody knew her. At night, in bed, if she strained, she thought she could hear the Pacific. She felt as though she was re-gestating; that for

those first months she was rerooting herself
via the cable matinees and pot, via late
afternoons strolling Abbott-Kinney, stopping on Main Street for a coffee and a book
or a *People* magazine. Watching movies
(*Titanic, Flirting with Disaster, Mannequin,
Thelma and Louise, Rushmore, The Goonies,
She's Having a Baby,* it mattered very little)
was a kind of prayer: She knew the charac-
ters as well as she knew herself, as well as
she knew anything there was to know, and
she could chart and rechart their movements and secrets and misunderstandings
endlessly, reflecting in any number of new
permutations on all of it, each time. Again
and again. They were acquaintances —
people she'd known her whole life and
understood well, people incapable of letting
her down by changing or disappearing or
offering up the unexpected. The *League of
Their Own* tears were purely for catharsis.
When she was done she would reemerge,
reborn. She would make new mistakes. Or
maybe none at all.

Okay, wait. Honestly? It wasn't *A League
of Their Own.* It was actually *Terms of Endearment,* but that just seems too easy, a bit
ridiculous. Reality's fucked like that. That
on the last day of her innocence Dahlia

19

Finger could be found sobbing on her couch, baked out of her head at 2 o'clock in the afternoon, watching *Terms of* freaking *Endearment*!?

What did you know before you knew?

No, let's just say it was *A League of Their Own.*

(But it wasn't.)

On some level you may not feel surprised. On some level you may have known Something was Wrong.

Anyway, the symptoms. Clear in hindsight, so obvious once their root cause is known. A headache, sluggishness, disinclination. She was tired, but she had done nothing whatsoever to tire herself. It was somehow perfectly acceptable as the result of — one could assume — having no direction, no desire to do anything but sit right where she was, crying, feeling *something* at least (even if it was about Debra goddamned Winger) in her perfect bungalow, the salty breeze fluffing her white curtains — curtains she had hung by herself! — just so. Bruce had been excessively proud of the curtains, and of Dahlia for having hung them all by herself. Bruce was excessively proud, always, of everything. The headache, et al., spoke only to the uselessness of Dahlia's existence — a life so relatively blessed and easy and bountiful that some festering guilt had to be thrown into the mix as well. Which quite plausibly added up to a consistent low-grade headache and the tendency to stretch out on the couch, stoned, napping in the breeze.

"Spoiled," she could hear Margalit spitting at her, running commentary. "Everything is too easy for you. You should have some real problems. You should know what real problems *are*."

Ben, the guy she'd been sleeping with, had wanted to get together that night for dinner, a movie, a drink, but Dahlia was happy on her couch, happy with her movies, happy with her weed. Ben exhausted her (like jobs exhausted her, like the GRE exhausted her, like her period exhausted her, like depositing Daddy's checks exhausted her, like going to the post office for stamps to pay bills with money she'd been given, no strings attached, exhausted her).

Dahlia and Ben had met at a bar party about a month earlier, a birthday of friends of friends of friends, on one of the unique evenings on which Dahlia had forsaken the couch, the weed, the movies, for a night out. A girl needed a night out every so often, and the infrequency of those nights out ensured Dahlia's total enjoyment of them.

She was the life of the party on those unique evenings. Why didn't she go out more often, she asked herself. Ben was getting his PhD in art history, bless his unemployable heart. He confessed to Dahlia that he didn't get out much, himself. He was the kind of guy she could easily imagine having had a crush on as an undergraduate, a goofy grad student with broad shoulders and thick, floppy hair, a messenger bag. If nothing else, imagining him as the object of someone *else's* undergraduate lust was attractive enough, and sealed the deal. She herself had never had the privilege of defilement by an academic superior. They kissed in the parking lot, his nervous smile endearing as hell, and his soft hands around her face like he actually meant the kiss. It was Santa Monica cold, the air wet and crisp. After New York Dahlia had promised herself, as an experiment: no more fucking on first meeting. Could she do it? Ben was sweet-smelling and cute and those soft hands held her face neither too loosely nor too insistently: Could she make it to a second meeting? No, she could not.

"Follow me," she told him before getting into her car. The shy, delighted look on his face briefly made her want to change her mind, but it was too late. Fuck it. Life, as they say, was short.

But over a month later, enough! She hadn't wanted a flipping boyfriend, for god's sake. She didn't want to hurt the sweet would-be-professor, but really. *"Dayenu,"* as Margalit would say when she was done with one of her men: *it would have been enough.*

This Ben character was so eager to spend time with her, to be her boyfriend, to see her on nights like this for dinner, a drink. Who had the energy? The fun part was meeting them, playing the does-he-really-like-me game, finding out what they were like in bed, getting comfortable enough to relax; after that they could go away. Usually this scenario ran itself out on about a three-week course. Don't get too attached to me, she wished she could somehow broadcast to the poor guy, I have no interest in being your girlfriend. And you might not realize it, but you have no interest in being my boyfriend. Have a nice life, etc.

By way of excuse, and in what turned out to be a fortuitous twist, Dahlia had told Ben she wasn't feeling well, that she would be at home that night, hanging out, lying low, "taking it easy."

"Okay," he'd said, sounding defeated. Surely he knew the jig was up; surely he knew she was blowing him off. She hadn't made any real effort to spend time with him in over a week, now. "Feel better. I'll call to check up on you later."

Don't, she almost said.

And as the afternoon gave way to evening Dahlia was a little confused: She really *wasn't* feeling so hot. Was this her punishment? Had her excuse made itself manifest? Because she really wasn't feeling so hot. Oh, well. She made herself a snack bounty (Brie, a sliced Fuji apple, garlic crackers, Oreos), arranged it buffet-style on her coffee table, and settled back into the couch for another bong hit. (Would it be over-the-top to mention that *Dying Young* was on cable? Probably. So let's split the difference and say it was *Steel Magnolias,* shall we? A Julia Roberts/untimely-death compromise; how's that?)

It is only natural to revisit the moment things went wrong, the moment our lives went from okay to not okay, from normal to problematic.

The last thing Dahlia remembered was taking a break from the movies to watch an *I Love the 90's* marathon on VH1.

She'd put a frozen pizza in the oven, made herself another cup of tea, flopped down on the couch, and begun the long process of psyching herself up for bedtime: the always depressing end to another failed day. But there she still was, after midnight, letting first 1993 and then 1994 and 1995 pass her by.

And then she had a grand mal seizure.

2. Understanding Your Diagnosis

Take the time to understand clearly and carefully exactly what it is you have. Look it up. Ask questions. Take notes. Read.

Margalit and Bruce Finger, split some twenty-odd years, came together with relative ease in crisis. Bruce was good in a crisis, always there for everyone — even his ex-wife, the woman who'd unceremoniously imploded their family decades earlier, not even a perfunctory glance over her shoulder as she'd skipped away. They sat vigil by Dahlia's hospital bed for six days, waiting for her to wake up so that they could find a way to sugarcoat — for her sake and for their own — the fact that she was a goner.

Things were looking grim, indeed. It would be misleading to suggest that Dahlia was "present" in any recognizable sense for any of this: She had been rushed first to the emergency room and then (after specialist upon neurologist upon specialist had been summoned and had weighed in) to surgery for biopsy of the lump — a tumor — they'd found in her brain when at last they'd MRI-ed her. She'd be out for a while, but she was stable. "Out of the woods," in the parlance of one or another of the swarm of doctors who'd passed through, their faces blurred into one authoritative, humorless mass. "For now."

Bruce called Danny to tell him that his sister was in the ICU, had just suffered a seizure and undergone a biopsy of a sizable mass in her brain.

"Is she okay?" Dan asked his father after a (too) long pause. What kind of question was that? No! She most certainly was not okay!

"Yes. Well. We're not sure, really," said Bruce. "She's out of the woods." He left out the *for now.* "We're waiting to hear more. They thought maybe it was a stroke, but now they're saying it's a tumor."

Danny heaved a sigh. His sister was *such* a mess. Oh, how weary he was of this world. "Well. Keep me posted."

Dahlia floated not "above" any of this, but sort of underneath it, within it. It's one of those pop-culture-validated fallacies of near-death that the near-dead are looking down on an unfolding reality and can watch it like a movie, albeit an oddly shot one. As if awareness of that sort is so lazy, so unimaginative, that the best it can do is sit back on some comfy cosmic couch, nestled with remote in hand, to *watch*. Really the near-dead are floating in an ether ("ether" as defined by the laws of physics as "a very rarefied and highly elastic substance formerly believed to permeate all space, including the interstices between the particles of matter and to be the medium whose vibrations constituted light and other electromagnetic radiation," but more on that later. Much.)

"She's got nine months," said the head of Neurology on the second day. It would be nice to think that he was just a supremely honest guy, the kindly doctor whose understanding of his role allowed for no understating of such news, a man who knew, at his core, that brutal, painful honesty was the only way to go. Really he was just a dick, a physician whose stellar performance in science classes and med school relieved him of the need for social skills, tact, or empathy. "Tops."

It was indeed a tumor: Glioblastoma multiforme (level four) in Dahlia's left temporal lobe.

"It's really not the best kind of tumor to

have," the head of Neurology said absently, to her chart.

Margalit was not taking any of this well. She sobbed, lapsed into Hebrew for dramatic effect ("My baby! *Motek! Chaval!*"), and generally spooked the nurses, who traded nervous glances with Bruce.

Bruce was all business, taking notes and notes and more notes. *Not worst possible place, not necessarily worst possible tumor,* he jotted in his notebook while the head of Neurology went on to explain that it actually was the "worst possible" tumor. But it was currently situated in a part of her brain that didn't affect too much neurological function and might be "addressed" by radiation and chemo alone.

"I have to tell you," the head of Neurology said before disappearing back out into the hospital flow, a river of indifference. "Glioblastomas are not good."

Bottom line, nobody survives a Glioblastoma. Kind of like how nobody puts Baby in a corner, dig?

Bruce Finger was not one to get angry when people invariably came up short. If you lied to him outright or with malicious intent he lost it completely — Dahlia had learned this the hard way at seventeen when she'd tried and failed to pull off a neat trick

29

of MasterCard embezzlement — but otherwise, whether you were callous, cruel, thoughtless, careless, harsh, neglectful, dismissive, lazy, unkind, and/or greedy, he let it roll off his back like water off the proverbial duck's. Simply put: He wanted to believe the best about you, about everyone, and about life in general.

This, perhaps, is what allowed him to calmly take his euphemized notes, to sweetly comfort his lunatic ex-wife, to call his unresponsive, ice-for-blood reptile of a son and relay whatever news came along. It didn't occur to him, as it would have to Dahlia — as it *did* to Dahlia, even in the ether! — to hold shit against Margalit, against Danny, against the head of Neurology, against the manufacturer of the hospital bed, which was not all that nice. To hold shit against, let's be honest, everyone. It didn't occur to Bruce to look sideways at the head of Neurology and mutter "asshole." It didn't occur to him to hurl his pad and pen across the room, to howl, to accept the implications of this news and react with commensurate fury and despair. His only daughter was going to die, and soon.

Neither Bruce nor Margalit had slept in days, unless you counted a heavy intermittent nodding in conjoined vinyl hospital chairs: her jaw gone slack and her forehead fraught, leaning into him, his chin coming to rest on the crown of her head until it woke her, at which point she jerked her head up — "huh?" — crashed into his chin, and made him bite down on his tongue — "ouch!" Which should have embarrassed them both (her for the impropriety of the affection and proximity, him for being such a goddamn doormat), but, because she, as a rule, took whatever she needed from everybody and he *was* something of a doormat, didn't.

The story of Margalit and Bruce began by the side of a dusty road near Arad, where she, at twenty, was hitchhiking in her army uniform on a weekend break. Bruce had picked her up (not at all a risky or weird thing in those days) and that, as they say, had been that. Nothing had been impossible then, not for a hot twenty-year-old *sabra* in her uniform, giant gun slung over her shoulder like a purse. Here was an American man, a lawyer-to-be, who, when she had leaned into his car through the passenger window to assess the character of her ride, had smiled, locked eyes with her, and won her over instantaneously. He was working on a kibbutz for a while after law school and the bar, exploring this amazing country whose birth and existence paralleled almost to the day his own. She could get into his car, she could fuck him senseless, she could marry him and move to the States and have babies and come back to Israel to visit her family and have affairs and bring the kids with her or leave them behind, she could marry again, then again; anything was possible. She would do all of it and more.

"Nu?" he'd said, waiting for her to open the door and get in. A catch-all — *So? What's your story? Well? What's it gonna be?* — handled expertly by this American man despite his ownership of hardly another word in the language. Margalit knew better than to take him for Israeli (there was the watch, first off, too shiny and old-fashioned — his grandfather's, she later learned — and there was the under-developed shape of his upper body, the softness of his hands: This was not a man who'd labored in the Mediterranean sun or done army service) but that expert *"nu"* stopped her in her tracks.

"Nu, *yourself.*"

They drove for a few miles in a hot, loaded silence, ardently smirking sidelong at each other, and not two hours later were embroiled in an altogether sordid, salty, desert summer rapture in the backseat. *"Nu,* yourself," they laughed with each other thereafter, frisky for a good long while.

Dahlia, in a creative writing class in college, had composed a poem entitled "My Parents Met Like a Porno," which had been poorly received. *(my parents met like a porno:/she standing in fatigues on the side of the road,/he driving by, horny as hell./her gun resting between them, huge and dangerous,/ turning him on./(though would he admit that?)/ pornos don't have epilogues, but here I am, writing this . . .)* It went on for a while, a bit of an epic really, to include a parallel in the form of her own loss of virginity, at fourteen, to a sweaty Israeli ten years her senior. A good poem, she thought, if admittedly somewhat awkward in its discussion of her parents' copulation. What did those idiot student poets know from lyric potential, anyway? Dahlia knew what was up. Dahlia was the *true* poet. Dahlia, it turned out, had cancer. Suck it, poets.

On the fourth day, in town to see friends, Rabbi Douchebag showed up empty-handed and alone. He slouched into the room with his arms crossed — defensively, instinctively — across his chest. His wedding ring glinted under the hospital fluorescents.

"Danny," Margalit cried out, her voice

breaking. "Oh, Danny! Danny!"

After allowing his mother to hug him (he participated in the hug as passively as possible, offering the side of his torso and one flaccid arm in accordance with his asshole rulebook) and sitting on the windowsill/air vent for a few minutes, listening to what they knew so far and glancing, frowning, briefly, at his unconscious sister, he left again.

"Keep me posted," he told Bruce, shaking his father's hand like a stranger.

It was not the weight of Dahlia's medical predicament, mind you, to which Daniel's dour countenance could be pinned. Do not mistake him for merely terse, concerned. Picture Jerry Seinfeld, but with thinner hair and without the native intelligence or easy smile. A perennial expression on his face that looked as though he was trying in earnest to stifle a large, unwieldy, and very smelly fart. His fingernails gruesomely gnawed, to the quick.

It should be noted that if Margalit and Bruce and Dahlia had not been Danny's mother, father, and sister, respectively, his vibe would have been 180 degrees from cold indifference. Rabbi Douchebag could be counted on by all and sundry in need. He visited countless ailing acquaintances, paid shiva calls to the most distant friends of friends. Attended weddings and baby namings and circumcisions galore. If Dahlia had been a lucky member of the all-and-sundry, Rabbi Douchebag would have brought cookies, played cards, told jokes, offered theological perspective, planted himself alongside the sick and held her hand, prayed. But Rabbi Dan was just Danny here, just the prodigal son of resented parents, the estranged, despised brother of the unwell.

Regardless, this was the hospital scene, which Dahlia inhabited only from within a deep unconsciousness (which is to say the *ether,* which is to say not really at all). Hours piled up into another day, then another. They waited for Dahlia to come out of her coma. Margalit went home to shower and change. Bruce barely moved. He called Danny twice to report that there was nothing to report.

Ben, Dahlia's quasi-boyfriend, the unlikely hero, had been the one to find Dahlia unconscious in her apartment some hours after her seizure, when she'd failed to return several of his calls. He loitered around the hospital for a few days, looking generally concerned and letting Margalit and Bruce buy him lots of coffee and cafeteria cinnamon rolls. He seemed, in the immediate aftermath of having found Dahlia unconscious and in god-knows-what state of fetid disarray (there had been vomit, there had been urine), to feel very much an integral part of this dramatic story. Never mind that Dahlia had been dating him *casually:* Margalit embraced him as practically part of the family, in her overwhelming way.

"Ben," she'd mew every so often, enfolding him in what seemed to be a painful embrace. Looking to be comforted. "Oh, Ben!" He was stricken, horrified to find himself in the position of providing some sort of solace to these random people in such dire circumstances ("Very nice to meet you. I'm so sorry," he kept saying). The nurses had somehow been led to believe that he was poor, sick, young Dahlia Finger's devoted fiancé.

"What do you do, son?" Bruce could be heard to inquire. And: "What do your folks do?"

Margalit and Bruce were just thrilled that Dahlia appeared to have a boyfriend. This happy news could almost elbow out cancer. How much more poignant to die an untimely death in the throes of a blossoming relationship! Love thwarted, etc. (Not that she was dying, though, no. Bite your tongue.) But for the fact that Ben was not even approximately her boyfriend (let alone her fiancé), and but for the fact that he hadn't gone down on her even once in half-a-dozen sexual encounters and furthermore seemed preoccupied with some prematurely dirty talk and a difficult legs-overhead-type thing which had felt mildly degrading and had kind of hurt and had led, Dahlia was pretty sure, to the recent urinary tract infection, it made for a good story. Oh, and: but for the fact that Margalit and Bruce were using a trumped-up romance to further refuse the reality of her undeniable doom. She had a *boyfriend,* after all, practically a *fiancé.* She couldn't die.

Ben was a nice guy, as guys went, but it wasn't long before he graciously bowed out of the whole shuffling-off-the-mortal-coil scene, nervously wishing everyone the best, leaving Bruce with his number and a request to be kept posted, which is what people say when they don't want to deal.

On the sixth day, Dahlia came out of her coma.

They welcomed her back to the land of the living. One of the nurses used exactly this phrase: "the land of the living."

She was Sick, they told her. Capital "S," Sick. Something very wrong with her.

"Something": ha! *A* thing. *The* thing. Cells, evil cells, multiplying like racial undesirables in a ghetto whose boundaries will soon expand to encompass even the best neighborhoods. The oncologist — let's call him Dr. Cracker — tried to explain it in exactly those terms when Dahlia could get up for the first time on the seventh day, a shaved-and-swaddled patch on the left side of her head, her suffering reduced, thanks to an ass-load of painkillers, to a vile case of anticipatory low self-esteem brought on by the bald patch, her sallow complexion, and the helpless indignity of sitting in a doctor's office with her freaking parents, as though she was *in trouble,* as though Dr. Cracker were the principal. There was something more than a little embarrassing about all this; the scope of it, the seriousness. Dahlia was never one who did well taking things, even serious things, seriously.

"I do not recommend surgery." Dr. C spoke to Dahlia. The patient. "As I've told your parents, surgery won't do anything to prolong life, and the risks to your quality of life are significant because of the location of the tumor. If you were to develop severe neurological symptoms later on, *maybe* surgery would be an option then. But we'll cross that bridge when we get to it." For

38

now, radiation. A six-week course. "Aggressive," said Dr. C. Followed by chemo.

"Although it is *not* a great tumor, it's in a relatively accessible part of the brain," Cracker added, nodding at Bruce, who liked hearing the latter. Accentuate the positive.

"What does it mean?" Dahlia wanted to know. Her voice sounded foreign, weird, like a down escalator on the left. Cracker made of his lips a long, thin line.

"It depends how treatment goes. It depends on your attitude, your individual response to treatment. I know of one patient who's had a tumor like yours for almost five years now and is fine."

Margalit snorted. "Fine?"

"It means," Bruce jumped in, "that it's in an accessible spot, and you're young, you're healthy. There's no reason for us not to be optimistic, here. There's no reason you can't beat this thing and have a long, happy life."

Accessible spot? Beat this thing? Long and happy life? Such vagaries! Like he was a mobster on a pay phone, talking about a hit. Don't oversell, Dad.

"But — *why?*" Margalit dissolved again into tears and directed this whine at Dr. Cracker. *"How . . . ?"*

There was no why, no how. Here was lightning, striking. Dr. Cracker only shook his head. "There are no environmental or genetic causes for this kind of tumor." He got up, switched on the fluorescents, and put up her MRI images. Gracefully, with a laser pointer held three inches away, he gave them the guided tour. There it was, a thing asymmetrical and off, blossoming in the left temporal lobe of the cauliflower floret that was her brain. Until now, Dahlia's biggest health woes had been tendencies toward constipation and ingrown hair. Insomnia, too. And the UTI.

Cancer is the abnormal development of irregular cells. Cancers are caused by a series of mutations. Each mutation alters the behavior of the cell.

When she was very small, her family turning and turning in its widening gyre, her parents headed for their pathetic breakup and cowardly Daniel fading so purposefully, so cruelly, out of the picture, Dahlia had indulged in occasional fantasies about illness, about getting Margalit and Bruce together again, united in a common cause against whatever was ailing their precious daughter. Later on, in high school, she had evolved into a bona fide self-mutilator. It was too late, now. Also too late was the realization that it wouldn't have worked anyway, that there was no better living to be had through sickness.

"What does it *mean?*" Dahlia asked the doctor again. She sounded not as forceful as she intended, considering the headache and all, but she wasn't going to let him off that easily. "Am I going to die?" Well, duh. "I mean, like, not of old age?" Well, possibly. "I mean, of this?"

Margalit blew her nose; Bruce looked down at his notes.

And all together now, without moving our lips or making a sound: Yup.

"Well," Dr. C finally allowed. "Statistically you have a one-in-three chance of living at least two years. It's very important that you think positively; there's increasing evidence that state of mind and force of will have a real effect on treatment and recovery." Dr. C recited this bit gazing up at her MRI images and then, taking them down, at the long manila folder they went in.

His countenance seemed to say: Give me a break, will you? Do not push me. As if Dahlia pressing him on the matter was its own kind of negativity, a gauche and unpleasant line of questioning that would, unchecked, somehow damage her. Further.

"But . . . realistically. . . ." She was groping. "What does it really *mean?*" Just say it! Say it! Say it!

There was a pause, taut and suspended as a bridge, a break from hysteria and note-taking. Bruce and Margalit looked at each other, at Dr. C, at Dahlia. Then Margalit resumed weeping softly and Bruce reached over and rubbed her back. Dahlia, fleetingly, was more upset by the way her parents were interacting — Bruce allowing Margalit to use him for his steady, reliable, generous brand of consolation — than by the fact that nobody would level with her, here.

"It's not helpful to think about a worst-case scenario at this stage of the game," Dr. C said. Ah: a *game.* A sort of battle, perhaps?

Dahlia waited for him to haul out further reassurance that it had been caught early, that it was highly treatable. On his desk, two framed photos grinned and bore it: one of a small, tow-headed boy peering up joyfully through too-long bangs, and another of an expensively high-lit woman fighting a losing battle on the seductive/maternal continuum. How many doomed Sick had had to sit where Dahlia sat, looking at those insufferable pictures? How many poor sap fuckers had had to process the physical manifestations of Dr. Cracker's physiological rightness (a fertile, pheromone-spewing wife, a fully functional kid, the implied healthy testicles that had allowed the former to grow the latter in her lush, plump little womb) while they processed their own total lack of physiological rightness? Little Cracker Jr. and Mrs. Cracker had surely borne the brunt of this paradigm a thousand times, holding grinning court over the process in which the hopes, dreams, and taken-for-granted future of yet another doomed idiot were deflated, cut up, burned, and scattered, ashes to the wind. *They* should be sick, too.

It occurred to her then, the words *environmental, genetic,* and *tumor* dutiful instruments in a marching band led by the cocksure, high-kicking, baton-twirling *Cancer,* that her parents and Dr. Cracker were presenting this to her as a front. She'd been unconscious for days, doped up nicely, and they had, of course, been over this already. They were gathered here to break it to her. It was like an intervention: You have cancer, you ridiculous screw-up, and we're all really worried about you. We love you. We want to help you. You can beat this, we know you can! How mortifying (in a word).

Finally, Dahlia arrived at "Am I going to get better?" A stupid question if ever there was one. She hated herself for asking, for tipping her cards: She *wanted* to get better,

43

and now she had let them all know it. So when she didn't, she'd not only be dead, she'd a loser, too.

"Yes," Bruce said, knee-jerk.

"There is a lot we can do," said Dr. Cracker. "And treatment is progressing scientifically even as we speak."

"It's treatable," said Bruce weakly. "You're young, and healthy. It's not in the worst possible place." The word "place" didn't quite make it out under the wire, though, and Bruce, bless his transparency, teared up and only got it out in a measly whisper.

Dr. Cracker leveled. "The average length of life for someone with a tumor like Dahlia's is 10 months. That's with radiation treatment. But she would probably be at the upper end of the curve because she's young" — not according to the alumnae magazine! — "the tumor is on the small side" — but the *worst possible* kind — "she's in good physical shape" — minus acute weed lung — "and she's not having any neurological symptoms just now." Other than the seizure. And the headaches. And the general misery. And so on.

Dahlia was twenty-nine years old. Too young to die, certainly, but old enough, surely, to be taking on the mantle of her own illness, taking her own notes, sobbing

44

histrionically at the imminence of her own demise. Instead she just sat there — not giving a fuck about the science of it all, the terms, the options; what did those words mean, anyway? And how would knowing help her? Looking at Cracker Jr. and Mrs. Cracker in those snapshots: Tow-head Jr. with those bangs and the Mrs. with her shitton of makeup and tight smile. It was always the same with these big life moments, these arrogant self-important moments demanding some purportedly innate, prefabricated response. She was to be sad, mad, sad, glad — well, no, not glad, but it rhymes, so what the hell? And then, after the predictable progression down the list, accepting. And then dead.

All together now: *Tumor, Cancer, Growth, No, But, Maybe, No.* No, no, no. No. Maybe. Yes. No.

Margalit again mouthed the word "why," but it wasn't directed anywhere in particular. They all sat slumped, spent. Dr. C folded his hands and looked toward Bruce for the commiseration of someone who was, as they say, dealing. For a guy who made his living telling people they had cancer, and outlining, in great detail, the fact of mortality, Dr. C was pretty crappy at it. Fucking amateur night at the ICU.

"Here's what we'd like to do," said Dr. C. Bruce flipped back to a previous page in his pad, filled with notes. At the top of the page he'd written OPTIONS. Margalit gave herself a hug. She wore her customary excess of accessories: two sturdy silver rings on each hand, enormous beaded necklace, wildly swinging pewter earrings from the Arab quarter. Margalit was never without a half-dozen too many pieces of jewelry. It was a look. She made it work. You could hear her coming from far away, soft clinks heralding the worst part of your day.

"Like I said, I recommend that you not have surgery. It can't make much difference in terms of length or quality of life, and the risks are just too numerous. The tumor is in a delicate spot — the temporal lobe is responsible for memory and speech and hearing and lots of important stuff."

"Much difference?" Dahlia said.

"The next step will be to start radiation treatment right away. We may recommend chemotherapy at the same time, or it may come later. We'll run some more tests. It's possible we may also recommend surgery at some later point, *if* she starts having severe neurological symptoms."

She hated to be talked about in the third person.

Dahlia didn't have it in her to hazard another hardly veiled Will I Live Or Die? If she pressed him, Dr. C had made implicitly clear, no way would she survive. She must be timid. She must take his answers. She must be satisfied and make do and ask little. And might this mean she'd make it? If she shut the hell up? If she accepted it? Might that somehow pass for positivity?

So Dahlia was on her own to contemplate death. And not in any detached, vague, stoned undergraduate manner, either: a real, protracted, horrific, imminent, unfair, and ugly death. Her *own* death: someone she knew. Like when her high school acquaintance Julia Grielsheimer had failed to wake up one Thursday morning in May, the victim of an undetected heart defect. Like at the schoolwide assembly that had followed, at which Dahlia felt worst about the fact that Julia had been an only child, that now her parents had nothing, not a goddamned thing, to show for the love and fear and sweat of having brought her into existence in the first place. Like the tears Dahlia had shed, when the girls' a capella group had launched into the most drawn-out, haunting rendition imaginable of Cyndi Lauper's "Time After Time." An ill-conceived reading of Yeats had followed, then some great Whitman, then the requisite Dickinson (it really was quite a rigorous, esteemed school). Dahlia was just outright sobbing, making a scene, people in bleachers around her snickering about how she and Julia *weren't even good friends.* It was true: She and Julia hadn't been good friends. But they'd had Spanish together, and once, just before the winter semiformal, Julia had described in loving detail the dress she'd purchased for the occasion. Royal blue, with an empire waist. Julia had said that she was going to wear her hair up, with a few pieces down. The word she'd used was "tendrils." She'd demonstrated this for Dahlia, holding a pile of hair at the crown of her head and pulling down two soft, light brown pieces around her face. Dahlia had been surprised by Julia's use of that word, tendrils, around which she could still vividly see Julia's lips shaped ("ten-drrrrils"), and by the whole conversation, which had ended abruptly when the bell rang and they'd parted ways for sixth period. Also surprising had been Julia's date, an outgoing drama geek embraced by practically everyone in school for his good-natured willingness to humiliate himself. They had made a fun couple. Dahlia had thought Julia sweet, and perhaps more interesting than had been assumed. Which just made Dahlia cry harder: They *hadn't* really been friends, and now they wouldn't be. But mainly: Julia's parents! Jesus Christ, Julia's parents. "Dahlia, god," even Mara had hissed. "Were you guys even friends?"

"At least I'm not an only child," Dahlia said suddenly, breaking the silence in Dr. Cracker's office. There followed yet more silence, and everyone seemed collectively to decide — Dr. C because he had no clue what she was talking about (these family scenes were so awkward!); Margalit because Dahlia was not, under any circumstances, to be indulged on the subject of her brother; Bruce because it was all too, too terrible for words — that she was best ignored.

Margalit was gaping like a hooked fish, her face upturned as though Dr. Cracker, Dahlia, God, or a small, winged, mystical animal might drop a dainty morsel of food (or hope) into her hole. Bruce, another bout of tears sufficiently conquered, continued to scribble away in his notebook. He asked Dr. C to please reiterate a few things, asked for the spelling of *astrocytoma,* the meaning, again, of *anaplasia* and *Glioblastoma multiforme.* He was writing these things down, ostensibly, in order to go over them later. But what, exactly, would he do with them later? Go online, double-check the diagnosis? Cross-reference Dr. C's medical knowledge on Google? Come up with some alternative miracle treatment that would turn the fundamentals of surgery and chemo on their miserable, deaf, bastard ears?

Margalit wanted to know *why?* Bruce asked Dr. C another thoughtful, ignorant question, took another thoughtful, ignorant note, disregarding as best he could his doomed daughter, his irritating ex-wife, ignoring as best he could the *why.* Margalit, for all her self-absorption and histrionics and redundant wondering, surely already knew *why.* Dahlia knew instinctively *why.* Dahlia had no confusion around *why.* It was kind of hackneyed, the *why* (no, it seemed, she couldn't face down even this most serious, definitive life-cycle experience without the generational-bred irony, the italics, the snarl). *Why* was the exclusive province of those on the run from the truth; *why* was for those stubbornly invested in the way things *ought* to be. *Why* was the realm of those who don't get the cruel basics of cause/effect. There was no *why,* there was just the reality, which was that this eventuality had been encoded in Dahlia's DNA from the moment of conception, like development of polycystic ovaries or acne or premature gray. Like her twin tendencies toward constipation and ingrown hair. It had been lying in wait, like the startling shriek of a set alarm, since conception, first steps, and that terrifying time she'd once been lost by Margalit in a shopping mall. She had been set spinning like a wobbly top toward this preordained destination of the worst kind of sick you can be, and her life had provided the ten million worm holes to bring her there. Asking "why" *was* why, goddamn it all to hell.

3. A Different Kind of Disease

Cancer is a disease unlike any other. Cancer is one of the most mysterious and elusive diseases known to man. There is no definitive cure and often no definitive cause.

After the seizure Dahlia had almost choked on her own vomit and died right on her new Shabby Chic couch, VH1 still counting up and up and up through the nineties and then back again, 1999 over and over again the end of everything, like in an outdated evangelical Christian mass market paperback. Lucky for her (this is what everyone says; Dahlia says, What's the fucking difference whether she now gets to live another few pathetic months, or years even, Sick?), Ben had taken it upon himself, after two unreturned phone calls, to come over and, when she didn't respond to his banging on the door, to peer into the window and finally break into her house early the next

52

day, the blackened-to-a-crisp remains of her pizza still smoldering in the automatic (thank goodness!) oven. He'd had a "sense" that Something was Wrong, he said, and was lauded like the Righteous Gentile he was: he'd saved her. It was even suggested that this sweet guy she'd been casually seeing might actually be *The One!*

"He clearly cares deeply for you, Dahlia," Margalit said, "and it is incredibly rare for a man to act on a sense like that." A not-so-subtle jab at Bruce, who was collapsed in the corner of the hospital room, having been an allegedly ineffectual spouse all those years before. Dahlia hadn't much energy at that point, with half her brain gone (well, not half — really, as Dr. C had demonstrated, just a biopsied nick — but fuck off, it felt like half), but the absurdity of Margalit playing Cupid did not go unnoted.

"Don't ignore me, *motek!* When somebody cares for you you don't just throw that away! How often do you think you get the chance? Unbelievable, this girl. Unbelievable!" (See also: What Is Your Battle Plan?)

It can be tempting to go over your life with a fine-toothed comb in search of a cause. Consider the personal roots of your illness, if only so you can put them behind you. We call this "narrative building."

53

Even douchebags with head colds have their narratives. How long they've been sick, how they first felt it coming on, exactly what their sinuses feel like. Then there's the subtle shift into prognosis mode: When will they be better? They can be sure they'll live — sigh, cough — but health seems so very far away, a land of taken-for-granted glory where unicorns frolic with thoroughly depilated nymphs on the Pill. Oh, how they'll rejoice when they're back there! Oh, how sweet it will feel, how *alive!*

And we're not talking about hypochondriacs; those freakshows are another kind of sick altogether.

Old people offer an interesting variation: they don't have long regardless, so they can bitch and moan all they want, pester overworked internists for new prescriptions until they stroke right out of existence, but they're still careening toward that great inevitability, they know it, and thus there's no when-I'm-better to cloud the issue. Dahlia's grandpa Saul, at 97 years old, wears most of his internal organs on the outside of his body and offers an introductory tour upon first meeting. There's no getting better where age is concerned. What a relief that must be.

Anyway, those were the facts of Dahlia's

story, her illness narrative (the one she'll be expected to relay self-importantly at parties for however long she fucking has left to live).

But as happy as Dahlia was to be alive (if sweet Ben hadn't found her when he did she'd surely have choked on her own vomit and died on her new couch and that would've been it, the end), she also felt mildly put out. Ben had broken into her apartment (they'd been, once again, only *casually dating*). What right had he had to do that? Now she'd been cheated out of the relatively quick, simple, catastrophic, and painless death fated her. Would she now be duty-bound to, like, "fight" for "her life" or some such? Worst of all, would she now be obligated to be in some sort of relationship with the shmo? Has it been mentioned that they'd been seeing each other only casually?

Telling your own story has to do with looking at things in your life that may have contributed to your illness, and which may now offer you a chance to proactively get better.

"You're young," everyone kept saying. "It's not in the worst possible place!" And: "If anyone can beat this thing, you can!" (Never mind that no one could possibly mistake Dahlia for someone who could "beat" it.) Also: "We'll get a second opinion."

She could let this talk permeate the membrane of the truth, *her* truth, which was that she was a dead woman.

So there you have Dahlia's illness narrative, sort of. The basic version, the watered-down, the immediate. The version people could hear, if they really wanted to, if they truly meant it when they asked "How are you?" or "What happened?" It was to be her party narrative trump, the ne plus ultra of *shut up and listen to me,* her script for when folks gazed pityingly at her, offered their awkward, premature condolences, or, worse, offered that oppressive optimism, pretending she was getting better. She's not getting better. There is no better. And this — *you listening, Dr. Phil?* — sure as hell isn't because she doesn't *want* to get better. It's not — *hear this, Oprah!* — because she lacks the sheer force of will to *get* better. It's not because — *talking to you, Lance Armstrong* — she isn't physically strong enough to get better. It's because — *fuck you all!* — she's Sick. Which is not a state one flits in and out of at will. It's a state of existence, concrete as race or shape.

Were you a smoker? Did you eat a balanced diet? Were you heavy into drinking? Did you hold on to a lot of anger?

But as to the real story, the true narrative,

an attempt to address the *real* why (which was decidedly unwelcome party talk anyway), Dahlia had to admit she's unplacatable. Seems she's Margalit's daughter, to the end.

Why?

Some gimmes: deodorant, birth control, processed foods, lead, cigarettes, smog, her cell phone. Any or all of the above.

She'd once become convinced, higher than ever (what was *in* that shit, Kat and Steph had asked nervously the next day), that the mole on her lower left check (often credited as one of her "best features" — but can a mole really qualify as a feature?) was growing. Getting bigger by the second, slowly and surely, aiming to overtake her face and then her very being.

"It's one of my best features," she'd tearfully informed her comrades, sucking on a blunt and marinating in the tragic unfairness of it (because it *was* her best feature, really, three coarse black hairs growing out of it notwithstanding).

Global warming, dirty politicians, social injustice, war. She was grasping. It was endless.

And there were the less-concretes.

The feeling of being submerged in a stew of humility when something stupid she'd said or done came back in a flash: told that one-night stand she loved him, brushed impatiently past someone on the sidewalk only to trip idiotically over her own feet not three seconds later.

The way she had heard her name mispronounced a hundred times a day over the course of her *entire fucking life*. Dah-la? Duh-lia? Da-ha-la? *Is that Spanish? Oh, like the Black Dahlia? Like the flower? Is that Jewish? What is that?* The way she'd just give her name to restaurant hostesses as "Doll" and be done with it. The way they'd squint at her then, wondering what the hell kind of name that was.

Margalit, leaving her children, running off to Israel to be "alone," to "think," to "find herself." To be the daughter of a mother who'd abandon her own children! And who'd failed, as well, to breastfeed. Oh, biological imperative; is it any wonder?

The paradigm of being pulled between two parents in two countries on different continents for fifteen years. That quality time she'd spent with Bruce, trapped, living alone with her father when he was a spurned, sad-sack, checked-out alcoholic wreck.

Daniel. Shittiest big brother since Cain, you'd better believe it, leaving her to her own devices all those years, whether out of simple dumbshit incapacity or maliciousness or a combination of the two it didn't ultimately matter in the least. He'd abandoned her to this, which had of course been lying in predatory wait all along. They'd all abandoned her to this. Kat. Steph. Mara. Jacob. Clark. Everyone. Support and love and devotion definitively, punitively withdrawn, nullified. Void.

That clichéd adolescent love affair with razor blades, the thinly veiled suicide threats. A handful of broken or nonexistent condoms, semen of unworthy men who cared not at all for her absorbed into her body, microscopic invaders. (Cervical cancer would've at least made some sense! But *brain?* What the fuck?)

And what about people who wouldn't let you hold their babies, who gave excuses about germs or attachment or whatever?

Locking eyes with homeless people and then giving them no change, none at all.

Reading in the paper about a schoolteacher in China who'd raped dozens of fourth- and fifth-grade girls. The sexual violence in the Sudan, blamed on its victims. A teenaged mother in Queens who had purposefully murdered her infant daughter by putting her *in the microwave.* To live in a world where such things were possible. All of it storm clouds gathering, gaining force, threatening claps of thunder amassing energy for the devastating downpour of *this.*

Why!?

Dahlia's propensity for grudge holding. Dahlia's inability, in fact, to do anything *but* grudge-hold. Dahlia's inability to do anything but everything-hold.

Why!?

Ever wonder where the accumulation of such shit, the *everything* holding — and holding and holding and holding and — goes? There are *consequences,* people, for the everyday shit she'd swallowed, so to speak.

The wrongs had piled up, a clusterfuck of wrong. In her brain.

The sound of one's own name butchered, environmental waste in the air, the immutable certainty at the age of ten that one *has no home:* All compelling, complex stuff, sure, but doesn't quite have the same immediacy as a simple "And I woke up in the hospital!" Well, hey: I told some frat boy whose last name I didn't know and who I openly (read: when sober) abhorred that I *loved him.* I never saw him again, but he carries with him a vestige of my health because for a fraction of a second I allowed myself to buy into the possibility that there was something beautiful between us, and *poof!* a pure, sacred, *healthy* piece of me, gone. In its place, something wrong, terribly wrong; something mortifying and sad and stupid and wasteful, mutating like crazy, taking over, making everything over in its own image.

You weren't supposed to eat nonorganic berries — raspberries, strawberries — because their enormous surface area was said to hold onto pesticides and chemicals better than, say, an apple. Every tart, cold berry she'd ever consumed: doom.

And Dahlia herself so much like the Dahlia flower: multipetaled, layered over itself, with enormous surface area. Doom.

Cause, meet effect. Effect, cause. You two have a lot to talk about.

She had felt The Towers fall in mighty rumbles from her bachelorette post in the East Village, and had emerged onto the street alongside a crowd of gasping, gaping thousands. And nothing — in New York or, indeed, in America, or, indeed, in the cellular makeup of Dahlia's brain — was Ever the Same Again. Might she have inhaled some pulverized steel-and-asbestos cocktail, some particularly rancid, corrupt particle of finance industry dust, some speck of flesh belonging to a wife-beating, child-molesting, hooker-raping, tax-evading banker? Mixed in with a mite of jet fuel and the evaporated sweat of a hate-pruned, suicidal fundamentalist? But no — then all of lower Manhattan and gentrified Brooklyn would have cancer, too. Then all the Park Slope boutiques hawking unpainted wooden toys and two-thousand-dollar strollers would by now have been replaced with wig shops and herbalists. (And the terrorists would have won.)

Also: There was the aftertaste she'd get, putting saccharin in her coffee. Metallic, dull, greasy, dangerous. Shampoo parabens! SUVs, carbon pile-up in the atmosphere, her bad attitude, antibiotics! The lead bib her dentist laid over her body when the x-ray machine was hauled out! The recycled air in hotels and airplanes! Real estate brokers! Pessimism! Potato chips!

People who read aloud to you from their journals; being sober in a roomful of drunks; being drunk in a roomful of sober people; having to turn down nice-seeming but unappealing men who'd had the courage to ask her for her number.

Going solo to see a band, initially feeling independent and happy, and then having to fight subtly and silently for space with some burly asshole in an untucked button-down and baseball cap, swaying freely with his arms around some pony-tailed match.com bitch. Dahlia would put her hands on her hips, widen her stance, too meek to actually say *hey dude, move the fuck over, I'm standing here,* too angry to just allow her space to be compromised, the show unfolding happily while she charted every minute movement, taking every opportunity to bump into the asshole, shoving passersby into him, the whole battle carried out without so much as eye contact.

Her cell phone ringing in the middle of a yoga class when she'd forgotten to turn it off. "Someone's phone is ringing," and Dahlia, mortified, simply rolled her eyes and shook her head: the nerve of some people, leaving their phones on in yoga. And for the remainder of the class Dahlia's anxious, a liar, waiting for it to ring again and out her as the inconsiderate piece of shit with the ringing phone.

Gossip. Some say your ears burn or your nose itches when you're being talked about, but Dahlia says you get a fucking tumor: omnipotent bad cells multiplying en masse to overtake every iota of truth, of goodness, of delicate singular light and beauty that might otherwise be allowed to proliferate and comprise your living existence.

Oh, and having been born in late June! Flipping eagerly to the backs of magazines and newspapers for some insight into one's emotional/financial/romantic possibilities only to find one's forecast filed under the word itself, a pen-and-ink rendering of that slow but sure crab: Cancer.

A woman in a parking lot not three weeks earlier had screamed furiously at Dahlia for accidentally cutting her off, and Dahlia had muttered something to the effect of "chill out, freak; you're going to get cancer." Because of the notion, handily bought, that negativity and hatred and ugliness and resentment became manifest within the bodies of such people and rotted them inside out. You're going to get cancer if you don't chill the fuck out. You're going to get cancer if you invest energy in being an asshole. You're going to get cancer if you judge and assail everyone around you, harsh and ungenerous, furious about perceived lameness and idiocy and general unworthiness. You're going to get cancer if you feel most alive when you're defining yourself in opposition to others. You're going to get cancer if you're incapable of "looking on the bright side." You're going to get cancer if you reserve a special place of hatred in your heart — right *in your actual heart* — for your dickheaded brother. You're going to get cancer if you stay up all night and sleep all day. Masturbate. Fail to pay off your credit cards. Eat sugar. Eat fake sugar. You're going to get cancer if you let others disappoint you just by being goddamn typical. You're going to get cancer if you expect too much. Ad nauseam. Ad infinitum. Ad mortem.

And it was just like you always hear, her life flashing before her eyes. Meet Dahlia Finger: emotional fly strip, hurt Swiffer, pain sponge.

4. THE BRIGHT SIDE

Something positive will come of this drastic turn of events. Believe that, and you will have the strength you'll need for the journey ahead.

Upon discharge from the hospital on the eighth day they went directly to the bookstore. This is what Jews do when the shit hits the fan: Go find books. Bruce and Margalit were revived in the search, some spring in their steps now, can-do crowding out despair. They'd whip cancer's ass, to be sure, with the help of Barnes & Noble.

They discussed Dahlia using the dreaded third person, like she was already dead, or at least no longer really there.

"She's not walking right."

"She's fine, she's fine, let's just take it slow."

"Is she okay?"

"She just needs to go slow."

In point of fact Dahlia was feeling a bit

dizzy (ever have a tiny hole drilled through your skull?), but Bruce was correct that taking it slow was the key. Bruce! Her dad. *Daddy Bruce,* she had called him when she was small, echoing that second strange name to which she had heard him referred. Where under normal circumstances he could sometimes appear dull, boring, dopey, he now revealed himself to be the solid sort of guy you could really trust and lean on when the going got tough. The kind of guy you were supposed to marry (and not later abandon with your children when you got antsy).

Dahlia observed her dad closely, looking for signs that he was reveling in this close, prolonged, intimate contact with Margalit. He was still a little bit in love with her, obviously. Dahlia couldn't begrudge him that. She knew broken hearts never really healed over. Hell, she knew it so well she had cancer. Let Bruce have this chance to comfort Margalit. To hold her close and reassure her and stroke her head and tell her it would all be okay. He deserved that much, poor man. Especially since now he would be losing his beloved daughter. Fuck, and we're back to the waves of grief brought on by thinking about Julia Greilsheimer's now-childless parents, who had not, in the more than ten years since her death, managed to select a headstone for their daughter's grave, which was in the same cemetery occupied by Dahlia's Grandma Alice, out by the airport.

Bruce's "she's fine" seemed almost to echo in the microscopic, newly hollowed out part of Dahlia's brain. You're young, it's not in the worst possible place! Her father smiled dazzlingly at her, tilted his head up toward the sky. He was a brilliant businessman, after all, and Problem Solving was a hallmark of any successful businessman.

"Gorgeous day!" he said, and it was. No visible smog, seventy-two degrees, perfect. Traffic and weather: the two safest topics of conversation available to postmodern man.

Dahlia kept her gaze resolutely on the ground. One foot in front of the other. Time after time.

"Are you okay, *motek?*" Margalit asked.

"She's fine," Dahlia spat. "She's young! It's not in the worst possible place! There's no reason she can't live a long, healthy life!"

The Health and Body section was alphabetized by disease: AIDS, Allergies, Cancer, Diabetes, and Diseases (Other): Arthritis, Asthma, Eczema, Epilepsy, Fibromyalgia, Heart, Migraines, MS, Sleep Disorders. And then on into History of Medicine,

Public Health, Medical Reference. Dahlia loved the word *Heart* listed in there, the way it stuck out from the others as a marker of things darker, more complex, and at once better and worse than anything else you might have wrong with you. Like having a heart at all — full, bloody, pumping, yearning — might just be the base problem.

Within Cancer there were subdivisions: Breast, Ovarian, Prostate, Thyroid. The whole section was riddled with the telltale yellow and black spines of the *For Dummies* series. *Prostate Cancer for Dummies, Ovarian Cancer for Dummies, Lung Cancer for Dummies.* Did Dummies get a different kind of cancer altogether? If only.

Margalit gaped at the diseasefest. There were some heartbreaking mis-shelves: *What to Expect When You're Expecting; The Precious Memory Scrapbook.* Had someone been carrying those around when they found out they were sick? Had they then wandered numbly over here, to Health and Body, only to be confronted with illness and mortality? Only to frantically ditch those books about life and head for the nearest exit?

Bruce got to work, down on his knees, pulling out one book after another. Dahlia lowered herself to the floor and leaned against the shelf, bravely facing all the illness. She glanced through Bruce's growing pile. *Heal Thyself. Why Me? The Bad Girl's Guide to Beating Cancer. The Cancer Sourcebook. The Cancer Answer. Eat Right and Live. The Organic Cure.*

"You guys realize this is all bullshit, don't you?" What were the alternatives? *Because You Suck? Unanswerable Questions? Eat Wrong and Die?*

Margalit squared her shoulders.

"You can choose to deal with this in a positive manner. Or you can choose to not." You had to love Margalit's syntax.

"Oh," Dahlia said softly. "Are those my choices?" She pulled out *What to Expect When You're Expecting* and looked up "breastfeeding" in the index.

"Yes," Margalit said. "Those are your choices." The book in her hands: *Positive Thinking for Life.*

Sure, the situation was bad, but Dahlia felt free, freer than ever, to do what she did best: muck around in the heinous reality of it. She was unimpeachable. She could say and think and feel whatever she wanted. She had cancer! There had been all that crying and carrying on between Bruce and Margalit in the days that came before and that

70

would follow, but Dahlia wasn't privy to much of it. She was almost incidental, somehow; this *thing,* this tumor, this cancer, this illness, was *the* thing. Margalit and Bruce were embroiled in their own private courtship of despair, whispering urgently to each other, clutching hands, embracing. High drama. When they addressed Dahlia directly they were all business, all pointed good cheer. They had already decided: It was up to them. It would all be fine. She was young, she was healthy. It wasn't in the worst possible place. Bruce flipped through *The Green Diet Cure;* Margalit through *Thyroid Cancer for Dummies.* "That's not what I have," Dahlia pointed out.

But when Dahlia caught sight of The Book — *It's Up to You: The Cancer To-Do List* — she was momentarily thrown off guard. It was slim and isolated, all by itself way over in Diseases (Other). It had a sort of amusing, harmless, captive dignity, like a Yorkie in a giant cage marked CAUTION.

The Book promised — a promise that, in contrast to words like *cure,* words like *answer,* seemed gracefully noncommittal — to help Dahlia *assimilate this shocking turn of events* (flap copy). The cover of The Book was an excellent bluish-green, which was also, apparently, the color of antimalignance forces she could learn to visualize and muster at will *against multitudes of bad cells* (back cover).

Gene Orenstein — Hey there Gene! — grinned out from the author photo, large, sunken eyes in a long thin face, looking suspiciously like that asshole who'd unleashed the Scarsdale diet upon the unsuspecting upper-class women of the Western world before getting shot by his lover two decades earlier. The grin came off as borderline shit-eating: wide, toothy, and determinedly positive under the big dorky Jewfro. In his two-full-page bio Dahlia learned that he'd been diagnosed with metastasized lung cancer and given six months to live but that *twenty-six years later he lives with his wife and three children in Elkins Park, PA* and had dedicated his life to *using what he learned in his own cancer battle to help others.* It was loathing-love, the only kind she knew about, like in screwball comedies from the thirties and Broadway musicals: She hated Gene with a passion and she was going to give Gene a hundred kinds of hell, but here they were, a pair, for better or for worse, meant to battle wits until the end of time (or until one of them died of cancer, whichever came first). Flirty duets twirled to mind, dance-offs, antagonistic banter, all a highball in one hand and a cigarette holder smoldering glamorously (if carcinogenically) in the other.

"Orenstein has helped thousands to face their illness with strength and the will to live," a TV news anchor gushed on the cover. "It IS up to you!"

"Gene Orenstein has given us a book of such power that all we can do is applaud," said a Howard Sellars, MD, before the title page.

"I don't know what I would have done without my *Cancer To-Do List.* It saved my life, and I hope it saves yours." An ageless soap actress whose name was familiar from Dahlia's unlikely passion for *People.*

"Everyone needs this *To-Do List,* whether or not they have cancer," according to JT Fortunato, the famous athlete whose triumph over testicular cancer had almost overshadowed his gymnastics gold sweep of the last four Olympics. Fortunato was such a badass, the logic went, that he had handily beat the crap out of cancer. He was just that strong, just that conditioned. For a time, it had been chic to wear the black rubber and silver "LIFELIFELIFE" necklaces sold — for two dollars said to fund research — on his website. They had sold out and out and out; gone on eBay for forty bucks apiece, worn stacked on the clavicles of starlets and socialites and mallrats alike.

Hello, said Gene in his introduction. *You've picked up this book because you've just heard the news that you have cancer.*

Hello, Gene. Yes, it's true.

In Chapter One, *Something Wrong,* Gene described his precancer self: two small children, a stressful job as a divorce lawyer, his oft-troubled marriage, a frighteningly large mortgage. His shelved childhood aspiration to become a pastry chef. *I was deeply, deeply unhappy, and Cancer was my wakeup call. Cancer was an opportunity to turn my life around. You now have the same opportunity. What's been troubling you in your own life?*

How much time do you have?

Cancer is the official end to all those troubles.

Sweet.

Actually, congratulations are in order.

Thank you!

You've just begun your life anew. Nothing that's happened up till now matters in the least.

Tell that to Chase Visa, why don't you.

Dahlia stared at the The Book while they were on line to pay, legitimately enthralled with the blue-green, which really was quite lovely and unique: neither cloyingly pastel nor insistently bright. Couldn't hurt. She almost felt better already.

Bruce held an armload of others, even a *Dummies Guide* (". . . to Cancer," nice and broad). This was Bruce's thing: Throw enough money at an issue and all will be fine. Witness the house in Venice. Witness his staggering generosity in the divorce. He'd not fought a thing, just handed over half (*more* than half, actually, basically funding Margalit's wide-ranging dilettantism of the past two decades), not a thought for anything but making problems go away. Go away, problems; here!

He was a mystery to Dahlia in this way: endlessly forgiving, generous, patient. He had grown up poor. Dahlia's Grandpa Saul had opened a menswear shop in Van Nuys in the fifties. Grandma Alice had helped with the books, and young Brucie worked alongside his father taking measurements and ministering to customers. Workingmen, ex-cons. It was a tough neighborhood in those days. They'd been held up once, a terrifying experience Bruce only once ever described to Dahlia in detail, warm on red wine one night in an Italian restaurant in the East Village.

"One guy jammed a gun into Papa's ribs

and demanded to know where the safe was. Well, we didn't *have* a safe, so that was terrible. Papa didn't know what to say and the guy started pistol-whipping him. The other guy had me pinned and a gun in my back. He put his face right up in front of me. I could smell the alcohol on his breath." Bruce's face took on a mournful cast in the telling. He'd shaken his head, neglecting his osso buco. "A few weeks later they hit another store a few blocks away and killed a guy."

"Were you scared?"

"Of course."

"What was going through your head?"

"I don't know. Time slowed down. My heart was racing. I couldn't breathe, almost. I was paying real close attention to the guy; it was like we were the only two people on earth. *'Where's the safe? Where's the safe?'* We didn't *have* a safe."

Dahlia had smiled ruefully, on her third glass of wine. "So, like, my whole existence hinges on the impulse *not* to shoot you of some drunk criminal in 1957?"

"Yeah," Bruce had said. "I guess it does. Mine, too."

So this whole current travesty had almost been intercepted, eradicated, trumped, by an earlier one.

The chunky teenager ringing them up, decked out in authoritative bookstore badges and the requisite nametag ("Holden," though she was female), stared them down mournfully, the pity — There it was! It was right there! — mixed in with surprise. She watched the three of them. Margalit busy grabbing whatever impulse buys she could, thrusting a magazine, a CD, and a box of expensive chocolate truffles into the checkout pile. Bruce going for the heavy Tiffany's money clip in his pocket, dutifully unfolding three crisp twenties, four, five, waiting to hear what was owed, ready and willing to spend whatever needed to be spent. Dahlia, leaning against a best-sellers display, was cosmically exhausted and, as expected, a tad headachey.

Holden looked them over as she scanned and repiled the books, trying to add up the clues. She was in the presence of someone with the big C! Which one of them could it be? The fiery, raven-haired fifty-something wearing dangly earrings, too much eyeliner, and a cape? The stoic square with the twelve-thousand-dollar watch, sweet, boyish face, and pleated khakis? Or the sad-eyed twentysomething with the dirty hair, nose ring and pilled Old Navy T-shirt? *Someone* here was clearly fucked, and how. Holden's cystic acne practically doubled the surface area of her face, like a berry, like a dahlia, which meant that her face held the pity better, longer. The pity: So here it began.

"One-forty-nine ninety-three," she said, her eyes coming to rest on Dahlia. Oh, yes, Dahlia was the one. That patch of shaved hair. Obviously. Tragic.

"Here!" said Margalit, thrusting a *Vogue* at her, as if to normalize things. "Add this."

"And this," Dahlia said, realizing that she had hidden The Book in her own embrace. Her fingers, sweaty and locked, ached when she let go of it. She lacked her usual energy to shoplift.

On the way back to the car, Dahlia took The Book out of the shopping bag — Hello again, Gene! — and held it close to her chest, half hoping, then hating the hoping, that that blue-green might radiate through her somehow, spare her chemo and the rest. What would happen if she dared to hope such a thing and it turned out to be not remotely possible? Could your heart break, on top of and even after death, from thwarted hope? This was a legitimate fear.

"Shotgun," she said to her mother. The small joys.

Bruce held on to her as they walked like he was determined to keep her safe, like he wasn't going to let anything, anything, anything happen to his girl. A little late and lame, but sweet, still.

In the car, Margalit flipped through *The Bad Girl's Guide to Beating Cancer* and started in with her whimpering again. On the cover of *The Bad Girl's Guide* was a cartoon rendering of a plucky chick with no hair, one absent breast, combat boots, and a leafy carrot held aloft, fiercely, like a weapon.

"This isn't for her," Margalit managed from the backseat. "This is not for her."

Right, no: because "she" was going to be fine.

Bruce watched the road, his face (Dahlia didn't even need to look at it to know this) that unique mask of phlegmatic bearing.

"Let's go to the Plum Core," Dahlia said, totalitarian: She was the guest of honor at the table of however long she had left. "I'm hungry."

Margalit picked up *Heal Thyself,* the cover of which displayed an abundance of leafy greens.

"She shouldn't eat crap."

"She can eat whatever the fuck she wants," Dahlia snapped.

The Plum Core was a dilapidated burger joint cowering in the shadow of a monolithic mall in west L.A., the inspiration for Aaron Spelling's famous TV hangout, the Peach Pit. It had already occupied the lot for some thirty years when the mythic shopping mall makers bought up the entire block in the early eighties. The entire block, that is, except for the tiny corner lot occupied by the beloved burger joint.

Rumor had it that all manner of pressure, legal and otherwise, friendly and otherwise, had been leveled at the Plum Core for years. The mythic mallmakers needed that corner lot, and they needed it bad. Their solid block of mythic mall was impeded only by the stubbornness of the storied burger joint. Op-eds were written, outrageously high purchase prices proposed; the Plum Core was offered a "plum" spot in the future mall's food court, rent-free, until approximately the end of time. Those mallmakers tore their mythic hair out. The rest of the block, in the meantime, lay fallow; the mall remained mythic.

The owners of the Plum Core — middle-aged brothers whose father, an old Hollywood propmaster, had realized a lifelong dream when he'd opened the place — weren't playing hardball. They weren't negotiating, they weren't holding out for a better deal. They just wanted to stay right where they were, in their dilapidated corner with its square counter and red vinyl stools and four ancient, tiny jukeboxes. They had a good life and a good business, which was all they needed or wanted.

So they didn't budge. The mall was eventually built anyway, minus the tiny corner lot where even still you can get a delicious (carcinogenic), greasy all-American meal. The countermen, middle-aged Hispanic men who'd been working the joint since they were teenagers, were famously curt. They took your order, they barked at each other with mock animosity, and they dropped before you with startling speed and accuracy exactly what you wanted, exactly the way you wanted it.

And in light of recent developments, Dahlia wanted just this: to be treated with gruff benevolence by paper-hatted old men who had valiantly held out against corporate, money-shilling mallmakers, whose operation in the shadow of said huge mall was unchanging and could be counted upon indefinitely. It was a small victory, a righteous mainstay in a world overtaken, block by block, inevitably, by malls. But not this block. Not this day. No sir, Gene.

She hadn't eaten meat in years (smoking, sure; alcohol, sure; psychedelics, sure; meat, *never!*), but today she wanted a cheeseburger with pickles and special red sauce, and a piece of banana cream pie. She overrode her own distaste for the sizzling, greasy patties on the open grill: It was time to rip shit up. This was bottom. Or top, if you're thinking food chain. *Eat it,* she ordered herself. Or be eaten, right? She made disgusting, feral noises when she tore into it, like the animal she was. It amused her, the first tiny, genuine giggle she'd had in what felt like forever.

"Mmmmmrgh," she said.

Bruce and Margalit weren't eating. They were frozen into a tableau of shock: Still Life with Untouched Cheeseburgers and Imminent Mortality. A counterman gracefully spun a plate of fries in front of them, whipped out a ketchup bottle and, with three decisive and graceful shakes of his arm, left them a neat swirl for dipping. Then he was off. Bruce and Margalit followed his movements with listless eyes.

Dahlia stuffed a handful of fries into her mouth, *grrrrr*-ing all the while, laughing at her own weirdness, her own weird sound effects. They were too hot, burned her tongue and the roof of her mouth. She swallowed them down regardless, reached for more, happy to be eating in this way, happy to be alive and eating at all, and she let her mouth burn. Living it up.

"Eat," she told her parents.

They dutifully picked up their burgers, held the burgers in midair, and then seemed promptly to forget where the burgers were headed.

"Eat!"

They took small bites.

"We need to get a second opinion," Bruce said. Margalit brightened.

"Yes, that is exactly what we'll do. That asshole" — she meant Dr. Cracker — "knows nothing."

"I have a call in to Barry Kantrowitz," Bruce informed Dahlia. "He'll know who to talk to."

And all at once the burger was too much for Dahlia. It was too rich, too salty, too juicy, pungent, dead. It was a piece of meat. She didn't eat meat. She hadn't eaten meat since high school, when she'd been on the receiving end of some persuasive vegetarian proselytizing (among other things) from Uri. She liked not eating meat. Not eating meat had become a part of who she was, what she talked about on dates. She gagged.

Motek! Margalit hopped off her stool to get as close to Dahlia as possible and proffer a paper cup of water. "Oh, *Habibi,* it's going to be fine. You're going to be fine. It's going to be fine." She stroked Dahlia's back, crowding her at an odd, uncomfortable angle. Margalit only offered whatever it was inconvenient to take.

"Stop," Dahlia said, pushing her mother back and holding her at arm's length. She just needed to breathe, was all. She just needed some air. From a crusty jukebox: *Did you ever see a dream, walking? Did you ever hear a dream, talking?*

"Okay," Margalit said. "It's all going to be okay, *motek.* You're going to be just fine."

Bruce nodded his agreement.

This was not unlike when they'd split up, the denial-happy bastards: everything under the table, everything swept aside, the possibility of facing difficulties head-on so terrifying, so unthinkable to these people that they'd rather endure any amount of excruciating silence instead. Was this why *they* didn't have Cancer? Because they'd made lives so fervently invested in *not* dealing, in looking on the purported bright side, in moving forward at any cost? In neglecting somehow to admit to themselves and their children that they were getting freaking divorced (for example)? Because, when it came right down to it, they didn't need to face it and face it and face it? (And then hold it and hold it and hold it?) Because they were capable of living this other way? All this time Dahlia had been convinced that she was superior: the kind of person who can face shit, who can stare it down and name it and live with it and regularly feel around in her pocket for the sharp edges of it. But all this time it had just been piling up, accumulating like lint in the dryer filter of the self. So now her mixed-metaphorical cup runneth over. With shit. From her fundamental devotion to dealing.

"No," Dahlia said coolly. "No, I'm not going to be fine." And here she was tempted to rip back into the burger for the tearing up of *other* flesh. "I'm not going to be fine," she said again, just for the sheer relief of seeing Margalit's face go all to pieces, irreparable. "I am not fine." *Fine* was not a lie she could live with. Clearly she had not been, was currently not, and would not ever be *fine*.

Margalit sat heavily back down on her stool. The countermen looked at them, briefly, concerned. One came over.

"The burgers is okay?"

"The best," Dahlia told him. He looked at the swaddled patch of her scalp. He looked at her face, at her parents, and then he walked away again.

85

"Let's stay positive," Bruce hummed. "There's no reason you can't get through this . . . not the worst possible . . . a second opinion." Margalit dabbed at her eyes with stiff, papery napkins from the dispenser.

The counterman danced back over with a piece of pie. "Banana," he said, "on the house! Beautiful girl! Don't be sad!"

"Thank you," Dahlia said to him, thinking: *yes*. Banana cream pie on the house was perhaps, possibly, curative. Gene? What do you say?

5. GET A SECOND OPINION

You *must* seek out a second opinion. Your vigilance and determination can make all the difference as to how you're treated, where you're treated, and how well your treatment addresses the problem at hand.

Bruce Finger and Margalit (nee Shuker) Finger had married and settled down to live and work side by side on her beloved Kibbutz Dalia, where they established an early, makeshift domestic pseudobliss eventually eroded only by such insignificant factors as reality and time. An old story.

The Shuker family's roots went wide and deep in Babylonian Jewry. They had fled Iraq in 1951 for the blooming desert of Eretz Yisrael, part of a mass exile, more than 120,000 Jews to leave Iraq between the years of 1948 and 1952, after martial law had been declared and the rise of Arab nationalism began to directly threaten the welfare of every Jewish man, woman, and child. Margalit's family had by all accounts been prosperous, established; her father an exporter and her mother a respected artist. "I had seventy-two first cousins," she liked to tell people. Like much else that came out of her mouth, this was an exaggeration. "We left everything behind. We were forced out of our homes." This was not. Margalit had landed in Israel with five siblings and their never-to-recover, by now long dead parents. Politically, she was slightly more Zionistic than even the hardest-line Zionists, which is to say completely insane. Israel's existence was divine right. Nothing else, *no one* else, mattered the way *Israel* mattered. They'd had nowhere else to go. They were making the desert bloom.

Enter Bruce, your typical third-generation American Jew: Zionism-infatuated and in the throes of what today might be known as a "quarter-life crisis." Margalit was heady, moody, hot-blooded, and "passionate." Bruce: Law Review. He loved the way she'd flip out on him for no apparent reason, thought it was sexy, interesting. She made him laugh. Her lack of perspective, her refusal to submit to calm. She was so . . . *Israeli!* So *Sephardic.* She was nothing like the mousy, materialistic Jewish girls he'd known.

Margalit was pregnant with Danny almost immediately, and Danny, it was generally agreed, had been horrendously difficult right from the start. Wouldn't sleep through the night, didn't verbalize a goddamn thing until he was almost three, and in general just needed so much — there was so much defensive, wounded, bottomless *need* in him — that Margalit and Bruce were utterly exhausted. They were shell-shocked new parents well into Danny's toddlerhood, when all the conventional wisdom had long since failed them; it wasn't colic, it wasn't teething, it wasn't (as they briefly feared) some form of developmental disability, it wasn't *just that age,* it was simply that their son was a fucking asshole. Nazi general in a previous life; or wife beater, or cheapskate moneylender, a crook of some sort, an animal abuser maybe, a fascist. A real asshole, at any rate, that kid. Always in a bad mood, always biting and hitting, always scowling. Hilariously bald as a paperweight well past infancy. They duct-taped his diaper on to prevent him from indulging in his favorite pastime: reaching in to finger paint with his shit. They had to carry him everywhere; he refused to learn to walk.

They had to entertain him constantly; he refused to take care of himself for even a minute. He screamed bloody murder if they left him anywhere, with anyone, for any length of time. Leaving him in the kibbutz children's house was out of the question.

Most kids, when engaged or smiled at or shown affection/attention, will eventually respond in some way: They'll smile back or blush or hide behind a familiar pair of legs. Danny was unflappable. There were precious few calculated smiles in him. Aunt Orly, Margalit's youngest, most beloved sister, would sing him songs, clapping and jumping around, to no effect. The kibbutz cook, Etamar, nicknamed him "The *Miezkeit*" (unhappy-face) and set about to try and elicit some response from the kid. Etamar would make food-people for Danny — celery bodies, raisins-on-toothpick eyes, beet breasts, orange-slice shoes — and watch, bemused, for any reaction at all. Danny would just look at the things, sometimes offer a controlled smile, and simply say, eventually, *"Todah."*

(Wasn't it Danny, really and truly, who should have the big C? Danny who should, rightfully, be Sick? Danny, who was secretly and then not-so-secretly and then sheepishly and shamefully resented and honestly disliked by both of his parents from almost the moment of his birth? It was Danny, truly, who should be wrong, inside out, rotted and doomed. Wasn't that just like life? Danny was healthy as a horse, Danny would live to procreate, Danny would outlive them all. Goddamn, the thought made her even angrier than usual, which was, of course, something of a snowball: The angrier she got the sicker she'd get, and the angrier that would make her. This was, according to The Book and by all other obvious accounts, not good.)

Margalit and Bruce had waited until their holy terror was almost six years old, when finally he seemed capable of living according to the kibbutz system — children bunked by age, apart from their parents — before it occurred to either of them to have another. Hell, they barely had the opportunity to entertain another conception, Danny clung to them so forcefully. Maybe it was the trepidation involved in their wanting Dahlia; maybe it was in the way they wanted another child, a sibling for the little shit, but couldn't help worrying that they'd end up with another Danny. Maybe at the moment of ejaculation Bruce had had second thoughts, had tried to pull out. (This is difficult, imagining one's parents' copulation and consequent conception, use of a colloquial like "pulling out" in reference to one's parents' genitalia, but this is required material, cannot be looked away from, avoided, ignored. Is that sufficient, or do we need to get into an imagining of grunting, faces, feet in the air? Because if anyone is looking away, wincing, or thinking *this is in poor taste,* we *will* go into it. We'll go into it and into it and into it and into it, word rape, until you, too, have cancer. Understood? Yes? Okay.)

Or maybe it was an inkling, taking root in Margalit's mind as the multiplying Dahlia cells (overlapping and multifaceted as a flower) took root, that this life on the kibbutz with a conventional husband and not one shit-headed tyke but *two* wasn't really for her after all. Maybe Margalit, at the very moment of becoming pregnant, had had a sincere and indelible moment of: *Oh, no.* Maybe this was all it had taken to set Dahlia wrong, her embryonic subdivision carrying itself out like mad, off kilter.

Margalit had been inconsolable when she realized she was pregnant. She didn't want another after all. Danny felt like a stone strapped to her back for the rest of her life. She couldn't imagine another Danny. Aunt Orly was about to get married and move to

Tel Aviv. The kibbutz, until then such a source of pride and happiness, was beginning to feel limiting and punishing, the work endless and the communal nature of things intrusive. Bruce began putting out feelers back in the States, looking around for some concrete reason — a job — to move back. He reinstated his membership in the California State Bar Association. This notion seemed to cheer Margalit up some: a house, privacy, a lawn. The States: okay!

So when Margalit was six-and-a-half months pregnant they packed up their awful six-year-old son and moved to Los Angeles, where Bruce had been offered a legal job with a huge real estate developer. Danny shook Etamar-the-cook's hand once, solemnly, before they left.

It was a bad move. The end of the pregnancy was difficult, worse than the first — bloating, moodiness, back pain — and Margalit found herself depressed and lonely, beside herself with longing for Orly and the kibbutz, unable to acclimate to her new surroundings. Bruce was under immense pressure to somehow make the transition and, indeed, life, okay for everyone. He spent huge chunks of time at his office, leaving his swollen, miserable, homesick wife alone with their dour son. Grim. And Dahlia gestating in it all.

But regardless: Dahlia had emerged into the world a seemingly beautiful, perfect, intact being, the light of their lives, the sweet baby girl they had wanted, needed, hoped for. June 27, 1978. For Bruce it was love at first sight, all the usual clichés, the requisite muck. A charming, fat, smiley, easy baby; the anti-Danny. She mirrored faces early, she grinned and cooed, she charmed passersby. She could happily play with a mobile or rattle or pile of Cheerios for hours. She was Danny's antidote, the universe's way of making it *maybe* possible for Margalit and Bruce to have a nice life together.

They named her Dahlia, after the longed-for kibbutz, the added "h" an affectation suggested by Margalit, who thought it feminine and lovely and floral. As if they might return. As if their connection would not be the least bit compromised by a stint of living in Southern California. Far away from Dalia, a place she had been all too willing to leave behind, Margalit idealized it, yearned for it, spoke of it to the vapid women in Mommy-and-Me as though it were heaven itself.

Still, Dahlia's birth was a kind of rebirth for all of them. Margalit's enormous dissatisfaction went temporarily on the back burner, her yen for adventures and freedom and her family in Israel and the kibbutz and *sabra* children who spoke effortless Hebrew temporarily assuaged. And even Danny seemed to perk up, shift slightly. He was fascinated by this new person, he loved the presents she got, and he regularly went so far as to park himself by her crib to watch her sleep. Margalit thought about taking the baby back to Israel to visit, about Danny's apparent maturity and positive development with regard to his new role as somebody's big brother, about her smart husband, whose big, important job had him making money hand over fist, her nice life. They bought a house in Pacific Palisades, a huge house. They took a lot of pictures, they laughed at their adorable daughter. For a time, things seemed to be working. It had been a difficult transition, to be sure. But now it would all be okay. Danny found his calling in comforting and entertaining his baby sister. It got so that Dahlia couldn't be put down for a nap or bathed or comforted after a boo-boo unless it was by Danny. Bruce and Margalit watched incredulously as their total prick of a little boy morphed into his sister's adoring caretaker. Danny would play dolls with Dahlia for hours on end. He read to her, he made up private, preverbal jokes with her, rushed home from school to hang out with her. And she, in turn, adored him.

As an adult Dahlia would reflect bitterly on this early bond — of which she had virtually no memory — as being a clear by-product of Danny's arrested prepubescent angst: He was allergic to dogs, so he'd made Dahlia his pet. He just wanted an excuse to play with her fucking dolls, the little shit. He was trying to adjust to a new life in a new environment and instinctively seized upon tiny Dahlia as a sort of proxy. She was surely the only person he knew who was even more helpless (and, on the rare occasion that she cried ceaselessly through the night, more terrified and enraged-seeming) than himself.

But no: Forget what came later. These were some positives, weren't they? An eventually wanted child, a happy birth, a nice early childhood amidst a revived family in a hopeful new setting? A big brother who adored her, whom she adored in return?

She called herself "La-La," the earliest, closest approximation of "Dahlia" she could manage, and it stuck. Danny shortened it to a simple "La": concentrated building block of a song with Dahlia at its joyous heart. "La!" he would call out to her. "La, La, La,

La!" She would laugh herself into a case of the hiccups, then laugh still more.

Dahlia loved him. She was, frankly, *in* love with him, her beautiful and smart and kind and loving big brother. He gave her wet kid kisses and played with her endlessly, tenderly. He mimicked a singing Italian man from a pizza commercial whenever she was sad: *Whatsa matter you? Why-a you look-a so sad? It's-a not so bad!* She loved him. (There: There it is. Doom.)

In her favorite of the proliferate home movies from that time, Bruce had simply left the camera on Danny and Dahlia for close to an hour while they watched *Sesame Street* together. A metafilm: a movie of two kids watching television (had that already been done or had Bruce broken new media ground?). Danny was technically too old to be watching *Sesame Street,* but he was clearly enjoying the hell out of it with Dahlia, because that's just how much they loved to hang. It was, to a casual observer, a fairly boring video: eight-year-old Daniel and two-year-old Dahlia curled up together in their jammies on the couch, a giant pacifier in Dahlia's mouth (no wonder the eventual need for such extensive orthodonture), occasionally giggling together, the sounds of loopy Big Bird and

97

dopey Cookie Monster and abrasive Oscar and the odd xylophone interlude running commentary. But there was something else there, if one knew to look for it: Dahlia's gaze, which she directed for brief moments away from the TV and up at Danny, her big brown eyes sleepy, dreamy, so full of worship and trust, so blindly loving, so grateful, at two, for her big brother's warm body next to hers, for the way he would surely love and protect her and be her friend forever.

Margalit, wandering through the den with a glass of orange juice and a book, could be heard to mutter at Bruce (right before the tape crackled and went black): "Who do you think wants to watch this boring shit? Enough with the video camera, for god's sake! Idiot."

As Dahlia grew older and life turned increasingly fetid, she looked obsessively back at that family, looked agonizingly often at those pictures and movies: It was like she had been a child star, part of something amazing, endlessly interesting and perfect, burnished to a reflective sheen. It was like looking at herself in a parallel universe, another existence entirely. It looked like Camelot. It must not have been, of course: Margalit was a moody bitch and grew more miserable with her choices and her life by the minute, always snapping at Bruce, always snapping at the kids, without warning storming around the house barking at everyone for no reason whatsoever other than that they were *there:* alive, comprising a life she wasn't made happy by.

Dahlia's inaugural drug of choice was family media; those videos, the photo albums so painstakingly and lovingly compiled by (who else?) Bruce. She had them all memorized, year by year, images burned into her brain, so it was almost like she had been there, really been there, cognizant. That was her! That little girl was her! Could that little girl really have been her? Yes. Yes, it was.

She obsessed over those pictures, over the gorgeous child she had been in the context of that gorgeous family. Margalit with her thick, black-red henna hair and giant sunglasses and regal Babylonian bone structure and hourglass figure — she must have been, what? thirty-one? thirty-two? — Bruce tall and broad, exceedingly proud of his family. He wasn't in too many of the pictures; he was usually behind the camera. There was almost a stop-motion effect to the albums. Bruce would crouch behind the lens for minutes, hours, snap-snap-snapping away at his beautiful children playing in their sprawling backyard. He was enthralled equally with the fruits of his loins and his state-of-the-art photographic equipment. The combination of the two was enough to fill at least a half-dozen albums per year.

The sight of them all, whole and real and (seemingly) right, evoked a strange pride in her: That was *me.* That was *us.* Look at what we/I had. Look at how effortless and normal and right it was. Dahlia had been an actual part of it, and there seemed to be a blessing of sorts in that, a benediction. Here was evidence that she was good, all was okay. Ample grace in evidence. And yes: That was *her.* She could not get enough of the baby pictures, an inconsistency throughout her adolescence and thereafter, which clashed with the drugs and the raccoon eyes and combat boots and the recreational arm-slicing. Hers was the only college dorm room in which Ani DiFranco posters and bong and Barbara Kruger postcards and misanthropic bumper stickers rubbed elbows so comfortably with frames and frames and yet more frames full of Finger family idyll, circa 1980.

It got so that the adult Dahlia would sleep with anyone who even feigned interest in her baby pictures. She'd dated a guy — Will? Bill? No, Will — who had, no shit, loved to watch her home movies.

What the hell was Will/Bill's problem, sitting with her in front of Kat and Steph's flat screen, cooing over the gorgeousness of that long lost family of hers, at the precocious verbal ability of little Dahlia, who, despite having some difficulty with her "r"s, could, at two, sing from memory all fifteen thousand verses of the itsy-bitsy spider? Will/Bill, a Greenpoint hipster with tapered jeans and a fucking handlebar mustache, would actually *request* to see the old videos: "Let's watch the one where you guys are playing tag and then you start to cry and your brother kisses your boo-boo and makes it better." There had been no other reason for Dahlia to stay in the relationship, but stay she did. For, what? Two months? Three? All so she could see, through someone else's eyes, the specter of her own long lost family and her own long lost self.

Dahlia was a fierce, funny child, vibrant and present in her own feelings, always feeling her feelings 115 percent. The capacity for joy and sadness and fear and boldness in their little girl was a revelation to Bruce and Margalit. They'd gotten used to blunted, joyless Danny, who was emotional in his way, sure, but whose moods were based not in genuine feeling but a *lack* of genuine feeling.

Dahlia was terrified of the carousel at Disneyland, and so guess what the photo album from Disneyland was comprised of? Why, snapshots of little La La crying her little heart out on round after round after round, that's what. ("I can't watch anymore," Margalit had said, in tears herself.) It was almost like Dahlia *wanted* to be scared, and angry, and upset. Like she *wanted* another round of terror and tears.

Dahlia would demand that *Saying Goodbye to Grandma,* an overwrought picture book about, indeed, saying goodbye to grandma, be read to her over and over and over again. She would sob every time; she would bury her tiny head in Bruce's lap and let loose with every square-inch of herself, but invariably she reached for just that book — for *only* that book — at bedtime. They tried to supplant it with *The Very Hungry Caterpillar, Pat the Bunny, Goodnight Moon,* name it, but Dahlia wouldn't hear of anything except *Saying Goodbye to Grandma.* She knew it by heart.

"Say 'bye Gramma," came the demand after a bath, first thing in the morning, last thing before bed. "Gramma happy life, Gramma time to go," she would recite to herself in singsong rhythm while she played with blocks. "Flower, doggie, kitty, birdie, Gramma, Grampa, too," she would list, all the things one had to say goodbye to in life.

" 'Bye, Gramma!" she would shout as a greeting whenever she saw her Grandma Alice, who, in her early seventies, was incidentally healthy as a horse.

"Well, hello, my girl," Grandma Alice would beam. "Where is it you think I'm going?"

Why would Dahlia demand to be read something upsetting? Why would she instinctively choose to repeat an experience like the carousel, which made her so anxious and uncomfortable? Why would she call upon her most disturbing and scary point of reference at every opportunity? For a time, she had taken to supplanting "hello" with "goodbye." Goodbye, Daddy! Goodbye, *Ima!* Goodbye, ice cream truck!

Why so eager to say goodbye, to reconcile herself with this most mysterious and painful farewell? For the love of god, Bruce and Margalit wondered to themselves, where had these two children come from? The first an emotional amputee whose capacity for feeling *anything* seemed to have been left behind in the womb, grafted like a third arm onto the second, his briefly adored little sister. If you combined the two, they almost made a normal, whole person. *Saying Good-bye to Grandma* was the only book Danny refused to read to Dahlia; it scared the living crap out of him.

"You're gonna get written out of the will unless you knock that off, kid," Bruce would teasingly admonish his cheerful, goodbye-obsessed three-year-old on the way home from a visit with Grandma Alice.

She might as well try it now: Goodbye, cancer! Goodbye, sickness! Goodbye, Dr. Cracker! Goodbye, death! But no dice.

So, a second opinion. Bruce had called up his old college buddy, the despised Barry Kantrowitz (Cornell Medical School, '68). Good old Barry (a fucking *dermatologist,* but never mind) agreed with Dr. Cracker: It was cancer, all right. This wasn't irritable bowel syndrome, for heaven's sake. A lump of malignancy in the left temporal lobe of her brain was a lump of malignancy in the left temporal lobe of her brain was a lump of malignancy in the left temporal lobe of her brain, to paraphrase Gertrude Stein.

For years, right on the fringes of Dahlia's memory, the Fingers and Kantrowitzes had been vacation buddies, annually forgoing their cushy lives from Christmas through New Year's for the well-groomed slopes of Aspen. The fraternal Kantrowitz twins,

Christianne and Rochelle, were two years younger than Danny and three years older than Dahlia. They thought they were such hot shit for being twins — "natural twins!" went the refrain, always unsolicited, from everyone in the family, as though this were an accomplishment not of Jane Kantrowitz (nee McManus)'s hyperactive ovaries, but of the Kantrowitzes' all-around genetic superiority.

The only person who hated the Kantrowitzes more than Dahlia hated the Kantrowitzes was Margalit. Dahlia hated them for their smugness, their golden tight-knittedness, the fact that, eventually, Danny seemed to prefer their company to her own; Margalit hated them for what they represented: banal American Jews with no real connection to or understanding of what it meant to be *part of the Jewish people*. ("Let him go and fight for the right to exist. Let him go and work the land. Let him put those ugly girls to use farming the land. Disgusting, these people. This is what our children will become if we stay here, Bruti. 'Christy'! *Chaval*.")

Margalit's general unhappiness about life in those days often focused itself on a GRE-worthy equation/comparison: The United States: Bad :: Israel : Good. She tried to speak only Hebrew to Danny and Dahlia, but had such an insistent, forceful attitude about it that both kids were compelled to avoid really hearing much. Hanging in Dahlia's childhood room was a huge, colorful, framed poster of fruits and vegetables, arranged like the periodic table and labeled jauntily in Hebrew.

Barry Kantrowitz was on the board of Cornell, and both twins went there, decked out in sweatshirts, etc. from birth (Go, Big Red!). One of the two, Christy, had met her husband there. Poor Rochelle, the runtier, had rebelliously remained single until she was — gasp — thirty-one. There was reason to believe that Danny had nailed both, though probably not at the same time.

Kantrowitz made them an appointment with his golf buddy, a renowned internist, who referred them to a neurologist, who threw *his* hat into the diagnostic ring: Yup, it was cancer, all right. They did some nebulous asking around as a favor and came back with the following: Dr. Cracker was quite well-respected in his field. Dahlia was in good hands. And sure enough, by the way: It was cancer. Yes, it surely was. Did we mention? Cancer.

Dr. C had prescribed an "aggressive" round of radiation followed by chemo, but the neurologist thought that it should go the other way around: aggressive chemo *first,* then radiation.

"Otherwise the tissue will just not be sensitive to the chemo. It's imperative that you do chemo first."

"No, no, no," said Dr. C when they called him to discuss this disturbing contrary opinion. "He has no idea what he's talking about. Radiation first is the best way. I've been doing this for a long time."

The internist threw his hat into the ring in a way Dr. C didn't dare, however, in admitting that it didn't much matter which course of treatment they went with: "Treatment can prolong survival, at best. But most malignant brain tumors are not curable," he told them.

(Margalit and Bruce, united in chorus for days thereafter: "Most! He didn't say *none!* He only said 'most'!")

Too often we are intimidated by the decisiveness and knowledge of medical professionals and assume we must simply take their word for law. Take the case of Melinda, a forty-five-year-old mother of three. Melinda was diagnosed with ovarian cancer and given three months to live. When she sought another diagnosis she was lucky enough to wind up in the office of an oncologist whose experimental

*treatment worked wonders. Today Melinda is
a proud new grandmother at fifty-three.*

Dahlia couldn't be bothered with the
opinions. Look: two experienced doctors,
two divergent opinions. Which meant that
no one knew a thing, really. Dr. C had
expertly displayed and explained that pretty
picture of her brain (a cauliflower floret: a
cruveet, according to her old Hebrew
poster) with its shriveled date pock in the
left temporal lobe (a *tamar*). They were going with Dr. C. First thought, best thought.
A tumor was a tumor was a tumor. A *tamar.*
In her *cruveet.*

They each had their reasons for avoiding
further proactivity: Margalit because she
was an irresponsible drama queen (due
diligence got in the way of hurling herself,
sobbing, at Bruce, at Dahlia, onto various
pieces of furniture), Bruce because he was
in some sort of strange hybrid problem-
solving and denial mode ("Okay, then, let's
just treat this thing and you'll be fine!"),
and Dahlia because, look: The Book she
could handle; it was pretty and blue-green,
finite. Let her parents parent. She didn't
want choices. She wanted this over with,
one way or another. She'd kick back with
Gene, let things run their course. Fiddle
dee dee, or whatever.

Bruce and Margalit could have at it: the decisions and scrambling and responsibility of hope. Annoying as it was in theory — Dahlia being not that far from thirty and having failed to come into her own as a separate entity from these goddamn parents or their financial support in the first place — it was actually a relief. She didn't really want to do her homework. The treatment options, the second opinions, the alternative therapies, the new menus; the hope and more hope pursuit of all that would entail. No magical thinking here, thanks. She was over and out.

When it was all done with, they could build her a memorial auditorium. Julia G. has a whole freaking art complex; Dahlia had glanced through the alumni magazine with news of the groundbreaking, the child-less Grielsheimers half-heartedly jamming shovels into packed earth; and then a few years later the description of a ribbon cutting ceremony, the childless-as-ever Griel-sheimers in their finest, talking about how Julia's spirit lived on in the ceramics studios and split-level, glass-walled gallery. The Julia Grielsheimer Memorial Art Complex.

Dahlia doodled in the margins of The Book: The Dahlia Finger New Media Center. The D. Finger Cultural Consumption

Fellowship. The Finger Archive of Early Childhood Documentation.

6. You're the Boss

Want to live? Roll up your sleeves. You, dear reader, are the master of your own fate. It's choose your own adventure, writ large. You're in charge. This is the biggest job of your life.

The news, speaking of alumni magazines, wild-fired its way to everyone she sort-of-knew and everyone they knew, gossip of the highest order.
 "A brain tumor!?"
 "A brain tumor!?"
 "A brain tumor!?"
 (Yes, she had a brain tumor.)
 Have you heard about Dahlia Finger? Do you know what happened to Dahlia Finger? Jesus. Crazy. Nuts. Do you believe it? Jesus fucking *Christ*. Awful. Rabbi Dan's sister. Bruce Finger's daughter. She was in our freshman dorm. Mara's friend. That girl Aaron/Clark/Jacob dated. She used to work here. That girl. You remember her. I know.

111

Shit. Can't believe it. She lived with Kat and Steph. How fucked up is that? I know. A brain tumor!?

A brain tumor.

She thought she'd have to tell people, break the news, but this turned out to be unnecessary. A, she'd burned most of her bridges anyway, and B, it turned out there was a mechanism already in place for getting this news out, an endless morbidity phone tree, branching off and blooming intricately around Dahlia at its center. Instantly, it seemed, everyone just *knew*. What the hell? Had they seen this coming? It didn't hurt, certainly, that Rabbi Dan served as the linchpin of several concentric social circles; the synagogue youth group circle, the parochial school circle, the summer camp circle, and on and on (and on!). Never mind that Dahlia Finger was mortally ill; Rabbi Dan's *sister* was mortally ill. Now was that a travesty, or what?

Funny that this was the only time you could be sure no one was passing judgment of any kind, whatsoever: They might or might not be thinking it, but this was the singular only time *in your life* you could be sure they'd be keeping their snarky judgments to themselves. She was unassailable. She was going to die.

She repeated her end of the same conversation over and over again.

"Oh my god."

"Yeah."

"Oh my god."

"Yeah."

"That's insane."

"I know."

"Wow."

"Yeah."

"Jesus Christ."

The undercurrent was simple: pity, in its purest form. Shock, awe, dismay, horror, all boiled down to hard, elemental particles: Pity.

These conversations were numbing and communicated nothing. People didn't know what to say. Lots of gods invoked, lots of profanity, silence by the truckload.

Dahlia's cousins in Israel called, but only after six, when the cheap cell plan kicked in. Rafi and Eitan, gruff, chauvinistic sweethearts both. And their wives, Talia and Neshama. Sobbing. Aunt Orly, sobbing. It was like a flash-forward of Dahlia's funeral. Truth be told, it was riveting. Was she supposed to match this horrifying pitch? Was she supposed to provide these shocked bystanders the requisite backdrop of hysteria? Would that make them all feel better?

No one from New York called; she had severed ties. Maybe she'd send out a mass email, like the ones she was forever getting in her old life: *My film is showing at this-or-that festival! I'll be performing this Tuesday at Hank's! The newest issue of Blah-dee-blah features my story about Whatever! My show is up at the Harry Balls gallery!* Sorry for the mass email, Dahlia's would say, but I just wanted you all to know that I have a brain tumor and a bad attitude and am fucked.

"What did they say?" Mara asked, shaken, quiet. She was in residency in Boston, at a prestigious teaching hospital.

"It's cancer."

"What kind?"

"The awesome kind."

There was a pause. *Dead quiet,* Dahlia thought. *Dead, dead, dead.*

"What are your treatment options?"

"Mara, I don't know. Call my dad. He'll tell you everything. I don't know. It's a brain tumor. I'm fucked."

"D."

"Yeah."

"Your attitude is going to be really important in how things go. There've been studies."

Then there were the conversations to which she wasn't privy.

Dahlia could so easily imagine these conversations, and would spend a good deal of her time — whatever time she had left, indeed — imagining these conversations. Conversations people were having about her. No one would be saying "prognosis" or "death," but they would all be thinking both, or some intimation of both: She was done for. "Fucked," in the parlance of the precious few willing to root around alongside her in the steaming mess of it. It would be on their faces, in their calculated grimaces. Poor Dahlia, how awful, oh my, oh no, et cetera. People could only unpack the truth about her — she was a dead woman — when she wasn't around. Otherwise it was shock and pity and pity's semi-contradictory corollary: forced optimism. *She'll be okay, right? Sure! She's so young!*

Privately, everyone would be wetting themselves with relief: Lightning striking nearby is humbling and scary, sure, but it definitively spares the unstruck. In this way they all owed her, big time. Their tea would be tastier than normal. Their beers colder, their movie-going more fun, their burritos spicier, their orgasms heightened. They would be thanking what- or whoever they believed in: Thank you God, thank you Jesus, Mohammed, Buddha, thank you John

Lennon: It's not me.

She both hated and loved the thought of these conversations, her narrative playing itself out elsewhere. She hated having her fate floating out in the ether, out of her control. Did these people think they knew her? Fuck them. But she also felt vaguely famous, an ersatz celebrity. Which was sort of fun. Didn't gossip mean that people cared, at least a little bit?

Remember that girl I used to live with? Dahlia? She has cancer. Oh my god. Hey, remember Dahlia Finger? She went out with Jenny's brother like six years ago? She has cancer. She had cancer. She's, like, dying. She died.

Everyone dumbstruck. Dahlia lightning-struck, and everyone around her dumb-struck. But of course, she reasoned, better cancer than dumb. Better anything than dumb. Throughout the visits that would surely follow, with the balloons and the bears and the immediate drama (which required a certain requisite amount of action and good cheer and optimistic tripe), they'd be struck dumb. What funny, disparate things we're all struck by in this life. Between cancer and dumb, which would you rather? A hard one. Take your time. Where, pray tell, was the very necessary *The*

Dummies Guide to Dealing with Other *People's Cancer?*

Look, it's not the worst thing in the world. She's still breathing, after all. Every moment of our consciousness might be a fitful sort of daydream anyway, right? So what if she's going to die? She could get hit by a bus tomorrow and die. She could outlive anyone, everyone. The old, old man on that bench at the mall is totally going to bite it before Dahlia does, and look at him there, licking his rapidly melting ice cream cone with such revelry.

It's decidedly bizarre, when the Worst Thing happens and you find yourself still conscious, still breathing. She was still blinking, still swallowing, still scratching the itch on her neck, still reminding herself to sit up straighter, still wondering what was for lunch, still coveting the pretty earrings on the girl who had made her latte weeks earlier. *Oh, but she was going to die.* Still, what was for lunch?

One was much more typically "upset" when it was happening to somebody else. Witness Julie G: Dahlia, to this day, speaks (and thinks, even) about her in reverential tones, with hushed respect and total terror at the thought of offering any condolences, of doing or saying the wrong thing, of making it somehow worse. How do you ever approach anybody else's travesty? Your own, though: with your own you could have some fun.

There is one given: With the right attitude you can live a much longer life. Maybe you think things are hopeless, and that's understandable. But try to remember, even in your darkest moments, that you can alter the course of your disease. It's up to you.

One quickly figures out that there are three kinds of people.

First there are the people who cower at all costs from trauma and loss and death. These people will say nothing. They will not come near.

Next there are those who are terrified of death but are still, it would seem, in possession of a semi-workable soul. These people will gingerly, fearfully approach in some utterly lacking way. They will stammer and hem and haw; then they will fail entirely to offer comfort. They will, in fact, make it worse. They will so ineptly attempt to address the abyss into which you are staring that you may even wind up comforting *them*. This is kind of funny and kind of tragic, but at any rate at least better than the first kind of people, who should be rounded up and shot, or, at the very least, get cancer.

Lastly there are people, rare, rare people, who can stare into the lonely, mysterious everlasting right alongside you, who can hold your hand, and who do not flinch from any part of whatever horrendous ordeal is at hand. Such people are precious and valuable. Here's hoping they don't get cancer (for a long time, at least).

Lucky for her, Dahlia had one of each prototype on display in her very own immediate family.

The first: Danny, a cowardly piece of shit. If shame were communicable by osmosis, he'd be stewing in a fiery cauldron of it, the fucking imbecile. (But here's the reality, out there in the ether, aimed squarely: You Are Going to Die, Too. Big time.)

The second: Margalit. Who might hang around emoting and whatnot so long as it was mildly entertaining. For which she gets a half-hearted pat on the back and directive to please, please fuck off.

One of the rare few: Bruce. God bless and keep him far away from illness.

But then again, Dahlia felt worse — more alone, more frustrated and desperate and sad — when it occurred to her that people might *not* be talking about her. That long lost elementary school classmates, people she'd partied with after college, people she'd temped with here or there, acquaintances, might not know about this, or might not care. Dahlia *who?*

Because: What if no one was talking about her? What if no one knew? What if she was to die and cause hardly a ripple in the lives of everyone she'd ever known? What if what she'd assumed were semi-meaningful associations built up over the course of her life were really just indifferent non-relationships after all? Was it possible that the horror of this wouldn't ruffle anyone else? If she'd had a significant other, a *dog,* an apartment of her own. Anything! But she had only bad credit, exes, and a small mortgage on a house that had been handed to her. So now she has cancer and it's back home to Daddy. Fuck, she thought. Over and over again: fuck. The only thought that made the least bit of sense: fuck. (Why so profane, ask the bookclubbers? Because we are talking here about death, and fuck you if you don't like it: You're going to die, too. This is *serious.* Fuck fuck fuck.)

She vacillated between feeling furious that her fate was gossip fodder and feeling furious at the possibility that there wasn't *even* gossip swirling about her, that no one gave a shit whether Dahlia Finger lived or died, that when it came down to it her existence

120

had been absent anything that would make anyone miss her. This was when people were supposed to emerge from the woodwork, the taken-for-granted tapestry of her existence, and surround her with love and support and the promise of heartfelt, devastated eulogies. But there was, in fact, only silence. Dead silence. Tick, tock.

Here was Dahlia, more than a decade later, still thinking about Julia Grielsheimer, for god's sake. Who would be thinking of Dahlia ten years hence? You were supposed to fill your life up to the brim with people who would be very upset when you died. It occurred to Dahlia that *that* — That! — was the whole *point.*

She wanted decorum tossed out the window, propriety trampled underfoot, all bets off. She wanted people illogical, unhappy, incapable of going on without her.

Briefly, shamefully, Dahlia allowed herself to wish that Rabbi Dickhead would show up for this, would resume his long-abandoned role as beloved big bro. She wanted him back, back the way he'd been before she could really remember him, anyway. Back before he'd existed in current form. Way back.

"Does Danny know?" Dahlia asked her father.

"Of course," Bruce answered.

"What does he know?" she pressed.

"That you're sick."

"What else?"

"That we're going to figure out what to do. That it's not . . . in the worst possible place."

"You told him everything?"

"Yes."

"And what did he say?"

"To keep him posted."

"Is that it?"

Bruce nodded.

When she was six years old, Danny had saved Dahlia's life. Bruce, as usual, was away on business, and Margalit had left the kids with yet another inept, apathetic sorority girl from UCLA.

Things were, by then, already badly deteriorated between their mother and father, but Danny and Dahlia pretended not to notice, or really *didn't* notice, or some unfortunate combination of the two. Maybe they could sense that they had precious little time left to live out the paradigm they'd taken for granted: life-of-the-party, legendarily edified mother, sturdy, loving father, each other. Maybe they just didn't really add it up: Bruce away and then away still more, Margalit out Israeli dancing every

Tuesday and Thursday, *Ima* and *Abba* barely near each other, scarcely speaking.

Margalit fell victim to increasingly terrible mood swings that year. It was with stomach-clenched uncertainty that Dahlia and Daniel and Bruce came home from school and work, respectively. Would Margalit have made dinner and be smiling, affectionate, inquiring about their days? Or would she be slamming drawers and muttering to herself about having to do everything herself? Or would there be some delicate balance wherein everybody sat on pins and needles, trying not to tip the scales by, say, failing to help set the table? It was generally hard to say. The only constant was inconsistency. *Ima*'s moods were capricious and terrifying.

They were eating dinner at the kitchen table, sitting catty-corner, the babysitter reading *Cosmo* at the foot of the table, bored, her blue-and-gold sweatshirt embroidered with a Delta, a Phi, and an Epsilon. They had been in the States for six years, and Dahlia had just started the first grade, not yet upgraded from lunchbox to backpack.

Danny was rearranging the food on his plate for Dahlia's entertainment, doing an excellent Swedish-Chef-from-the-Muppets imitation. ("Dur-dee-dur-dee, Froogleoogle-argle-oo, darf-dee-darf") and Dahlia was giggling and giggling and giggling still more. She was also continuing to eat as her laughter mounted, and, after swallowing a mouthful of peas and rice, suddenly found that she could not breathe.

She could not breathe. Not in, not out. She could not breathe. She tried to make a noise. She could not. Breathe. She panicked, still, strangely, laughing. She panicked more, embarrassed now, and trying to laugh (with no air) at her own dumb self. She kicked her legs, eyes bulging as she tried to take in air. She could not breathe. She understood instinctively that she had done something stupid, something wrong, and that it ("it": *this*) was her own fault.

The babysitter looked up from *Cosmo.*

Danny reached over and smacked Dahlia on the back, saying "Come on," and rolling his eyes. There were already limits to his compassion, faint, Etch-a-Sketch boundaries beginning to make themselves clear. The year before, Dahlia had slipped out of her kindergarten classroom and shown up at the door of the sixth grade, homesick. Danny had hustled her back to her own classroom impatiently, annoyed, and just given her a hard peck on the top of her head, meant to last her the rest of the day.

She couldn't breathe.

"Shit," said the babysitter.

After what felt like a lifetime, Danny went around to her back and hugged her, hard. She still couldn't breathe, but now she felt calm; Danny loved her, Danny was with her. It was okay now, it didn't matter whether she got air again or not. *Thank you,* she would have said, had she been able.

Later she would hear the name of what Danny had done: *the Heimlich Maneuver.*

A mushy clump of rice and peas came flying out onto the table, and air, sweet air, came rushing back into Dahlia's body. It was the most delicious thing she had ever experienced. Heaven. The gold standard to which every high she'd ever have would be held.

"Eww," said the babysitter.

Later, with her parents and Danny carefully arranged in the living room, Dahlia had put on a special pageant for them, a hero's reception, in which she lip-synched and performed her own choreography to "Holding Out for a Hero" by Bonnie Tyler, which had recently been featured in *Footloose* and was all over the radio. *He's gotta be strong and he's gotta be fast and he's gotta be fresh from the fight!* She presented Danny with a drawing of herself choking (complete with enormous green peas floating over her face) and him behind her, saving her.

"He *saved* me!" she crowed to Bruce and Margalit, who sat far apart on the couch, equally annoyed and stricken, and feeling, individually and collectively, like the worst parents in the world. They traded a single, commiserative glance, momentarily aspiring to try and be happy together.

Anyway, again: this current travesty almost superseded by an earlier one.

According to Gene, Dahlia was the CEO of her own wellness. Fuck the GRE, man; she was starting at the top.

Leadership and delegation distinguish a good CEO from a poor one. Your oncologist is your VP, your right hand man, your go-to guy. Your family and friends are your sales reps, your middlemen. Remember: You are in charge. Inspire a can-do attitude in yourself and your team.

A good CEO would surely get her director of publicity on the horn and send out an all-points bulletin: It's not in the worst possible place, she's young, she's healthy, and she's going to beat the crap out of this. Spin it. Get people talking. Buzz.

She'd heard about some schmuck who'd recently accepted twenty grand from some lame Internet company to tattoo the company's name on his forehead. Her advertising people should get on that, find someone even more pathetic than Dahlia herself to get a "Dahlia Finger, 1978–?" put somewhere visible. You had to be creative with marketing. Let's go, people!

Dahlia considered her "team." Margalit alternated between hysterics and stunned silence, her face raw from weeping, her eyes preternaturally puffy.

"*Doda* sends you a big, big kiss!" Margalit would yell (she was being positive, Gene) before getting off the phone with Aunt Orly in Tel Aviv.

"I cannot believe this is happening," she said.

"It'll be okay, *Ima*," Dahlia told her.

Margalit just stared into space, the wind gone from her sails. It was amazing to see Margalit without words. These were Dahlia's favorite moments. So *this* is what it took to shut the woman up. A lifetime of listening to her mother go on and on and on, a lifetime of watching her gesticulate and over-dramatize and use, emphatically, *the most hyperbole of anyone, ever,* and all it took, it turned out, was a soupçon of mortal illness to finally shut her the fuck up.

Bruce was businesslike and dependable, as ever. He toted folders, a binder, clippings, website printouts.

They decided she was to move "home for the time being," which was funny: both the "home" part and the "time being" part.

"What does that mean, do you think?" she asked Bruce.

"Just until you get back on your feet," he said. Treatment would be brutal, that much was unarguable. She couldn't realistically be on her own.

"Home" was Bruce's house. After Margalit had skipped off to get actualized or whatever, they'd sold the Palisades house and Bruce moved to Brentwood with Danny and Dahlia while Margalit stayed with Orly, made earrings in Jaffa, and screwed her way through the Israeli Defense Forces.

"Do you mean my cosmic feet, Dad? Because unless you heard something different, I'm dying."

Here Margalit snapped into furious focus. "You are *not.* STOP THAT."

They went to Grandpa Saul's. Saul was determined to hit a hundred and talked about little else. Dahlia wondered how he'd react to news of his grandchild set to beat him through the pearly gates, if he registered it at all.

The retirement community smelled like it was full of rancid babies, which, in fact, it was. Grandpa Saul had lived there, first with Grandma Alice and now on his own, as long as Dahlia could remember. It was not a happy place.

Surprisingly, she now looked at the guy — ninety-eight years old and shuffling around behind his walker with great, heaving grunts — and wanted to beat the hell out of him. Okay, so old age wasn't a walk in the park. Okay: It must've sucked to wear diapers again and run out of energy on the way to and from the dining room. But what did you expect? Life lasted only so long and then you died. Was this not the mother of all truths? Was Grandpa Saul really to be pitied for making it to the very end of a very long life?

They sat around his cluttered coffee table. Large-print presidential biographies aplenty.

"Pops," Bruce said to his father. "We're here to tell you a little bit about what's going on with Dahlia."

"Why is *she* here?" He pointed at Margalit. Saul had never forgiven his ex-daughter-in-law for her carelessness, her abandonment of his son and grandchildren. Dahlia loved that about him.

"Hello, Saul," Margalit said.

"Pops," Bruce said, louder this time, almost shouting. Saul's hearing was pretty much nonexistent. "We have to talk to you about Dahlia!"

"Hiya, Pops!" Dahlia yelled. "How's it going?"

Saul made a liver-spotted fist, pretended to aim it at Dahlia, grinned. "Why, I oughta . . ."

"I'm really *sick,* Pops," Dahlia yelled.

"Dahlia's got a little *problem,*" Bruce shouted. "But everything's going to be *fine.*"

"Good," Saul said.

"Pops," Dahlia yelled. "I've got ——"

"Don't," Margalit hissed. "That's just not nice."

"He's not a child," Bruce reasoned.

"He can't hear me anyway," Dahlia pointed out.

"How are ya, my ever-loving one-and-only? Got a boyfriend?"

"This is stupid," Dahlia told her father. She turned back to Saul, and reported the facts as best she could. "Got a brain tumor. *Fucked.*"

"I'm almost there!" Saul went on, referencing his favorite subject: longevity. "I'm gonna make it to a hundred! You gonna stay for lunch?" Shameless, really, in light of recent events, that he persists in the *gonna make it past 100!* shtick.

Lunch was saltines and chicken soup.

They sat with Saul amidst the clinking spoons and slurping in the dining hall.

That night, Bruce and Dahlia went to the Venice house to gather some of her things. Toothbrush (was she supposed to keep up with the flossing, now?), XL Lemonheads T-shirt she'd stolen as a token from Clark, the novel she was in the middle of (*The Magic Mountain,* if you can believe that; actually, well, no, sorry, honestly? *The Death of Ivan Ilyich*), and the small tin box containing her weed.

On their way back "home," Dahlia requested a stop. The day had been long and exhausting, her head hurt, her eyes were itchy, and she was spent. But she wanted some normalcy. She wanted a cup of tea. She wanted to be a part of the world and knew no better way than to drop by a café. Her café.

Bruce would wait in the car.

"Want anything?" she asked before getting out. "Sure," Bruce said. "Whatever you're having. Tea, right? Tea sounds good." It was such a banal moment, such a normal, everyday moment, that both were momentarily suffused with a refreshing okayness. Then it went away again.

The counter guy, who'd been flirting shamelessly with Dahlia for weeks and with whom she had decided she'd sleep when the time was right if he continued to gift her with free pastries, said "Hey."

"Hey," she said back. "Can I have two green teas? How's it going?" A rhetorical, for fuck's sake.

"Oh, whatever, I dunno. Been trying to write this spec script with my writing partner and his wife is, like, having a baby now, so our script is fucked. But whatever. It's so hard to find the time. I get so antsy when I'm not writing." He was a real brooder, this one. The type for whom everything was a huge headache, a depressive vortex, all the little pains in the ass life threw you. Kind of like Dahlia had been until last week. (Fine: kind of like Dahlia was, still.) He didn't follow this up with "How are you?" but she offered anyway.

"Yeah, well, I have a brain tumor." She put three dollars down on the counter and smiled, left him there with his brooding jaw unhinged. "See ya."

Your life is a train that is being rerouted. Where would you like it to go from here? Consider the slate wiped clear: You have the chance to start all over again. Nothing that came before matters now. You're free.

Gene said to make a list. This was the A-number-one best thing to do right away, apparently. Because once she'd made a list — a list of good things, things she's grateful for, a list of things she wanted to do in life — then she'd have herself something(s) to live for! And then she'd live! That easy?

A list. List, list, list. A la-la-la list. She loved the Venice house. She loved her television, her cable. She loved her baby pictures, especially the wackier ones, like where she's cracking herself up with a solo game of hide-and-seek in a patch of yard covered with gold afternoon sun. She loved strolling Abbott-Kinney, the way gentrification nestled right up against a thriving gang presence, the way she was mostly secure in the knowledge that she wouldn't bump into anyone she knew. She'd love the wind chime she'd hang when she got around to it. She loved the mental list of great names for kids she'd been keeping since she'd started menstruating (*Rafe, Asher, Chaia;* if any of you lucky reproductive fuckers steal 'em, she'll haunt your dreams forever). She loved thinking about the possibility that someone would learn everything there was to know about her and would love her anyway, would not blink when she picked her nose or said something mean about a relative stranger. She loved the breeze by the water. She loved, loved, loved eating toaster pastries, methodically, in quarters. She loved the thought of being a capable professional, of talking someone out of a heroin relapse, of being the only person who would not flinch at the deepest, darkest reaches of others. She loved watching *Thelma and Louise* over and over and over again and being moved, every time, again. Ditto *National Lampoon's Vacation.* Ditto *The Shawshank Redemption.* Ditto *Pretty Woman.*

And, if she could possibly look both ways and relax into top-secret sappiness for just a fleeting, private moment (but don't get used to it), there was life itself: just the state of being alive, which was all she knew and so was quite precious indeed. The familiarity of it, even of its myriad miseries: precious. Whatever happened after and whatever had come before was surely, at the very least, different. Better? Worse? Neither? No way of knowing, and anyway, it mattered not at all.

She did not love the thought of her likely subpar performance on the GRE. Nor did she love the thought of the life she'd led up to this point: New York, Kat, Steph, the men, the burned-through cash, oh Jesus. Her ruined credit, the nights she'd kept drinking even after she was already drunk, then puked on her floor and had to clean it up herself the next day, the people she'd grown up with who worked as lawyers and i-bankers and served as bridesmaids in each other's weddings and sent out "Happy Holiday" cards every year with sickly sweet photos of their ever expanding families, the imminence of the inevitable announcement by Rabbi Dickhead and his wife, the dreaded Velociraptor, that *they* were expecting.

Shit, Gene! See how it worked? See how the list of things she should hold on to with both hands, to which she should cling ferociously and pull herself back from the brink, morphs into the other list, the anti list? See how this means it's all moot? There was no first list without the second list; there was no second list without cancer. And there was no cancer without these goddamned lists, it seemed.

This progression was the normative unfolding, the only way her brain worked. See? So she made other lists.

Alongside the obvious (growing old), here is a partial list of things Dahlia wouldn't get to do in this lifetime: Go to India. Be in a band. Be in a good mood sober. Have a three-way. Give birth.

The last of which she's especially pissed about. To die after you've had the chance to reproduce, well. On some level that's fair enough.

She compiled that list not so she could spend the however-many-months she had left (this prognosis would differ, maybe, doctor to doctor, day to day, lie to lie, and her folks would continue to bullshit about the possibility of her "making it," to which she says: HA) running around frantically checking them off so she can die with some measure of satisfaction and dignity, some illusory control over what went down. That would be another book altogether (and one that might have a shot at a flipping film option). This was not a draft for the Make-A-Wish Foundation. Though she does wonder what would happen if she wrote to them requesting a three-way. Did they honor those kinds of wishes? Might she find a couple of unemployed porno stars, hung like horses, wearing nothing but giant gift bows and cowboy boots, on her doorstep? And might they then fuck her as though she were healthy? With none of the pity, the *god-awful pity?*

She compiled the list so she could beat everyone else to the punch. It was like calling yourself ugly, stupid, fat; a matter of making sure to get there *first,* to declaw the terrible truth. Sickness was hard enough;

the pity would fucking kill her. Pity was the flip side of the *you can fight it* bullshit. Both were dishonest. Both failed to even vaguely approach the reality of this, which was that her life will have come and gone on earth and meant nothing, have left nothing, have created nothing, and she'd never have had the experience of two men at once in the meantime.

What cliché. Torment. She wanted something new to feel, something organic and original, something unique. The Book also said to make a list of what she *has* gotten to do, what has meant the most. And surely she's lucky compared to Julia G. Certainly she's had a nice run of things in these extra ten or so years, some nice afternoon lattes and moments of clarity in listening to her favorite music and those precious minutes when someone — anyone — spooned her in a clean room under a fluffy duvet and kissed her where her neck and shoulder met and told her she was beautiful (which, she estimated, totaled maybe seven minutes in twenty-nine years), some genuine laughter, the way it had felt to try Ecstasy for the first time, and some possibilities which had seemed, at the time, wonderful.

Okay, so: a different list.

She's excused from life. She's free! No

worries about her performance on the GRE!

Wait, though. No. She's had her heart broken half a dozen times — and we're talking *broken,* man. Shattered. She's developed a kind of disdain for her only sibling usually reserved for despotic political regimes and perpetrators of genocide. She's aimless, she's broke. Ben wasn't remotely her fiancé; and besides which, he'd fucked her like a jackrabbit. Recently, some lady backing out of a parking space had screamed at her ("Get out of my way, you stupid bitch!") for no good reason at all. The world was a terrible place. She hadn't gotten to know Julia G. when she'd had the chance and now Julia G. was dead. She had assumed there was lots and lots of time during which her life would right itself, that she'd wind up one of those eccentric and self-possessed older women with a doting, bemused partner, a late-in-life child or two, and a well-carved niche in the world.

No business plan? No battle plan? She was fired.

7. Trust Your Treatment

The more you believe in the healing potential of your treatment, the more effective your treatment will be. Get excited about it! Embrace it! Chemo is your friend, radiation your pal, surgery a straight-up opportunity.

She kept getting it mixed up. There was the problem of her rapidly degenerating left temporal lobe. But she was also, to begin with, imprecise and distracted, and so found it difficult to focus in on any coherent narrative of what was happening, what was about to happen. She played catch-up, held brief recap sessions, but even those were broadly sketched and blurry, words floating untethered to any reality she could own: *high grade astrocytoma, glioblastoma multiforme.* Biopsy, neurological symptoms, treatment. Radiation. Chemotherapy. Alternatives. Fight it! Let go. Fight! Let go. She was baffled, mostly, and allowed herself simply to be chauffeured, daily, to and from radiation, floating passively along. Then chemo piggybacking, per Dr. C's insistence. But Dahlia was living minute to minute, focusing on the one-at-a-time moments that made up her days. She had delegated, like any good CEO. Bruce was in charge of the binder. He carried it around and updated continuously. Margalit was in charge of crying and raging. Danny was in charge of denial and avoidance. From each according to his abilities, to borrow part of an old chestnut.

The drives to the hospital. The stops at Starbucks, uniform and comforting, the DVDs on hand (Margalit was also in charge of entertainment, always proffering new picks as soon they walked in the door), the trips to Whole Foods for the expensive, organic ingredients in the simple meals they prepared at night. The cast they'd made of her head, meant to hold it in place while the radiation went in at precisely the right angle, at precisely the right spot. The different nurses she saw on different days — Reba, Shelli, Sharlene, and Archie, on a rotating axis — in their different scrubs and clogs. She entrusted herself back into the care of her parents and let herself be carried on the tide, driven to and fro, put into bed at night and awakened in the morning. It was like a vacation, really: new and foreign and removed from regular life.

She wondered: Might she have brought this all about with sheer force of wish? Her inept attempts at adult independence brought so neatly, so powerlessly, to a close? It was bliss (the obvious aside) for the simple fact of taking her life out of her hands. She'd never been good at it — her life, that is — and now something larger than herself had seemingly dismissed her. Her proverbial wheels now spinning in reverse, miles flying off her life, sending her back and back and back.

The car rides to and from radiation recalled being taken to and from school. She sat slumped in the backseat as Bruce and/or Margalit drove. Riding along, twice a day, there and back, passive and sullen, Dahlia could recall car pools, various permutations of backseat comrades, Margalit unhappily at the wheel, driving like a maniac (or an Israeli), and then Bruce for a stretch, and then any number of sympathetic car pool moms ("That poor man, doing it all on his own," they must have said, deciding to include little motherless Dahlia Finger in car pool without forcing her sweet, sad sack single Dad to do his share of the driving.)

She leaned her head against the window and imagined herself being taken to and from Temple Israel Day School, the site of her thorough, non-denominational, formative Jewish education. She tried to will the formation of a time pocket, resolved that when she finally opened her eyes at the end of the ride her Dad would be putting his forest green Jag in park and tapping her on the knee: "Okay, La-la, we're here. Have a great day! I'll see you at three."

Now, just as then, she dreaded having to share alone time in the car with her mother. Bruce-chauffeur days were endlessly preferable to the alternative. Margalit would melt down at any moment, Chernobyl-style. It was no fun being her passenger. Some days you got sunshine and best wishes for a great day, some days you got *get the fuck out of my car,* the vehicle barely stopping for your exit and then screeching into motion again immediately, burnt rubber drawing stares from a sizable assortment of K-through-sixth-graders and their horrified caregivers.

But when Bruce drove her to radiation, as to school, Dahlia felt calm and safe. He brought her tea and helped her into the car, sat with a book, came up with cheerful suggestions of where they might go on the way home: the Plum Core, the Novel, Baskin-

Robbins. He knew how to be silent, how to look over at Dahlia from time to time, smiling in a way she could almost feel at the side of her head.

Margalit, on the other hand, was a stressful pain in the ass: the running commentary, the constant chatter, the mood swings.

"They're doing incredible things with acupuncture. You need to look into that. Have you read the book about the grass juice yet?"

And "Shoshanna knows a woman who does hypnotherapy. Why aren't you interested in this? This is your life, Dahlia. *Your life.* This is serious! This is as serious as it gets! What is the matter with you?" (Uh, cancer, *Ima.*)

And "You need to relax, Dahlia. *Relax.* That is the most important thing: relax!"

And then of course, the favorite track, on a loop: "Do you have any idea how lucky you are?"

It was unbelievably stupid that Dahlia had been irresponsible enough to walk around sans health insurance, but Dahlia had, indeed, been walking around sans health insurance since college.

"Why, yes, *Ima,* I'm probably just about the luckiest girl I know!" She'd never had the kind of job that came with benefits;

she'd never bothered to insure herself. Who did? Certainly no one Dahlia knew. Dahlia, like a lot of people who have everything handed to them ("values" notwithstanding), couldn't be bothered to worry too much about money. She didn't "care" about money. She didn't think about it. It existed. It wasn't her problem.

As it turned out, Bruce had seen to it, unbeknownst to anyone, that Dahlia was in fact fully covered — comprehensively covered, safe. Which was, in light of the whole cancer situation, a really fucking good thing. If slightly demoralizing. She'd been borderline proud of her lack of health insurance. Health insurance was for pussies. She tended bar, she did drugs, she dated inappropriate men, she bought expensive, exquisite Italian leather boots instead of paying rent, she ran up credit card bills she forgot to pay. She was not someone with a 401K or IRA or frigging health insurance. Health insurance would have undermined Dahlia's efforts to be something other than the JAPpy little lemming she feverishly feared herself, way deep down, to be. Purchasing health insurance would have been like giving up. No health insurance: the only way to live. (So long as Daddy secretly had your back, just in case.)

"You're incredibly lucky," Margalit would spit, all adorable Sephardic rage. "Lucky, lucky, lucky! This is not funny! Why do you think this is funny?"

"Yes, *Ima*, I feel very blessed indeed," Dahlia repeated with a sugary smile. "I'm the luckiest girl alive!" Jazz hands.

"Who doesn't have insurance? Who thinks like this? This is a joke to you?"

"You're really sexy when you're all pissed off, *Ima*. Has anyone ever told you that?"

"But she *does* have insurance," Bruce squirmed in a vinyl hospital row chair, with his let's-use-our-indoor-voice voice. "She's covered. It's fine."

"So irresponsible."

"Margalit."

"Your *Abba* is there to save your tuches, as usual."

And yours, Dahlia thought. Who, after all, funded Margalit? But save his *own* tuches, was more to the point. Because Dahlia would eventually be dead and dear old dad would have had to foot the bill anyway. The emergency room and initial hospital stay and radiation and chemo and god only knew what else down the road would've run Bruce some tens (if not hundreds) of thousands of dollars. *He* was certainly a wise businessman to the bitter end: the foresight to cover Dahlia — without fanfare, without even mentioning it — would end up saving him big. A good investment. CEO Dahlia was very pleased, indeed. Bruce would certainly get a promotion in the wobbly metaphorical offices of Help Dahlia Survive, Inc. Pretty amusing that he'd correctly deduced that she wasn't covered in the first place. Of course she wasn't covered. He knew her so well and he loved her anyway. She was one lucky bitch.

She knew how lucky she was. Lucky! It wasn't a matter of not getting into the fantastical car wreck in the first place; it was a matter of having been *wearing your seatbelt* when you got into the fantastical car wreck, see? Because no one was spared the fantastical car wreck.

Monday through Friday, for three weeks, Dahlia was chauffeured to and from radiation, where she was strapped to a table, harnessed into her headgear, and zapped (well, radiated) with a machine that knew just where to beam into her head. Side effects weren't too big a deal. Just total exhaustion and the missing patch of hair, where the bald skin became sensitive and irritated, red and raw.

Radiation treatments are painless. External radiation treatment does not make you radio-

active. It's important to get plenty of rest and to eat a well-balanced diet during the course of your radiation therapy.

Every day one of the nurses expertly arranged Dahlia's radiation setup. They were businesslike and friendly and distant. Every day they asked her how she was doing.

"Any nausea?"

"How are you sleeping?"

"How are we today, Miss Finger?"

Sharlene was her favorite: a bosomy black woman who never wore the cutesy scrubs. It was always solid blue or solid lavender. No dancing puppies here, no ma'am.

"Sharlene, it's *Ms.* Finger. We don't distinguish between married and unmarried women that way anymore."

"Um-hmm," Sharlene would say, making a note on a clipboard and moving along.

Reba was the worst: All dancing puppies all the time, all false cheer. "Well, *hello, sweetheart.* How are we *feeling?*"

Dahlia felt like one of those ancient Greek statues: weathered by time, placid despite (or perhaps because of?) the missing arms and noses and anything else that stuck out, silently begging the tourists to please, please put down their goddamn cameras and just *look* at her for a minute. Stop taking pictures and just *be there,* in the room with her. For a minute.

In the aforementioned idyllic days, the Fingers went back to Israel every summer, and stayed at Kibbutz Dalia or in Tel Aviv, worked and played and hung out and almost forgot they didn't live there. Their albums were thick to bursting with sandaled and sandy Mediterranean candids. Dahlia remembered the aunts and uncles, kibbutz families, swarms of them, yelling. Young, by-then-divorced, gorgeous Aunt Orly. Where in theStates they had only a few random pockets of second- and third-cousin Finger family dregs, whatever faint familial ties a couple generations of assimilation and apathy and diasporatic movement had not thoroughly eradicated, in Israel there were first cousins galore, and *great* aunts, *great* uncles, second cousins, beyond. And everyone *cared,* everyone existed well within the borders of a family identity, everyone hugged you, laid giant smacking smooches on your cheek, happy to see you coming and sad to see you going. Those summers were like rafts; surreal and precious and buoyant, inflated with the fulfillment of every primitive fantasy she'd ever since conjured about family, about community, about love and belonging. Then they would return home to L.A., where things were progressing rapidly down the shitter.

Dahlia could remember feeling smug — once school had started up again and her "real" life stretched, thin to breaking, ahead of her — that she had had that happy life in Israel. She spoke elementary Hebrew with her mom like it was a private gossip language, in public whenever possible, preferably in front of people who couldn't understand them. In car pool she would ask Margalit inane questions about dinner, about the weather, just so the other kids wouldn't understand. She was part of something different and exclusive! She knew something they didn't!

"Kaama ze oley?" *(How much is that?)*, pointing as they passed a big, beautiful house, or "Lama ma kara?" *(What happened?)*, when another driver honked. Margalit just squinted at her, and murmured back in English if she responded at all.

At the Hollywood Bowl one August night, right before Labor Day wiped clean the delicious slate of Israel in favor of the dismal specter of back-to-school, Dahlia had joined Margalit in refusing to stand for the national anthem.

"It's not *my* anthem," parroted seven-year-old Dahlia, her little chest puffed out indignantly. "This is not *my* country."

She could sense that Something was Wrong, something barely perceptible and profound, slow until it was immediate, like the melting and breaking apart of glaciers, between Bruce and Margalit, and in their family as a whole. In the middle of Dahlia's second-grade year, Margalit went to Israel to be alone, unprecedented: to "think," to visit Aunt Orly, leaving Danny and Dahlia with Bruce, who got lost in his own escape of work and wine-in-a-box.

For a good while, Dahlia was actually relieved to find her mother gone. All that unpredictability, all that rage. All the times Margalit was an inconsolable hurricane of fury, lashing out at her husband, her son, her daughter. Whew: Things were relatively so calm with her gone. Exhale: all that intensity, all that vitriol. And sure, Bruce seemed terribly distraught and distant, but at least he was *nice.*

Bruce had brought from his office a giant, blank, month-long calendar, and he gave Dahlia special stickers to affix to each passing day, marking time until her *Ima* returned home. Soon the stickers were all gone and the calendar full, but still *Ima* did not come home. They got letters as her trip turned into a "long visit," then a longer one, and then an indefinite stay.

Ima loves you so so so so much! I need to be here now. Doda needs me here and it's so wonderful to be back. Maybe you will come to visit when school is over! This summer we'll have a wonderful time!

All the letters were more or less the same. Dahlia searched them hungrily for clues as to what the real deal was; she may have been a child, but she was no fool. Her father drank nightly, looking lost and terrified, never, ever mentioning the 25 percent loss of warm bodies in their household.

Dahlia looked long and hard at the words in her letters from *Ima:* Love. Need. Wonderful. Maybe. Wonderful. These words, divested of meaning, made her sad. Her stickered calendar, moot, seemed to mock her.

Danny would hoard his own letters from Margalit jealously, locking his door, pushing Dahlia out of the room, refusing to talk to anyone. She yearned to see what his letters said. Did he, being older, get different information? Was the answer in them? Did he know something she didn't?

And that was precisely when Danny soured, fermented, acrid as if left indefinitely in bad vinegar. He turned monosyllabic, pissy. Where had her sweet pal gone to? Whither her beloved bro?

"How was your day?" Bruce would venture, playing at fatherly involvement.

"Fine."

"I wrote a book report! Look!" Dahlia would say, knocking on Danny's perennially locked door.

"Fuck off."

"Teenagers!" Bruce would shrug pseudocheerfully when Danny took dinner to his room and locked the door.

"Teenagers!" It became Dahlia's refrain as well, along with the hope that this was only a temporary state, as Bruce intoned: a *phase*. Fine, another hurdle. They'd get through it. And *then* they'd be happy.

When he did bestow upon Dahlia the great gift of his engagement, Danny's attention took the form of pure torment. He would moon her, and hold her down, hard, in order to sit on her face and let loose a torrent of flatulence. He would leave fresh piles of his own human waste in the toilet, unflushed, so that she'd lift the lid in order to pee in their shared bathroom and find a dump of epic proportions staring up at her.

She did her best to assimilate this dynamic, but she was mightily confused. What had *happened?* No one was talking. Was it *her?*

This phase of your struggle will be perhaps

the easiest. You've done the hard work of facing and accepting that you are sick, of searching out the best possible treatment, of surrounding yourself with the right team. Now you get to let your hard work heal you. Trust that it will.

The basic effect of Danny's burgeoning assaholism was that Dahlia, in turn, began treating her unsuspecting, insipid, whole-happy-familied elementary school classmates with the same brand of violent disregard she experienced at home. This is what psychologists sometimes call *transference,* Gene.

There was trouble in car pool. Dahlia morphed into an enormous bully, the Tony Soprano of elementary school. There had been lunchtime collections. She'd somehow forced several kids to hand over their "treat": whatever was most delicious and sugary in their packed lunch. Fruit roll-ups, granola bars. Her favorite was a brand called *Dipps;* essentially a granola bar covered in chocolate. Oh, what lies and manipulations and scare tactics she'd revert to for a Dipps bar. Dahlia was allowed no junk food. The Finger household lacked the junk-pantry omnipresent in the kitchens of her playmates. There was no candy, no chips, no fruit roll-ups. There were certainly no Dipps.

"See the window?" Dahlia had inquired of a car pool mate, circa third grade, gesturing to the open window. "If you don't give me your [Dipps/Rainbow Brite/sticker collection] right now, I'm gonna throw you out of it."

"I just heard this huge wail from the backseat, this little boy so upset he could hardly speak! And there's La-la, happily holding this doll that doesn't belong to her! Unbelievable," went Bruce's fond, amused recollection. "I tell you, kiddo, it's not too late for law school."

A note from one of the many babysitters employed during that time, found tucked into Dahlia's baby book (!): *Mr. Finger, I think it would be best if you found a different sitter for Dahlia. I have too much self-respect to allow myself to be subjected to intimidation by an eight-year-old child. Thank you.*

"I'm gonna kick you in the balls," was her favorite retort. And "shut up," the old standby. Also the grandmaster turn of phrase, cribbed from Danny: "Fuck you." She became a horrid child. You'd think someone would've said *time for a psychologist,* right?

But it wasn't just intimidation and assault that characterized school-aged Dahlia; she was also the foremost expert under ten on matters of the adult body, with all of its fascinating attendant pastimes.

The ineffable moment had come when, surreptitiously looking through Danny's things — in blatant violation of the KEEP OUT stamped on his oft-locked door (hey, all bets were off: anarchy!) — she had stumbled upon an issue of *Hustler* and a pile of *Penthouse*s. It was the most exciting moment of her life: eight or nine years old, confronted with images so forbidden, so thrilling and dark and secret and dirty, alive with inappropriateness as jarring as the lingering vibration of an enormous internal bell. She'd been relieved: She was looking, for all she knew, at the basest thing there was. What joy. She had gotten to the bottom of things. She knew, now, what it all came down to. Her heart pounded, pounded, pounded some more. Here, at last: some answers. Her hair stood on end. In *Penthouse* there were women with giant teardrop-shaped breasts and soft bodies. It was seventies porn, and thank *goodness* for that — no surgeries or piercings or eradicated pubic hair — photographed in soft light. Some wore garters and heels, some bent over or squatted. All had that same look on their faces: terror and deadness and shame masquerading as seduction. She may have been a kid, but again, she wasn't a goddamn moron. Dahlia could see it in their eyes, every single one of them: There was something *the matter with* these ladies. She loved them.

She never could find the real source of her searches through Danny's room — the one thing that had justified the danger of being in there at all: Margalit's letters to him. But somehow she was sure that the magazines — and the baseness therein — were connected to that so-central, as-yet unacknowledged absence. Her mother had disappeared, and here was this baseness to contend with in another realm entirely. In Dahlia's mind, Margalit's absence was linked inextricably to the magazines. But how? And why? More questions, alas, and scarce answers. Regardless. It was comforting to face these things squarely, especially in the dark corners of Danny's room, when he might or might not walk in and crack wide open with a torrent of fury. Better to face these things than not, was Dahlia's default understanding. She fancied herself a keenly invested detective, of sorts: What were the Rules of the Adult World, and how might she best proceed according to those rules?

Dahlia was the advanced, "precocious" (private schools euphemize a lot during conferences with parents who pay full tuition) kid, the go-to girl for sexual knowledge.

"Do you know what a blow job is?" she'd lecture a nervous, rapt group who'd each handed over a Dipps bar or fruit roll-up or package of cookies in exchange for information. "It's kissing wieners. The man licks the woman, too. If they do it at the same time, that's sixty-nine."

"Why's it called that?" a brave soul would venture.

"Because."

"Women don't have wieners."

"No duh."

She demonstrated tricks on the calculator, such as: 1 girl, who was 16, did 69 three times a day (11669 X 3). What was this girl? When you hit the equal sign and turned the calculator upside down, you could read the sum (35007) as LOOSE. There was also a complicated way to come up with 55378008 (aka BOOBLESS).

"What's a hand job?" a prepubescent classmate would ask. Or "What's an orgy?"

"Give me your Dipps," was always Dahlia's stone-faced reply.

In the fifth grade, the school rabbi had

appeared to provide sex-ed fundamentals, offering up official versions of things Dahlia was already all too happy to describe in occasionally misinformed minutiae (for a small fee or trade). The thing that stuck out most in Dahlia's mind was his description of an orgasm, which she had hitherto not begun to contemplate: "It's like a sneeze," he said, a common analogy that was to remain with her, absurdly, for the rest of her life. "You're just walking along and, *wham! — a-choo!*"

So Margalit was in Tel Aviv more or less indefinitely, living out another existence entirely, seeming to have forgotten she had children. By fourth grade, Dahlia had not seen her in two years, despite oft-repeated assurances that they would visit with each other soon, here or there. Bruce was buried in work and his supermarket alcohol. Brentwood had become a theater of confused pain and silence. Life was like a postmodern performance piece: Was Dahlia just dumb or was it totally impenetrable? There was no *Ima and Abba can't live together anymore but we still love you and Daniel and each other* talk. Okay, so *Ima* needed to be in Israel. Surely that couldn't last forever. She'd have to come home eventually, right? Right? Hello? Anyone?

Her parents checked out and oblivious, Dahlia turned to Danny, clung to him fiercely. Ever tried to give a cat a bath? That's how desperately Dahlia clung to Daniel. She trusted him, Gene. All evidence that suggested trust was not in order aside. This was her central, original, disastrous mistake: a leap of faith, a near-religious belief in something not easily proven, at best, and quite unlikely at worst.

But she'd take what she could get. He mocked her, pushed her, laughed at her, tripped her, mocked her some more. Or just ignored her. Transference, again: She was paying for Margalit's sins.

Dahlia didn't immediately care, though. She just got very good at falling down, pratfalling. She let herself be mocked, teased mercilessly, pushed around. Any attention, any interaction with Danny was better than none at all. She became a regular nine-year-old Lucille Ball, aiming to entertain: dumb and clumsy, but in on the joke, at least. Which she understood even then as preferable to being outside the joke. Anything was preferable to being outside the joke.

Ima can't visit with you this summer because I'm going on a big trip with a new friend! He's a commander in the IDF! Maybe soon we can all have a visit. Ima misses you and loves you!

Five days a week for three weeks, to and from radiation, no distractions, no one in the car now to torment or blackmail. She missed those poor car pool saps, those dumbshit kids who didn't how to stick up for themselves, who hadn't been broken in and hardened at home, who weren't as advanced in the art of intimidation as was little La.

The radiation rides were heavy with the weight of the past and the unavoidable heft of the present, the questionable status of the future. With no one else around, no one weaker or less knowledgeable than Dahlia, no one on whom she could act out all her terror and powerlessness, no one who might thus swing the balance and help her feel less, well, *fucked,* she bore the weight alone.

The summer before the sixth grade, Bruce had had some stressfully referenced "work" to do ("meetings" and such, though likely he had simply exhausted his capability to maintain a valiant air of normalcy in their disintegrated household), Danny was off to the sleep-away camp his friends all attended, and Margalit remained mysteriously and capriciously unwilling to plan Dahlia's umpteenth promised summer visit to Israel. So Bruce packed Dahlia off to camp, too.

Camp sucked ass, a misery she had hitherto not imagined. Dahlia was homesick. Sick for home and sick because of the reality of home, a sick precursor that, when she thought about it now, made perfect sense. In the first few days she had desperately sought out Danny in the older boys' *shetach,* tent area, a terrifyingly pheromone-and-boom-box-charged enclave out by the edge of camp, near the road to town. Her heart slamming in her brain, she realized only once she was *in* the boys' *shetach* that she had no idea where exactly she could find Daniel. There was a forbidden thrill in her being there, a sheep in the wolves' den.

"Do you know where Danny Finger is?" she shyly asked a group of boys. They looked her up and down. She was eleven and starting to develop, little boobies budding.

"I'll Danny finger you, if you want," one said. The boys erupted.

"Yeah!" said another, lunging for her and making an awful face.

"C'mere!" they yelled after her, laughing, when she bolted. "Where you going?"

In the dining hall that night she caught sight of her brother, relief and adoration swelling in her like the anticancer.

"Danny!" she called, running to him. She grabbed on to him like he was her mother, hugged him like she yearned to be hugged. "Danny!" He pushed her off, looked around casually.

"What's your problem?"

She beamed at him. "Hi!"

"Hi."

She opened her mouth to speak to him of her homesickness, her extreme loneliness, her longing to be *home,* home, pleasegod-home (but a home, *bevakasha,* that didn't resemble the home of late), the scary tent-area encounter of earlier. "I'm in bunk five," she said instead, so he could just come find her later.

"Good for you."

"What bunk are you in?"

He was being watched by a couple friends, boys who struck yet more of that same, soon to be familiar, unabated unease into her, that same unease still just beginning to weave its long and complex way through her life and through her body.

"I'm in bunk Fuck You," he said, laughing demonically, a barking dog's laugh, like ammunition fire, much to the delight of his friends. Then he put his hand full on her face, palm to nose, and pushed, hard, so she stumbled backward, before allowing himself to be carried off in that nauseating cloud of Boy.

Dahlia could feel tears welling, a storm cloud moving fast and dark over her, but there was nowhere to go until it passed, nowhere to escape the throngs of hungry kids arranging themselves according to age and gender to get fed.

Can you imagine that, Gene? Do you get the kind of asshole Danny was? Okay: He was sixteen, fine. Sixteen-year-old boys are well-known assholes. But she was *eleven.* How on earth could he not have sought to take care of her even a little? Was it because he was, himself, so un-cared-for? Was that really how human beings worked? That simple?

And by the way! Now she had cancer.

Be kind to yourself, Gene said, treading water. *Let your treatment do its work. Trust that it can and will.*

The next summer Dahlia had patently refused to return to the horrific camp, and tried to insist, instead, on visiting her mother in Israel, a place that had, over the course of those few years, become as unfamiliar and shadowy as her own intact family. Margalit's response was swift and decisive and familiar: *Ima loves you so much, but she needs to be here on my own for now.*

"She means go fuck yourself," said Danny, snatching the letter from Dahlia with all the viciousness he could muster. Which was a lot.

Danny had gone back to camp on his own, to be a Counselor-In-Training and ball eighth-grade girls. As a consolation prize, and because he finally, finally saw that his La La was having a "rough time." Bruce treated her to a special trip, just the two of them: ten days in New York City, seat of dreams and wonder, Dahlia's ancestral home, screw Eretz Yisrael.

It was becoming clear that Margalit was gone for good, and Bruce wanted to do something nice for Dahlia. She was hurtling toward her own adolescence now. Soon enough she'd surely sour, too.

They stayed at the Plaza, in a double suite, and saw eight Broadway shows in seven days (Saturday there was a matinee *and* an evening show). Bruce went to a few business meetings, slept late, read the paper in his bathrobe, and gave Dahlia room service carte blanche. They paid respects to the portrait of Eloise in the lobby. They ate sundaes at Serendipity. Bruce let Dahlia have his credit card and roam the streets freely. She went to Bloomingdale's and bought herself a small bottle of Chanel No. 5.

"Is that for your mommy?" asked the saleslady, unfazed by the gold card proffered by a twelve-year-old.

"Yes," Dahlia had replied.

She bought herself an Esprit sweatshirt, the height of fashion.

She bought herself maroon lipstick at Barneys.

She bought herself a silver ID bracelet at Tiffany.

She returned via taxi, tipping extravagantly, feeling calm and mollified, safe and hopeful. The Plaza doormen smiled, winked at her, bowed at the waist.

At *Sweeney Todd,* there had been two actors whose scene called for a make-out session, staged in the aisle, not five feet from where Bruce and Dahlia sat. Dahlia watched her father continue to watch these entangled actors even after their spotlights had dimmed and the action commenced elsewhere in the theater. She could plainly see that he was "horny" (as once defined in exchange for a strawberry Pop Tart as: "when you really, really, really want to have sex a lot").

The specifics might have been swept under the rug, the reality of her parents' marriage and separation and attendant adult complexities just out of reach, but Dahlia understood at least that much. And thus came to a close her formative education: *Hustler* magazine, awful adolescent Danny, vanished Margalit, and now her horny father, twisting all the way around in his seat to get a better look at the embracing, prone actors in the theatrical haze of dry ice before collecting himself, smiling blankly at Dahlia during curtain call as if all was well, and suggesting they go get some dessert.

8. Choose Life

Decide that you are going to overcome this illness. Decide that you are going to live a long and happy life. It's just that simple.

Fuck you, Gene.

9. FIND A SUPPORT SYSTEM

Don't shut out old friends or avoid making new ones. Let your loved ones support you, help you, and love you. Now is the time to let yourself be supported, helped, and loved.

Living With Cancer met twice a week (once was hardly often enough for people whose weeks were thus numbered). Rick, their fearless leader, demonstrated intimate familiarity with The Book. Dahlia wondered if there were some sort of party-line cancer shtick, a well of pat bullshit from which everyone drew. Had Rick and Gene pledged the same mortal-illness-is-all-in-your-head fraternity? They echoed each other eerily.

"We're here to help each other win the hardest fight of our lives," Rick began. They sat on a giant L-shaped couch and several folding chairs in what served, during the day, as Rick's Santa Monica psychotherapy practice. "At home, we may not always be able to get what we need. Our families are dealing with their own emotions. Here we can be free to experience our feelings without worrying about how we're affecting our loved ones, or what they might be going through."

Living With Cancer (much like, well, life with cancer) wasn't the same from week to week. People came and went, got better or worse, got sicker or less sick, disappeared altogether, reappeared looking gaunt and gray or ruddier and fortified, brought macrobiotic cookies to celebrate another milestone passed, the dawn of another day.

The rules were clear: Anything went so long as one kept one's face turned resolutely toward the aforementioned Bright Side. One could acknowledge sorrows and difficulty, sure, but one was not to end on a sour note. One could not put out unhappiness untempered by positivity. One could say *I'm so tired I want to die,* for example, but only if, after a beat, one added, brightly, *but I know I need to fight hard to get through this!*

Dahlia was the youngest. Ovarian Carol, Ruth Ann, and Carlotta passed around pictures of their grandchildren and wept for the possibility of not seeing them grow but offered thanks to God for the time they did have. Silver-haired Lung Arlene and Double-Mastectomy Francine reported symptoms and next steps in treatment with a steely reserve and a kind of endearing, understandable, appalled disbelief that this was actually happening to them. Compact, forty-something Testicular Bart, the only male, said he wanted to "beat this thing," which was funny, since he was talking about his genitals. He wanted very much "to start a family." He spoke often of his recently frozen sperm — a step he'd had to take before chemo ravaged every living cell in his body — and of "finding the right woman." Dahlia pictured tiny creamy ice cubes full of diminutive Bart's cartoonish spermatozoa, stuck in a permanent tableau of refusal and shock. She imagined Bart bashfully proposing with a cum-cube perched in a velvet box.

"I am going to kick the living shit out of this thing," he'd say. "I am going to *fucking kill* this fucking cancer."

Dahlia was going to write a heart-wrenching grad school admissions essay about this when all was said and done.

Research has shown conclusively that those patients who avail themselves of a regular support group system during treatment and recovery can live up to twice as long as those who do not.

"How about you, Dahlia?" Rick would gently prod at the end of each session. The group looked to her with a mixture of pity (so young!) and protective tenderness (so young!) and puzzlement (so young!). Rarely could she bring herself to communicate much. *I do not belong here,* Dahlia repeated to herself. *This is a purely anthropological exercise.*

"Radiation is almost over," she said, the only non-negative she could think of. A simple fact.

"And is there anything about that experience you'd like to talk about?"

"It sucked," she said. "But not as much as chemo's gonna."

She kept going because there was the need to break up the monotony of life at "home," of life interrupted, of time stopped. And she did, she had to admit, like being there, even if she mostly kept quiet. She'd been hoping to broach the topic of medical marijuana. Specifically, where she'd be able to get some. In the spirit of positivity, after all.

Six weeks of radiation had left her exhausted to her core. It was the utmost in tiredness, the gold standard of fatigue. She had that angry pink bald spot, about an inch in diameter, like a treatment badge on the left side of her head. It was perfectly smooth and worn, like the strangest pattern-baldness ever. The radiation beam, which always attacked just the same spot en route to the tumor, had marked her. Ah, yes. Let us not forget the tumor. The out-of-control rocker trashing the hotel room of Dahlia's existence.

"Do not Google your cancer," Rick told them. "Listen to your doctors, listen to your body, listen to yourself. Save your energy."

Twelve weeks after the end of radiation it was on to chemo, in pill form, which was everything one hears: brutal, unhappy. It made her sicker than sick. She was to take one Temozolomide pill a day for thirty days, then a thirty-day reprieve (a medication vacation), then another thirty days on. And then? And then, and then, and then? They would have to wait and see. And then. And then.

Dahlia could feel herself getting foggier. Polluted, blurry, lethargic, blunted: She was tired. She wasn't hungry. Her bowels were a mess.

Her mother urged Dahlia to get dressed up for chemo.

"What are we wearing today?" Margalit would ask, like they were sorority sisters.

The Bad Girl's Guide to Beating Cancer

(Margalit's book of choice) insisted that even the sickest Bad Girl take pride in her appearance ("When you *look* great, you *feel* great!"). Gene, at least, made no such claim. And thanks, Gene, at least, for that. Because hell, no — Dahlia had been a Gender Studies major. She understood all too well what "Dress Up for Chemo!" really meant: that it wasn't enough to Understand Your Diagnosis and look on The Bright Side and get A Second Opinion and Trust Your Treatment and (ha!) Choose Life *and* Find a fucking Support System, for starters. If you didn't look cute, you didn't deserve to live.

Margalit could also be counted on to relay tale upon tale of how others — people who were, it was implied, somehow *better* than Dahlia — faced down their doom. Acquaintances of the Fingers, Helene and Arnold Mendel, had had a son who'd gotten cancer. Dahlia remembered Helene and Arnold only vaguely; their son had been a shy boy, a year ahead of her at Jewish day school, who'd been unable to keep his hands off his penis.

"Bone cancer," said Margalit. "The most painful thing you can imagine."

"Yeah, that sucks," Dahlia said, eyes closed, riding the chemo pill hard. She imagined her nausea as a mechanical bull she'd once seen in a cheesy bar in lower Manhattan; you had to throw your body around in opposition to *and* imitation of the thing in order to stay on, to survive.

"You know what Helene and Arnold say?" Margalit asked.

"No. What do Helene and Arnold say?" You had to anticipate it, to fight surprise, to take for granted every buck and wave. You could even, if you were a particular sort of badass, pretend you were having fun.

"Helene and Arnold say that Andrew never once complained. Never."

"Sounds like a trouper." The minute you let it get to you, the minute you said *whoa!,* you were a goner, which then would come to seem an inevitability you'd wasted a lot of humiliating energy battling.

"Never once."

"So, what, are you fixing me up on a date with him?"

"He died. Last year."

"Oh."

"He wrote poems about enjoying every minute of his life, every minute given to him. Helene and Arnold sent me some when they heard about you." Margalit brandished a sheaf of printed emails. "They're very beautiful."

Dahlia could see herself flailing, her boobs

flopping unbecomingly, the thing hurtling in place, a crowd of strangers hooting and hollering for her to fall off. To, as they'd say, *bite it.*

"Listen: 'I learn from the sky and the stars. They know not how much time is left, but they shine, shine, shine, their beauty for all, inhabiting the sky like jewels. Reminding us that life is precious.' "

"What the fuck is that?" If you let it surprise you, you were screwed. Then you fell off, and it was someone else's turn.

"It is a *poem,* Dahlia." Margalit frowned, her chin cocked as if ready to discharge the diagnosis: *negativity!* The nurses would come running and administer a shock to Dahlia's soul.

"I'm no expert, but it's not a poem just 'cause Helene and Arnold's dead son says it is."

"I think it's beautiful. It is a beautiful poem." Margalit's eyes were brimming. "This young man *died,* Dahlia. Show some respect."

Dahlia sucked in a surfeit of air. "Bullshit," she coughed out.

"I think he had a wonderful attitude about life."

"It isn't a poem just because he's dead, either."

175

"That's not the point! The point is that he had a wonderful attitude about *life*."

Margalit took the liberty of dressing up on Dahlia's behalf. If Dahlia insisted on sweat pants, that was her problem. If Dahlia didn't really "care enough about living to put a little effort into [her] appearance," then that was her loss. Margalit made it her mission to face Dahlia's chemo with aplomb. Cancer was no excuse to look bad. She wore her Turkish jewelry, her rhinestone-encrusted, turquoise cat-eye reading glasses on a beaded chain, voluminous cashmere ponchos, delicate, exorbitantly priced suede flats, dark red lipstick (a Chanel shade called, Dahlia could hardly believe it, *Deadly*).

Dahlia felt slightly girl-who-cried wolf now, because chemo was brutal. Even if she *had* had any of that gold-dust positivity before (which, fine! She hadn't!), she would have had a hard time rising to this challenge. And at least there was that: She was now definitively entitled to feel like ass. Who could blame her? Gene? Double-dog dare you, man.

She was exhausted. She was nauseous. She wasn't hungry. She wanted to die. Her hair was thinning in great clumps; her skin was dry, itchy, flaky, peeling. Margalit bought her some fancy-shmancy La Mer lotion wrapped up with a pink and green ribbon.

Dr. C, breezing through the treatment room weekly, asked her about these symptoms, hardly glancing up from her file. When she made herself clear — um, no, she was *not* okay — he finally took leave of the file and looked up at her, his oh-so-valuable gaze cool and comforting as lotion from France made from disenfranchised minority placenta.

"Are you opposed to using marijuana?"

"No," she replied, clicking her internal heels. "I am not opposed to using marijuana."

The pot was outrageous. No complaints there, Gene. It was the best shit ever. She smoked it and smoked it and smoked it. At the house they watched Dahlia's favorite, repeat-viewing movies. Dahlia passed her joint to Bruce, who recoiled, refused.

"Did you ever think I might like some of that?" Margalit asked.

Dahlia passed it to her.

"I used to be very into this stuff. Orly had a boyfriend who sold it. Once we went to Amsterdam with him, but he found a Dutch shiksa and fell in love and never left. Orly was heart-broken." She held it inexpertly, like a cigarette, with a grating, mischevious smile, before sucking too hard and blowing smoke out too quickly. "But I don't think it really works. I feel nothing."

Dahlia took the joint back and held it out again toward her father. "Dad."

"I don't want it, La," Bruce said, laughing.

"Come on." She shook it at him.

"No, thanks," he said, weakly.

"Here," Dahlia said again.

Bruce, blushing, lost but amused, looked at Margalit. "I don't think I like that stuff."

"It's true," Margalit said, as if just recalling it, a curl on her lip. "It's true: he doesn't. He wouldn't ever do it with me." They looked at each other, the sum of every fondness and resentment and betrayal ever perpetuated between them condensed into a moment. She'd urged him to try pot while camping in the Galilee in 1971, he'd demurred, she'd gotten high without him and flirted for hours with another man, then Bruce had relented, smoked some, and spent the remainder of the night flipped out and paranoid on the outskirts of a campfire, watching his wife chatting up the other man. And all this a million years ago, it seemed.

"Try it," said Dahlia. "For me." She affected her best I-have-cancer face. "Please?"

It was a ridiculous manipulation to pull, one absurdity among many. But really: No one "didn't like" pot. Anyone under the impression that they didn't like it just needed to chill out and like it. They were watching *Crimes and Misdemeanors.* Jerry Orbach looked *exactly* like Bruce, and Anjelica Huston a lot like Margalit. For the first time Dahlia could see how Woody Allen had used the heavy-handed repeated metaphor of lights going out to accent moral failings and murderous impulses, lives ending.

Bruce took the joint. "How do I do this?" He smiled haplessly, game. Dahlia wanted very much to share this with him. Get Stoned with Your Dad and Watch Good Movies, she would have advised anyone still mired down in Understanding Your Diagnosis or Trust Your Treatment. She wanted to watch movies high with her sweet dad Bruce right on into eternity. Insert misadvised Freudian misquote here.

Tenderly, she took it back. "Like this," she said, showing him how she held it between her thumb and forefinger. Not taking her eyes off him, she took a drag, held it in, lowered the joint, waited a beat, and then exhaled the long gray tunnel of okayness. Then she nodded encouragingly and handed it back. Bruce sucked down a good hit, like a pro.

"Good!" Dahlia told him. He smiled ruefully, but held in the smoke heroically before coughing it out violently. Virgin lung.

"It doesn't do anything, *nu?*" said Margalit. "I feel nothing. I feel *nothing.*"

"Yeah," Dahlia laughed. "We know."

Twenty minutes later they were circling the kitchen island and raiding the fridge like a bunch of teenagers, Dahlia half dancing to a dopey melody only in her head. High, Dahlia felt normal. She felt like herself. She felt fortified and ready to do all the things one had to do to survive. Ah, yes, she thought. Support. A system. Okay.

"I want some of this," said Margalit, reaching into the subzero for a tub of hummus and one of black olives. "And some of *this,*" she said, removing the twisty tie from a plastic bag of salty, thick fresh pita chips. "Oooh, *yaffe me'od!*"

The way Margalit enjoyed life, the way she took it all, whatever she could, more and more: one had to marvel at it. She had caused Dahlia and Bruce (and fine: Danny, too) immeasurable pain and suffering with this greed, this hunger, this single-minded pursuit of whatever she wanted, whenever she wanted it, but one had to admire her just the same. What might life be like if one

180

just shamelessly did *whatever one felt like?* No recrimination, no shame, no holding back. Dahlia esteemed her mother, almost. What a creature.

Margalit snuggled up to a half-uncomfortable, half-besotted Bruce.

"Here," she said, picking a grape off its stem and holding it up to Bruce's lips. "*Bruti,* want a grape? Have a grape."

And just as suddenly as she'd felt okay (as suddenly as that long, gray tunnel of exhaled okayness), Dahlia stopped cold with a mouthful of cookie, realizing that a) she had a brain tumor and b) any illusion of support was just that. Illusory. Her father was laughing strangely and backing away.

"Fine, don't have a grape," Margalit said. "You're boring. You're both boring! You bore me."

Bruce shrugged his aw-shucks shrug and took a step forward, grabbing the grape with his mouth. Then he stood up straight and chewed it, grinning.

Dahlia, incredulous and annoyed, watched him pick another grape and toss it into Margalit's mouth, then toss another in the air and catch it in his own. They giggled, looking ancient and goofy. Bruce had lost some weight, and the craggy valleys in his face seemed especially pronounced. Margalit's

hands were — how had Dahlia never noticed this? — beginning to look liver spotted and veiny. But there they were: giggling.
Dahlia felt left out, a child again.

Danny (by then he'd made himself over
as monosyllabic, pissy, hateful "Dan") was
off to college when Dahlia was twelve, but
of course he'd already been long gone for
years, lost in his own fog of free-for-all
adolescent contempt, a loathsome stranger
to his parents, his sister, and most likely
himself, too, though that was no kind of
consolation at all.

Poor Dahlia was like a stupid puppy, the
kind whose fierce loyalty and idiot optimism
keep it dutifully in line with an owner who
delights in pummeling it. She wrote him
letters. She sent him collages and funny fake
diaries (*A Week in the Life of a Seventh-
Grader,* by Dahlia Finger). She made him
mix tapes, trying to prove that she was cool,
that she was smart, that she was worthy of
maybe even a *little* of his attention and affection. Where had all that attention and affection gone? She believed in it entirely,
regardless — it hadn't disappeared, she was
sure, it had just ducked behind a rock or a
tree, still there for the finding, surely. This
was true faith, real, actual religious belief:
persistent in the face of no proof whatso-

ever. Dahlia refused to revise her definition of their relationship. She was his darling, his baby, his favorite person on the planet. He was her best friend, all evidence to the contrary notwithstanding. Okay, so he'd spent the past few years becoming rather a huge sadist, tripping her only to point and laugh that mad-dog bark of a laugh when she was down, when she was hurt, even. And sure, the closest he ever came to demonstrativeness was the old "I'm not touching you!" shtick, in which he'd hold his hands inches from her face, her body, refusing to tire and leave her alone ("I'm not touching you! What's your problem? I'm not touching you!"). Well, and yeah: He delighted in making her feel/look stupid, in trapping her so she shot herself in the foot. His fail-safe method — she fell for it *every fucking time* — went something like this:

"Hey, dumbfuck, did you like *War and Peace*?"

Of course Dahlia hadn't read it — she was twelve! — but she very much wished she had; it wasn't every day that Danny opened a conversation to her. She would do whatever she needed to do in order to keep his attention. He was her pal, goddamn it! Her ally! Her beloved big brother!

"Yes."

"What was your favorite part?"

Shit.

"I don't know."

"Did you like the part when they all jumped into the river and splashed around?"

Oh thank you, God.

"Yes!"

"That never happened, you stupid ugly piece of shit." Cue the mad-dog laughter. The upshot was that Dahlia became about as precocious as any preteen you've ever met: She read anything and everything she could think of, expert at casing Danny's room and following up on anything she found — the musical oeuvre of U2, the canon of John Knowles, even Danny's high school *yearbooks,* for the love of god. She swore she'd be ready, ready for whatever he had in store, ready to provide the right answers and references to earn back, once and for all, his affections. She would know more about what he knew, more about his life, than he did. Surely then he'd have to stop tormenting her. Surely then he'd have to revert back to being her pal.

If she referenced herself as a fucking loser, as dumb, ugly, stupid, clumsy, might then he deign to shine his big brother light back on her for even one more minute? If she made him a mix tape? If the mix tape contained artists she'd sleuthed out on her own, seemingly obscure musicians even *Dan* had never heard of? Mark Knopfler, Taj Mahal, Brian Eno?

Margalit had been reduced to her left-leaning handwriting on airmail paper. She had returned to L.A. a handful of times, each visit more difficult than the one before. She would come over to the house, waltz back into their lives as though she'd never been gone, and then get furious when they seemed ambivalent or aloof. "It's no wonder I don't want to be around you! You're awful children!" she had said, in tears, the last time, when Dahlia had expressed slight hesitation at giving her mother a hello hug.

Bruce remained in bad shape. It had become what passed for a family joke: At the end of Danny's senior year of high school, waiting for a table at the Hamburger Hamlet with Grandma Alice and Papa Saul, Bruce was so thoroughly checked out that he did not, for several moments, recognize the sound of his own name.

"Finger?" the hostess had said. "Bruce Finger? Party of five?"

Bruce had not registered.

"Dad," Danny said. Still, nothing. "Dad," Danny said again.

"Finger?" the hostess repeated. "Finger party?"

"Dad!"

Bruce's eyes glazed, his mind elsewhere, Grandma Alice and Papa Saul blissfully hearing impaired, Dahlia confounded and scared.

"Dad. DAD. DAAAAAAAD!"

Bruce snapped to it, calmly. "Oh," he said, eyes focusing. "Yes. Finger."

Danny went to UC Santa Barbara, where he continued his same friendships with his same camp and high school buddies, the same guys who had floated through the house for years: strange pubescents, his baseball teammates, his camp co-counselors. She could hear them still, shouting their favorite benediction: Whenever something was remotely favorable it wasn't just "cool" or "awesome" or "great." It was "suh-*weet!*"

Their voices echoed off the walls, ghostly, passing through the cavernous Finger house, omnipresent and mysterious at once, from behind closed doors.

"Suh-*weeet!*" The Dodgers were "suh-*weeet!*" *Star Wars:* "suh-*weeet!*" The fact that Debbie Dash's parents were out of town: "suh-*weeet!*"

They sounded like pigs ("suh-*weeeet!*").

186

Scary, menacing (*I'll Danny Finger you,* she kept hearing them say). But they hardly acknowledged Dahlia, never looked at her as she lingered nearby, hoping to be invited into some sort of social discourse. How stupid she must have seemed to them, if they considered her at all. A weird girl, no question. "Old for your age," she was forever being told.

What had happened to her family? (Simple: Hairline fissures had turned eventually to enormous cracks, splitting apart those aforementioned arctic glaciers and creating altogether new cliffs, ice floes floating catastrophically off into the sea.) Precocious Dahlia understood many things — the definitions of "fellatio" and "horny," *A Separate Peace,* theories about the impetus of the Beatles' breakup — but not the simple facts concerning the main issue: What had happened to her family?

Margalit had made an appearance at Danny's high school graduation, then disappeared again just as quickly, trailing perfume and kisses and promises in her wake. *Ima loves you! Ima misses you! Ima needs to stay in Israel this spring/summer/fall. Ima can't wait to see you soon!*

Come fall, when "Dan" (sorry, it was hard to get used to) had gone off to college, Margalit announced that she'd be staying in Israel straight on through until Dahlia's bat mitzvah. She could help plan it from Tel Aviv. Aunt Orly needed her. Aunt Orly had left her second husband and was trying to start a business making jewelry and sundries; her pins and eyeglass cases and pillboxes occasionally arrived in the mail. Dahlia had dozens of them: ugly shellacked objects made from old newspapers with screaming Hebrew headlines.

"Just you and me, kiddo," Bruce had said after they watched Dan drive away in his loaded-down Jeep, a bright UCSB sticker already affixed to its bumper. "Wanna see a movie?"

No, she did not want to go see a movie. She wanted to be dropped off at the mall with his credit card, left to her own devices to comfort and console herself.

Bruce disappeared into his trusty haze of work. He had branched off and started his own firm, and was poised to put his old employer to shame. "The Firm" was ubiquitous, like an invisible third child with a rare genetic disorder, in need of constant attention and care. But he was better than he'd been — no more wine-in-a-box all the time, no more staring hungrily, like a silent starved animal, at women on the street. He even "socialized" more, which meant, Dahlia knew, that he had himself a "lady" friend.

She came along for dinner one night, this lady friend, all hyper-attempted chumminess, hooking arms with Dahlia on the way out and asking "Do you like any boys at school?" and "What's your favorite subject?" *Dorel* was the lady friend's name, which sounded like the kind of obscure brand of duty-free cigarettes you buy by the carton at the airport. Dorel was too young for Bruce, but not scandalously so. Thirtysomething, just at a stage when she was beginning to keep an open mind about dating older, divorced men with kids.

Dahlia enjoyed entertaining the notion of Dorel as parental figure/ally, and made the shrewd, pre-adolescent decision to just take whatever the hell she could get.

Without Danny in the house there was a new, startling silence to get used to. No echoing "suh-*weeeet,*" no odious adolescent males stomping through the house and drinking milk from the carton, no baseball games on high volume.

At Bruce's urging, Dahlia had applied to and gained acceptance at the Westwood School, Los Angeles' most prestigious, competitive bastion of social/academic assaholism, and so had begun seventh grade there, leaving behind legions of scared-into-submission elementary school classmates. No public school for Bruce Finger's precocious princess. Her new classmates were icy and blond and rich — *rich,* mind you, not just well off, not merely "comfortable." They had their *own* credit cards. They wore their pleated uniforms hemmed to the hilt with witty patterned boxer shorts sticking out from underneath. They had older sisters who got brand-new BMW convertibles for their Sweet Sixteens. Delicate Tiffany solitaire diamonds in white gold rested on their sharp clavicles. She'd been a big fish in a small pond; now she was a small fish in a decidedly big pond. Her reign of terror and intimidation was over, definitively. Her new classmates didn't need Dahlia to educate them; the seventh graders had boyfriends with whom they had already done things even Dahlia couldn't begin to explain or imagine. Their mothers bought them designer clothes and booked their spa appointments. They never wore the same witty boxers twice.

And there was Dahlia: in the early stages of severe early-onset adolescent hirsutism, newly fitted with braces and headgear (which she only had to wear at night, thank

Jesus), motherless and sisterless and diamond solitaireless and living alone with her dad, who had "values" and so would only give her the credit card on occasional, careless, guilt-ridden afternoons. She persisted in writing Dan letters, calling his dorm to say "hey." In his absence she could recast him, absolutely, as her friend. She wanted to tell him about Dorel. She wanted him to explain things to her, give her some perspective and insight. There were no magazines left in his shell of a bedroom in which she could ferret out her own understanding of life now. Though he had left behind a crumbly copy of *The Catcher in the Rye,* which she devoured in a rapture. Okay, so he hadn't technically *given* it to her, but she chose to believe that he *had,* in his way. That leaving it in his room was a purposeful gesture on his part. She was his Phoebe. That bond was theirs, the book was definitve proof! He might act like a fucking asshole, but he couldn't help it ("Teenagers!"). She'd never been surer of their unshakable bond. Old Danny. Old Dahlia. She was not alone, no sir.

"Is Danny there?"

"Who?"

"Dan. Dan Finger."

"I don't know." Silence. "Hey, faggot!

Where's that motherfuck Finger?"

Then dorm noises in faint cacophony, doors slamming, ("DUDE!" "suh-*weeet!*") until Dahlia would give up.

When she did get to talk to him, Dahlia offered tidbits and facts — "Dad has a girlfriend" — hoping to rope him into some sort of shared familial experience, which he, in turn, faithfully resisted.

"Good for him."

"Her name is Dorel."

"Huh."

"Westwood School is kind of hard." Her voice breaking.

"I have an idea, dumbfuck. Why don't you call someone who cares?"

She had no friends. Most everyone else at the Westwood School had come up through elementary school together. There were no Jews. There were people who were technically *Jewish,* sure, but there were no Jews. The Kantrowitz twins were a few years ahead of Dahlia and, for their sixteenth birthday, got a single BMW convertible to share, which was a hardship, but they made it work. And even if they'd wanted to throw Dahlia a social rope (which they didn't), they were too many grades ahead and too politically mighty to be of any real help. That was their tenth-grade year, and they were embroiled in battling an insidious rumor that they had taken turns blowing a star basketball player from a private school in the valley. Times were hard all around. Dahlia couldn't fault them. She was probably beyond help, anyway. She understood. She accepted her fate. She had a Tiffany ID bracelet at least, but she was a loser and would have to make do.

Saree Lansky was the closest Dahlia would get to a "friend" that year — a scholarship kid whose class awareness and keen sense of wild injustice were already so sharply honed at the tender age of thirteen that she could tell you exactly how much everyone's outfit cost, how much money her parents made, how much her house was worth in the current real estate market. Dahlia was semi-forgiven for being, as it happened, semi-rich, because she was ugly and unpopular and had a bona fide burgeoning mustache and no cute clothes and a left breast that was already noticeably larger than her right. She posed no threat. Saree was part of a different breed of Westwood Schooler; misshapen, brilliant, lumpy girls with fiercely enmeshed Ivy League aspirations. Julia G., it must be acknowledged, was one of these, too. Dahlia didn't much fit in with these girls, who spent their weekends taking PSAT practice tests, enjoying quality time with intact families, and studying Italian. But as a useful life-skills tool, all the more applicable in junior high, it was important to take whatever you got. Beggars can't be choosers. Dahlia tried to act normal, had passing friendships with girls she disliked, and deeply coveted straight hair and a mother (in that order).

Saree was willing to invite Dahlia over and spend Friday nights with her at the movies, and Dahlia was willing to take what she could get, even though Saree Lansky was really no fun whatsoever, what with the early-onset halitosis and the kind of shoulder chip that should, goddamn it, probably have resulted in cancer.

Take What You Can Get: Dahlia Finger's Tips for Surviving Early Adolescence.

Dorel was excessively solicitous of Dahlia's friendship, and that was also something, while it lasted. They went shopping. They saw movies. It was a relief to have an adult female around; Dahlia needed some serious advice about how to handle her goddamn facial hair. No way could she ask Bruce, who actually seemed increasingly fragile as time wore on. Her heart bled for her father, and she didn't want to lean on him, couldn't bring herself to saddle him further. He looked so sad, so haggard, so wrecked. She feared toppling him altogether. "Dan" was trouble enough; implicit in her father's basset hound eyes was a plea that Dahlia *please, please* cut him a break. He didn't ask her questions so much as he commented on her life. "School is starting," he'd say. Or "This weekend is Halloween." This had to suffice for parenting. He was bashful around her, too, his sweet little girl morphing before his eyes into this ugly, misaligned, mustachioed *thing.* He was embarrassed not only by her changing shape, but also by the constant, unarticulated knowledge that he was somehow failing her. He knew he was failing her. She knew she was being failed. Nothing was spoken. Yet another failure. And so it went, layers of silence and failure and silence about the failure, until eventually every conversation they had was conducted as if via tin can and wire across a deep ravine of shame. Still, she wanted to cut her father a break. The poor man couldn't deal.

Dahlia's bat mitzvah was her way through that year, the event toward which she focused all her living hope. She had the sense that junior high was just a nasty phase, anyway, a fever dream. Margalit had no plausible excuse for missing it, and Danny's presence would be required, too. Her whole family, together again. All would be right with the world! She could get through the seventh grade only by clinging steadfastly to her vision of this great, singular, healing event. Her vision of it felt almost like the presence of an actual family. She wrapped herself in it like a blanket.

"Close your eyes," Rick said at the end of every group meeting, and Dahlia couldn't help but sneak hers open to see if anyone else was disobeying like she was. But no: Everyone else's eyes were shut. "When was everything in your life exactly as you wanted it? Go back to that moment and remember the way it felt." Dahlia just sat watching them all, wondering: What was behind all those lids? What were they remembering? Where in time had they gone? The best she could do was to imagine the ideal moments flickering on the movie screens of *other people's* memory. "Carry that feeling with you when you leave this room and continue your fight to get well. We'll see you next week."

The day of the magical bat mitzvah had arrived the week after seventh grade came to a merciful end. Bruce had spared no expense, "values" notwithstanding. Dorel took a giddy and grateful Dahlia to her Canon Drive hairstylist, who created a

196

spectacular blowout with excellent, intricate poufy bangs, and to a brusque Armenian lady in white scrubs, who, within fifteen seconds, miraculously, if painfully, eradicated the hellish mustache. Dahlia looked not at all like herself, which was a very, very good thing. Margalit flew to L.A., Aunt Orly in tow, only to lay down the law at the very last minute: If Dorel would be sitting at the "family table," Margalit would not be attending. "It's inappropriate for her to sit with family, Bruti," she'd said sweetly, firmly.

Bruce had tried, in his way, to gently break this news to Dorel, who in turn got very angry indeed, and chose to skip the event and end the relationship once and for all. If the man wouldn't stick up for her, then to hell with it. She didn't need this. Bruce had hovered on the fringes of the party: spectral, flattened.

Dan, at least, had seemed somewhat excited. He knocked back a few rum-and-cokes and got Dahlia up on a chair during the hora. With the help of three others, Dan delighted in thrusting the chair high and hard, roughly jerking her around until, inevitably, Dahlia fell from that great height and landed — wham — in her bat mitzvah finest, on the side of her face against the checkerboard dance floor, amid silver streamers galore and a veritable army of hysterically amused Westwood School nonfriends. In the days following, a purple bruise had faded to blue and green and yellow before it finally went away.

10. EVALUATE YOUR RELATIONSHIPS

Who is a helpful, loving presence and who is a taxing, unhelpful one? What makes you feel good and what makes you feel rotten? It's time to let go of anyone who isn't plainly good for you.

Not that Dahlia had too many people in her life to begin with. Where were her ex-pals, one might wonder? Her ex-acquaintances? Her ex-roommates? Her ex-lovers? Where, indeed?

In Living With Cancer, talk turned again and again to marriages, divorces, affairs, near misses. Children, spouses, friends. And how most of the above were simply not cutting it.

"I'm having terrible night sweats," Ovarian Carol would say, and they would all nod. "And I keep getting the sense that Tim's patience is running thin, you know? Like, he wants to be supportive and good to me, but in the middle of the night I can tell that he really just wants me to settle down so he can get a decent night's sleep for the first time in god knows how long. And I guess I don't blame him, really, because this must just be awful for him."

"Sounds like it's pretty bad for you, too," Rick would say.

Or Ruth Ann would start by saying, "I'm drafting my will," only to wind up, ten minutes later, concluding that "Allison hasn't been over to help out *once,* and Jamie's been there every *single* day, and is it really right that I leave them both equal shares? I mean, I don't even feel like Allison's my *child* anymore, and she's married to that horrible prick, while Jamie is just *there* with me all the time."

"It's normal to be angry when our loved ones let us down," Rick would say.

Cancer will throw your relationships into sharp relief. People you thought were good friends may turn out to be distant and unsupportive; those you may have taken for granted may come through in ways that will surprise and amaze you.

Dahlia had thirty days off chemo before another thirty days on. A medication vacation.

Testicular Bart suggested they go have

sushi in Malibu.

"You're such a sweetheart," he told her. Her appetite was returning slowly but surely. "I know you're going to make it." He reached into his briefcase after miso soup and edamame and pulled out a copy of The Book. "Read this, if you haven't already. I'm serious. It's the best."

"Know it well," she told him.

"Really? Good! Where are you?" He flipped to the table of contents, laid the open book out on the table. He was wearing a magnetic energy ring on his left pinky.

"Evaluating my relationships," she sighed, averting her gaze.

"That's a total turning point." He beamed at her. "That was the most amazing part for me. I made peace with everyone I know, and I've never felt better. You are so going to beat this thing, Dahlia."

She spent most of her time hanging out alone or with Bruce, fending off overweening offers from Margalit to "get mani/ pedis!," indulging in the activities of the wealthy, the wealthy unemployed, and the ill: surfing the Web, getting high, walking around the Third Street promenade, the occasional matinee, structuring afternoons around procurement of a latte or two from a cushy chain purveyor of lattes, sleeping late, buying herself presents. The group, twice a week. Shopping for fancy organic groceries every other day and snacking like a queen. Her orders, per Dr. C, the group, and Gene, were quite clear: rest, be kind to yourself, take it easy. Hey, can do.

Bruce was tender and indulgent.

"What shall we do today?" he asked. "A walk on the beach?" The chemo vacation gave Dahlia a false sense of well-being. Her awareness rested on the fact that she had been through something bad, that she was sick, that there was Something Wrong with her, and stopped there: cancer purgatory. She had nothing to do for a whole month but take a big, deep cosmic breath.

They existed in a timeless bubble, she and her dad, worldly concerns eradicated; there was only the life of the body and mind. Did she want to go to the movies? Did she want to read the paper? Did she want to see the Hockney exhibit at LACMA?

"Whatever you want, my girl," he said. "Whatever you want."

Mara called to check in. Dahlia had liked to joke, way back in her former life — so very long ago, in its way — that she didn't need health insurance.

"I got *you*, baby!" she would say in whatever abbreviated phone calls Mara could manage between rounds during medical school. "You can take care of me if I get sick. I'm so glad only one of us is a fuckup. How's school?"

Mara invited Dahlia to Boston. A vacation from her medication vacation.

"You still have a few weeks off before the next round of chemo," Mara said. "The leaves are changing."

Dahlia was reminded of a doomed Debra Winger, heading to New York to visit Patsy, only to be carted around on display: Sick Lady, object of pity and fascination. *Terms of Endearment* was still fresh in her mind. Should they rent it? Might be fun to watch with Margalit, see Margalit weep.

"I don't want to."

"Dahl, come on. It'll be fun! I talked to some people who would be totally willing to check in on you while you're here. Mass General is one of the best places for your kind of tumor. Why not just talk to people here, explore some other options, see if anyone has any different ideas? Can't hurt."

Oh, but couldn't it? Dahlia didn't want to go anywhere. She wanted to do nothing. Doing nothing felt, finally, okay. Back in the day, back when *nothing* was Wrong, before *something* was Wrong, she was plagued by guilt and shame structuring an afternoon around procurement of a latte. Now it was perfectly fine! And she wasn't about to wreck that with any amount of productivity. Hell, no. She looked to Gene for benediction. Maybe a *Do whatever the hell you feel like!* Or *Don't let anyone come at you with an agenda — your time is your own, and precious.*

The closest she got was *What do you feel good about, and what worries or upsets you? Make no room whatsoever for anything that's not unabashedly positive, anything that doesn't feel* great, *or, as hard as it can be, anyone who doesn't add to your wellness.*

"I'm happy here," Dahlia said. "I'm tired." Mara wasn't going to argue; when had Dahlia ever claimed to be "happy" anywhere? There really was no arguing with a cancer patient, anyway.

Mara wasn't bad, per se, but the hard truth, Gene, was that, in the end, Dahlia found *every* relationship "taxing" and negative. Every attempt to relate. The problem of having to accommodate another human being: ultimately impossible. Living with other people, trying to get whatever it is one needed at whatever given moment: unfeasible. Add to that the expectation that Dahlia somehow actively participate in combating her illness, talk to someone at Mass General, and thanks, but no.

Mara had materialized at the Westwood School halfway through their ninth-grade year, just when Dahlia might otherwise have accepted her lot: passing friendships with girls she hated. Saree Lansky, when she wasn't obsessing about straight As, talked endlessly that year about getting her hair permanently straightened.

"Why are you just starting here now?" Dahlia had asked Mara in Algebra, spring not being a typical time to switch schools.

"Because my dad died."

This was a great answer, without really being an answer.

"Oh," said Dahlia. "Sorry."

"Whatever."

Dahlia assumed that Mara would fall in with some crowd — ostensibly even a cool one, given her cute, compact body, her piercing green eyes, her jaunty veil of straight, shiny hair — but Mara had remained a loner well into March, seeming not to want to be friends with anyone, and she breezily accepted Dahlia's overtures. Saree Lansky and her lumpy, frizzy, eczemaed, future-Ivy-League ilk were suddenly, happily, part of Dahlia's past. She had a *real* friend! Here combing Wasteland on

Melrose Saturday afternoons for embroidered silk Chinese blouses and used Levi's, there crank calling Joey Tanenbaum late on a Friday night, now talking smack, in endless late-night phone calls, about their math teacher, who had the worst B.O. of all time but was perversely kind of hot.

Mara never spoke of her dad's mysterious death, or of him, or of life with her polite, distant mom. Something was off. Any mention of dads, or of fatherhood in general, was strictly off-limits. Once, at the start of tenth grade, Dahlia had made the mistake of referring, obliquely, to the situation with "your dad and all," and Mara's eyes had narrowed to knife-wounds, her face shrunk instantly into itself. "Sorry," Dahlia had said, groping, clueless as to what she was apologizing for but keenly aware that she had transgressed. "Whatever," Mara had said, but they'd grown noticeably apart soon thereafter. The fact that Mara's father's cause of death was a secret was far sadder, somehow, than the simple fact of his being dead in the first place.

"Okay," Mara told her from Boston, defeated. "Whatever you want. Keep it in mind, though, will you? The offer stands." Mara obviously disapproved of Dahlia's passivity, her lack of affect, this horrible inaction.

But Dahlia didn't want to go anywhere. And she certainly didn't want to get mani/pedis with Margalit. Fuck Margalit.

"Let's go to the Golden Door! Or, what's that one in Mexico? Remember, *motek?* That one we went to the week after you finished high school?" They had spent five days in a shithole resort, getting eaten alive by bugs and picking at egg-white omelets and lounging by a greenish pool and pretending the chunky girl from Chicago wasn't later barfing up everything she put in her mouth. The trip had been Margalit's gift to Dahlia. Nipped in the bud when Margalit had deemed Dahlia's attitude "unpleasant." ("You're an ungrateful little bitch, do you know that? I'm so sorry that this spa isn't to your liking! Disgusting, this girl. The whole world owes you something, does it?" It hadn't been worthwhile to try and argue any of these points. The spa *was* a shithole; it wasn't an issue of gratitude. Dahlia was well aware that not everyone got to go to a shithole spa after high school graduation. It's not like Dahlia would've preferred to be at a nice spa; she wanted to be *home,* lying on her bedroom floor, listening to the Indigo Girls and reading *Prozac Nation.* They had left two days early.)

Say what you will about her maturity and self-awareness, but Dahlia had at least learned to avoid taking trips with her mother. It had taken her an awfully long time to figure that out, though. She'd not been the most apt at evaluating her relationships for most of her life, admittedly. And now she has cancer.

She had been scheduled, at long last, to go spend the summer after ninth grade with Margalit (her disappeared mother! remember Margalit?) in Israel. Monumental, especially after years of thwarted visits and hardly seeing her mother at all. Okay, so it had become clear that her parents were split up. She got it, finally. ("No shit, Sherlock," Dan had spat at her when she'd worked up the nerve to talk to him about it: "I guess *Ima* and *Abba* are broken up, huh?") Maybe her brain had just been consumed and distracted with the task of getting her menstrual cycle up and running. Her body had had a lot to do those days. Big jobs. A comprehensive understanding, without having ever been told a goddamned thing, of her parents' un-marriage couldn't have been a priority for the subconscious of a fourteen-year-old on the womanly seesaw.

When at last she had wrapped her doddering awareness around the fact — Oh!

Her parents had split *up!* That was why her mother had run back to Israel! That was why there was only the distant memory of a family! That was it! Of *course!* — it was, obviously, old news. The kind of clear, long-standing reality that leaves one indignant and humiliated for not having grasped it sooner, like the fact that smoking, asbestos, and synthetic hormones cause cancer. (And parabens, and smog, and heartbreak, and selfish mothers, and ineffectual fathers, and sadistic big brothers, and private school attendance, and PSAT vocabulary drills, and self-pity. Especially self-pity. But we've been over this already.)

In the months leading up to the epic journey, Bruce and Dahlia had communicated only haltingly, as usual. His technique for dealing with his absent still-wife (they had not begun any divorce process — to do so would be to admit, first off, that they were no longer a couple) was to ignore, ignore, ignore. His face, though still fairly destroyed, a thinned-out echo of the visage he'd worn in the all-important home movies, had taken on a new cast of resign and resolve. "This summer," was what he said, if he referenced it at all. This summer. Her *real* bat mitzvah, make no mistake. A divide she would cross into definitive adulthood.

Always the benevolent figurehead, be-grudging her nothing, Bruce ached for his daughter's lack of a mother, and had tried to do everything in his power to distract her. She got her own credit card that year, joining the ranks of her classmates, finally. She used it to shop like mad for things she imagined she would need in Israel. Jean shorts, "fish" hair clips, slip dresses. She daydreamed about all the things she would buy *in* Israel.

I can't wait to have you here! Margalit's let-ters said. *We are going to have such a good time! We will go everywhere, do everything! Aunt Orly is dying to see you. Your Hebrew will come back in a matter of days, just wait and see. Why won't Danny come, too? See if you can convince him, yaffa — you're his favorite person. Love always, your Ima.*

Danny, college man Dan, had of course been given the option of a summer in Israel with his mother and sister. He bark/laughed at the suggestion, and refused to address the possibility thereafter. Regardless, Dahlia was dying of excitement. That was how she spoke of it to anyone and everyone through-out the ninth grade: "I'm *dying* to go."

That summer was a fulcrum: all this murky childhood behind her (what had hap-pened to her family? what had happened to her darling brother? whither her beautiful, dark-haired *Ima?*), and ahead of her a life over which she hoped she'd have some measure of control. (She would buy herself a pair of Doc Martens! She would go on a cantaloupe diet! She would get a boyfriend! She would develop a marvelous, even tan! She would spend an hour a day on the treadmill! This summer she was going to Israel!)

She sat in class making lists of what was good about her life:

I have a full lunch card.

Mr. Warren was friendly to me today.

I am wearing my Doc Martens.

Brian smiled at me on the steps.

I am going to Israel this summer.

My brother is coming home soon.

My brother loves me.

It was almost spring break, and Dan would be rolling up to the house in his Jeep, U2 blaring. He would be lounging around the house, watching movies and eating late-night bowls of cereal. And here was the thing: Dahlia was almost a grownup now. She was a woman. She was his equal. She was in high school; driver's ed in her sights; puberty almost (please, God?) done with her. She planned to hang patiently around, waiting for him to emerge from his assaholic stupor, the sun breaking through the clouds. He'd say something like "Hey, La. How's it going? What's happening with you? Come here and give me a hug, little La." Because now was the time. Any day, now.

It was never explicit, but her real motive for these lists was simple: Each good thing was a reason to refrain from killing herself on that particular day. They had, truthfully, been reasons-to-live lists, compiled ritualistically in her notebook.

In addition to the lists, Dahlia found cutting extremely useful. She had conceived of it organically, too — a fact of which she remained exceedingly proud. A few years down the road it became a trendy issue, lumped in with the whole media-saturated Girls' Self-Esteem Crisis of America, replete with memoirs and memoirists' talk show appearances. To this day, Dahlia felt incredibly, strangely validated to learn that her own bloody coping mechanism was a not-uncommon one, a club of which she was a rightful member. She'd thought it up all by herself, sitting on the floor of her bedroom, listening to the Black Crowes' "She Talks to Angels" over and over again, liking that line about how "the pain's gonna make everything alright." That was totally it, fuck yeah, the pain really *is* going to make everything alright. She'd fondled a pink Daisy Gillette razor and dragged it slowly, carefully, over the skin on the side of her wrist, too far from veins to mean much. Those first few times she'd hardly drawn blood, but still. The adrenaline rush calmed and clarified her. She didn't yet have the balls for a suicide attempt, and she didn't actually want to die, anyway. She just wanted to feel something; to push herself right up to the edge, familiarize herself with it. Because she knew that one had to prepare; these things took practice. It felt like letting air out of a stretched-to-breaking balloon. She felt great for days afterward, elaborately bandaged herself so someone would notice, though no one ever did. She had faint scars: tiny, almost invisible lines of keloid tissue where her thumbs swelled out into palm. She'd been chickenshit: never cut too deep, never pushed too far. She was just experimenting, getting ready for the possibility that one day the lists wouldn't be enough and she'd have to cut deeper, longer, harder. Surely that day was out there. She let it bolster her.

She made her lists and sliced her arms diligently all year long, as though marking off calendar days until she could go to Israel.

The plane was packed to the gills with corpulent orthodox men, apple-cheeked young mothers in long skirts and head coverings, the odd hippie-seeker, and, since it was June, a raucous group of high schoolers on a summer trip. The gate attendant took Dahlia's ticket and murmured, *"Nesiyah tova,"* mistaking Dahlia for an Israeli, wishing her a good trip. Someone had mistaken her for Israeli! How fucking cool was that? She *was,* she figured, sort of Israeli. National pride blossomed in her heart. She wanted to sing "Hatikva" against a slo-mo, flag-waving-montage backdrop. She wanted to spear Yassir Arafat in the heart with a plastic fork. It all fit perfectly. The way, when El Al touched down at the airport in Tel Aviv, everyone applauded and the PA played "Shalom Aleichem." The way the whole planeful of passengers sang jubilantly along, clapping. The way the customs agent was gruff and tender; rude and funny and polite and harsh all at once: Israeli!

"Bevakasha," he said when he took her passport, and then, looking her up and down, glancing at the American passport, a jumble of Hebrew she couldn't follow. "Ah, so you are not a *sabra* after all," he said, amused. *Oh,* she would have argued if she'd had the presence of mind, *but I* am *a sabra!* I am I am I am I am!

214

How could she have so delayed journeying back to her homeland? It had been five years, almost, since their forever-ago last trip as a family, and almost two since her bat mitzvah, when she'd last seen her mother. Dahlia had forgotten Margalit, a little. She'd forgotten the mood swings, the verbal attacks, the caprice. These two shadowy, mythic entities — Margalit and Eretz Yisrael — had come, like pillars, to assume the weight of Dahlia's every longing. What could they do then, in reality, but give way?

Margalit wasn't at the baggage claim with flowers and shrieks of joy like Dahlia had envisaged. Dahlia got her duffel off the carousel and sat down on it to wait for many long minutes before she saw her mother bursting through the automatic doors and running toward her. Those minutes fucked her up, Gene. Those minutes (had it been three? Ten? Twenty?) drained her of every idealized hope she'd had for the whole summer. It was then that she remembered her mother. Her *actual* mother, the one who eventually greeted her with a simple smile and "You got so fat."

Dahlia had had the urge then to turn around and fly back home. Bruce was alone at the house for the whole summer. Dan was building houses in Guatemala with a

Jewish youth group. She felt herself in the eye of a force-five loneliness tornado, afraid to move.

But then Margalit had descended in typical fashion: "*Motek!* You're here! You're here! Aunt Orly and Uncle Moshe are going to meet us for dinner! Are you hungry? Of course you're hungry! Oooooh, it's so good to see you, *haruti!* Ooooh, so good!" The embrace hurt.

Margalit's five siblings (Uncles Rafi, Yoni, Nissan, and Moshe, and Aunt Orly) were scattered all over the world. Respectively: Australia, New York City, Italy, Kibbutz Dalia, and Tel Aviv. Dahlia knew them all, vaguely, from those Dalia summers, when everyone had seemed to converge on the kibbutz, collapse into each other's lively chatter and laughter. But they had all gotten vague and further removed as time passed. Uncle Moshe was the only remaining Shuker at Dalia, a senior member of the community, a gruff and (if memory served) earthy man, slow to affection and short on words, but not a bad guy.

Margalit pointed things out on the drive through Tel Aviv: There was the boardwalk, there was the King David Hotel, there was the dairy restaurant, here was Sheinkin Street, here was George HaMelech.

"What's wrong, *motek?* You're very quiet." Dahlia was shy and stunned, overstimulated and exhausted. Her eyes burned.

Details came clamoring back, little things from her earliest memories in Israel: Bisli snacks, Israeli ice cream bars covered in rich, delicious, melty chocolate, feeling safe and free, her feet tanned in sandal-strap pattern. "Everyone here *looks* like me!" she had exclaimed as a tiny girl, ecstatic in her sense of belonging. She and Danny had romped in the warm waves off the boardwalk.

"What's the matter with you?" Margalit wanted to know.

"Nothing, *Ima,*" Dahlia assured her.

They went for dinner and ate fancy hummus and tahini and couscous and baklava.

"Look at the appetite on this one!" laughed Moshe. Dahlia immediately ceased eating.

"Shut up, she's beautiful!" Orly yanked on a lock of Dahlia's hair. Well, no, not exactly true, that. Dahlia was too mortified to speak.

Margalit had failed to mention the fourth person joining their dinner party, a tall man who'd introduced himself brusquely as Gil ("I am Geeeeel") and said nothing more all night, his hand resting on, alternately, Margalit's shoulder, knee, and lower back. "Gil" refused to speak English, though he clearly understood at least some of it.

"Why doesn't she speak Hebrew?" he asked Margalit in Hebrew, indicating Dahlia as though she were a deaf mute. Margalit just shrugged, rolled her eyes as if to say *she's a dumb American; what do you expect?*

Dahlia was jet-lagged beyond capacity for thought, but had the correct impression that seeking refuge in sleep so soon after dinner would be a disappointment to her mother. So she tried hard to stay up, "having a good time" or whatever it was Margalit wanted from her. They went walking by the beach, Dahlia slack-jawed with tiredness, hallucinating flashes of light. "She's tired, I guess," Margalit said to Gil finally. As if it was a betrayal. "We'll take her home."

Margalit was chummy and overwrought in fits and starts those first few days — Let's go shopping! This is my daughter Dahlia! *Yaffe meod, ken?* Isn't she pretty? — but after a week or so of intermittent smothering affection and attention, she had run out of both, and gave Dahlia a key to the apartment, more or less leaving her to her own devices.

So Dahlia had wandered, mostly, by herself. Bliss. Down Diezengoff Street, past the Agam fountain, through the giant mall, where she took a huge, relieving crap, the first in days, her body seeming to recognize immediately the safe haven of a mall. Along Sheinkin. Into Old Jaffa, where she bought pastries at Abulafia, the hundred-year-old Arab bakery whose sweet aroma greeted you forty yards off. Through a park, overlooking the blue Mediterranean. Down into winding stone alleys and stairways and paths, all the doors painted blue to ward off the evil eye. Stray cats everywhere. She thought: One day I would like to live in a house with a blue door. And the thought that followed: One day I *will* live in a house with a blue door! An instinct to look toward a time when she'd be able to shut out all that was bad, protecting for herself all that was good. A teeny-tiny instinct, but an instinct all the same. Where had it gone? Why had it not persevered?

There was a pretty good flea market in Jaffa. She bought a wrap skirt made out of two scarves, and a silver ring encircled with an intricate, knotty pattern. A tiny, ornate, wood backgammon set, with mother-of-pearl inlay, for Danny. And, on second thought, one for her father, too. She stopped for another sweet croissant at Abulafia, where the boy behind the counter winked at her and refused her money.

And the Tel Aviv beach! She had almost forgotten it. The most fabulous beach in all the world, arguably. It ran along the whole length of the city and was inhabited in the best possible spirit — crowded but clean, fun and safe, hopping and relaxing. Groups of beautiful people playing some sort of table-less game of Ping-Pong, with rubber balls. She plopped herself down in the fine, soft sand day after day to watch the sunset. She dipped her feet into the warm sea. She returned home every night to Aunt Orly's crumbly Bauhaus apartment with an ever-deeper tan. (Oh, and tanning: We all know where that leads.)

But after about two weeks of wandering, Dahlia felt choked with the whole summer ahead of her. What was she doing here? Her mother was helping Orly run her little jewelry store, selling those ugly shellacked *Ha'aretz* pieces to Americans. Every night there was the option of dinner with Gil, who — with his silence and refusal to speak English and his stare and his hand always near/on her mother — gave Dahlia the serious creeps. She had purchased, with her trusty credit card, at least two of everything she could possibly want. She had pasted so many temporary tattoos on her ankles that there were no more patches of unadorned skin. She had let a hot guy with a stall near the boardwalk pierce her belly button with a needle and watched it get infected under layers of generic Israeli bacitracin. She had had small pieces of hair wrapped in colorful string. She had learned how to communicate effectively using her limited Hebrew: *How much is that? Thank you. I don't have any money, sorry. Excuse me! I don't speak Hebrew. Where is the nearest bathroom?* She was bored.

"What is your problem?" Margalit demanded. "Always a *miezkeit,* this one," she said to Orly, making a mock sour face.

She called her father from pay phones around the city. Her birthday came and went. "Fifteen!" said Margalit. "But *I'm* only thirty-two! How is this possible?!"

It was Bruce who, sensing Dahlia's loneliness, offered the suggestion that Dahlia spend July at Dalia with Uncle Moshe, who also left her largely to herself but at least didn't yell at her for frowning. Perfect.

She worked, as did all volunteers, eight hours a day, six days a week. From 6:00 a.m. to 2:00 p.m., with half-hour breaks for breakfast and lunch.

"This is my niece," Uncle Moshe told the volunteer coordinator, grinning. "Make sure she works her ass off."

"*Bruchim HaBa'im,* Dahlia!" said the loud-speaker at dinner the day she arrived, to a rousing chorus of *Dahlia, Dahlia, Dahlia! Ooooh-ahh!* Which was, she gathered, the chorus of a once-popular Israeli song. The kibbutz was sort of familiar from those Finger family summertimes of yore: the soap factory, the heated soccer matches, the orchards, the sheep.

Dahlia stayed in a dorm room with a Dutch woman named Mariejke who'd come to volunteer after her boyfriend had died in a car accident.

"That's so sad," Dahlia said.

"So it seems I am alone," Mariejke said, late at night, when they had what she told Dahlia were "our heart-in-heart talks." "But when you're alone you are also free. It's the good and the bad."

"But don't you wish he hadn't died?"

"Yes. I wish he hadn't died."

"But he did die."

"Yes, he did."

"So you have no choice."

"No, I have no choice. Most things, we have no choice. Everything, really."

"Like what?"

"Go to sleep, you."

Dahlia's job, in the avocado orchard, was to cut still-hard fruits from trees and place them in a canvas picking bag, wearing gloves and using the utmost care — avocados, like people, are terrifically easy to bruise and mark. It was tiring, mindless work, but it was finite, and rhythmic, and the knowledge that it was her job only through the first week of August made it seem straightforward, simple, and fun. She wore a white cloth hat with a brim and worked happily, the switch of her mind turned off, off, off. She was glad she hadn't been tapped for work in the soap factory, kitchen, dining room, or laundry room. No grimy conveyor or women's work for her.

She had come to Israel to be with her mom for the first time in years, but was instead harvesting avocados on Kibbutz Dalia: such a disparity between what she'd imagined her summer would be and what in fact her summer was. But it was a relief to fit in here, a cog. And the kibbutzniks accepted her warmly. They asked about her beautiful *Ima* and very smart *Abba*. Etamar, the cook, graying at the temples, wondered "How is your *miezkeit* brother?" ("Still a *miezkeit!*" Dahlia had giggled.) The newer ones remarked on her name, and grinned when she told them that she'd been named for Dalia. Her belly button piercing was healing nicely.

"I am Uri," said a tall, thick-necked young man with a crew cut one night in the dining hall. "I remember you from when you came here long time ago. You were a small child, only." He held out his hand at the height of the little girl she'd been. He'd grown up here, done his army service, and was back.

"No one comes back," he said. "They leave. They go to New York. But I come back. To come back is important." He was a man of few words, but when he had something to say, watch out. He seemed to think hard before he spoke, though his range was not huge. "You want to see *Die Hard* tonight? They are showing it after dinner. I watch it before, it is fantastic." Uncle Moshe, watching from a few feet away, winked.

"Okay," Dahlia had said.

Uri followed her everywhere, which was, she had to admit, flattering. Even though she was fifteen and he was twenty-five, and even though he was, at his best, sweaty, lumbering, awkward. At fifteen you don't stop to wonder what the fuck is the matter with the kind of adult who'd try to get into your pants. She called forth the confidence and assurance with which she'd once edified an entire generation of her peers on the workings of the body. She was so far from what she considered her actual life; nothing seemed to matter. She understood enough to know that Uri was into her — he made this clear by lecturing her on topics large and small.

"When you eat the animal, you are eating every fear and — *eich omrim,* how do you say? — anger they have when they die. Exactly when they are dying. And all of this is in their body. And then we eat this."

"Nasty," Dahlia said obligingly. She had a tray full of dining hall sloppy joe.

"It is the reason human beings are unhappy in the world."

This made okay sense, actually. And she was enjoying the attention.

At the end of the summer, when it was time (alas) to leave the avocado orchard and return to Tel Aviv to reunite with Margalit for a few days before heading back to the uncomplicated embrace of her father in L.A., after Mariejke had left the kibbutz and wished Dahlia "a very, very nice life," Uri had knocked on her door and jammed his lips up against hers, his sluggish tongue reaching — quite inexpertly, she would come to understand later — into her mouth. And then, on her last night, in her twin bed, Uri had relieved her of her virginity. It had hurt, she would tell Mara a few weeks later — leaving out the near asphyxiation, her non-participation, fear — like a *"mother-fucker."* It was nothing she'd had the presence of mind to fight off but certainly nothing she'd wanted. She hadn't expected it, had not been ready, had not effectively prepared herself for the event. It was over before she could articulate what was wrong with it, just a memory by the time she'd figured out how to formulate an appropriate emotional reaction. There had been some blood, which had had the positive effect of, at least, lending the terrible pain some tangible confirmation. She had wept briefly, a couple of embarrassing, surprising, convulsive sobs before she could gain control. This had irked Uri.

"You are okay?"

For some reason, she had wanted him to think she was. She nodded, biting the insides of her cheeks.

"Okay?" he asked again, and she nodded harder: *yes, yes, yes.*

She ached for days, hardly able to sit in a chair for any length of time, fidgeting left-butt-cheek/right-butt-cheek all the way back to Tel Aviv, through another unmemorable dinner with Aunt Orly and Gil and Margalit ("What is the matter with you? Fidgeting, Jesus Christ! It is so unpleasant to be with you!"), and through the entire eighteen-hour plane ride home, where she found Bruce waiting for her at the gate.

"Hi, my girl," he had said, and with palpable relief held his arms open to her. "You look great!"

11. Heal Yourself

Participate actively in your wellness. Pursue whatever seems to instill calm and positivity. You can actually heal *yourself.* Believe it is so and your capacity for wellness will be limitless.

You were making some sense for a while there, Gene. Bright side, whatever. Support system, fine. But honestly, this shit isn't going to fly. Dahlia's supposed to heal *herself?* You think she can *heal* herself? It gets dumber with repetition, an intellectual tongue twister, like *she sells seashells by the seashore* or *Peter Piper picks a peck if pickled peppers.*

Choose life? Okay, then: life! And she lived happily ever after. Guess we're all done here. Thanks.

If she could *heal herself,* you infuriating shitball, then why, pray tell, was Dahlia about to embark on another brutal thirty days of brutal chemo? Even Margalit, with her Kabbalah string and Hamsa charms and daily raw garlic clove, would never make a claim so obnoxious as *heal yourself.* Is Dahlia *Jesus?* Let's talk logic, shall we?

If Dahlia could heal herself, would it not stand to reason that she could have kept from getting sick in the first place? Like when you don't eat right or get enough sleep and then come down with a cold, was that it? And then, on top of feeling like crap, you have to feel stupid for having run yourself into the ground, to blame for your own suffering, right? What could I have done differently, you're supposed to wonder. If only I hadn't X, if only I had Y. And sympathy is hard to come by, since you are expected not to *allow* yourself to get sick in the first place. On top of which, no one wants to catch whatever it is you've brought on yourself.

And if she *doesn't* heal herself? If she *can't* heal herself, what then? She *wants* to be sick? She *deserves* to be sick? What made *you* sick, Gene? You mention only briefly those oh-so-generic troubles: your large mortgage, your spastic kiddies, your high-stress job. But come on, now. What's the real story? Were you messing around on your wife? Was she messing around on you?

Did she make you feel small? Were you disappointed in your kids? Were they ugly/stupid? You were a bad lawyer, too, surely. Never won a case, sloppy with the contracts, mistrusted by your firm, a laughingstock. And earlier? Did you get married because you were facing down the gun of thirty and felt you "should"? Did it occur to you only later that you had married someone lame? That your whole life was a dumb race toward a finish line you hadn't even acknowledged, let alone chosen? Did you daydream about taking off? What went through your head while you wrote out those giant mortgage checks? How often did your house require some sort of physical maintenance? Did it wear on you, those lightbulbs burning out? The leaves choking up the gutters? Did your parents love you, Gene? Did they??

Fresh, local, organic fruits and vegetables should be your staples. Whole grains are your best option. Avoid caffeine and alcohol entirely. The sulfur compounds in garlic seem to block the synthesis of certain carcinogens. Garlic also promotes the body's production of natural antioxidants, which protect healthy cells from damaging renegade cells known as free radicals. Shark's cartilage, wheatgrass, and kombucha can all also potentially be help-

ful. See the supplement diagram on p. 139 for a helpful chart of vitamins and minerals essential to your wellness.

Just say it: She's to blame. She eats Oreos by the palmful. She loves sourdough bagels and sugar cereals. She couldn't ever have just one Jack-and-ginger; she had to have *four* Jack-and-gingers.

Dahlia's tumor had not grown, but it had not shrunk, either.

"After we see how the tumor responds to this round of chemo, we'll evaluate our options and think about our next move," said Dr. C. *Our:* as if it was really a collective problem. Flipping her file shut, he offered an appalling, self-satisfied nod and smile.

Bruce scanned his notes while Dr. C shifted his weight and looked obliquely at his watch.

"So," Bruce said. "Would you say that radiation and the first round of chemo have been successful?"

"It's generally hard to say. She seems to be holding up well, which is encouraging, though I do wish I could see some shrinkage in the tumor itself." (*You* wish we could see some shrinkage!) "The MRI after this round of chemo will tell us a lot. Right now we can be glad the tumor hasn't spread. But I'm not thrilled with her lack of appetite, and the depression can possibly be attributed to her antinausea medication. Let's try a different one. Keep using the marijuana as long as it helps."

Bruce scribbled, scribbled, and scribbled.

"Oh," Dr. C went on. "And she should get a flu shot immediately."

The cancer was in limbo; Dahlia's entire being a sort of fulcrum. Which way would it go? It was up to her.

You have the power to banish this illness from your being. Treatment takes you only so far. The rest is up to you.

Sure, it may seem weird that Dahlia was so laissez-faire about her illness, her treatment, her second opinions, her options, her progress, her prognosis. Weird, but only if you're the type of person who *doesn't get sick in the first place,* dude.

Harumph. Fine. She went for acupuncture and shiatsu, ate Chinese herbs and guzzled wheatgrass. She took specially prescribed dosages of vitamins A and C and E and selenium and milk thistle and echinacea and she let her mother wave burning sticks of white sage around the room. She dutifully sipped from Margalit's proffered bottles of kombucha, miracle mushroom rot juice. She ate fresh ginger. These things had an admittedly pleasing air of luxury to them; they made her feel relatively okay. She even got a colonic, like a movie star. (Like a *regular* movie star.) She sampled quantities of day spas with indoor waterfalls and raw nuts and free green tea, which, if she didn't think too hard, could almost seem like good, old-fashioned hedonism.

Except for the daily chemo pill, that is. But she was, she had to admit, somewhat less nauseous this time around.

"It's because you're finally doing the stuff that can actually *help* you," Margalit said. "Of course you feel better now. You're taking charge!" She held her fist up against her own head and knocked sternly. Margalit was in her element. She booked herself massage appointments alongside Dahlia's, and carried on like they were two ladies of leisure, whiling away their afternoons in pampered bliss. Eating expensively, drinking five-dollar voodoo concoctions from the health-food store.

"This is the life," Margalit would say, lowering herself into the Jacuzzi at Bruce's and/or sucking on one of Dahlia's joints. "Ahhhh, yes."

Dahlia let herself be poked, prodded, rubbed, pressed. The body certainly did hold stuff; that much was clear from the knots in her right shoulder and in the hip she favored when she sat. Or the way she burst out laughing — tearful, uncontrolled, intense, followed by an embarrassing gasp which seemed to come from nowhere — when a masseuse put one thumb firmly down on the right side of her midspine. As though a trigger were being pulled, something seized and released at the same time.

"What's going on *here?*" the masseuse asked gently, not letting up at all. "I think we've found your trouble spot, sweetheart." Oh, sweetheart: that's so nowhere *near* Dahlia's trouble spot. When Dahlia stood up at the end of a shiatsu, a Swedish, acupuncture, a hot-stone, she'd find herself moving unsteadily, slowly, like a newborn deer: utterly vulnerable and wobbly on unsure legs, dreading the moment when she'd feel steady and bipedal and old and herself once again.

"I'm doing all the woo-woo shit, now," Dahlia told the group. They forgave her her refusal to present cheer, though occasionally they took it upon themselves to present it for her.

"You look much happier this time around," said Lung Arlene.

"I think you're doing amazingly well," agreed Ovarian Carol. Rick seconded that. Double-Mastectomy Francine had disappeared entirely. Rick read aloud a note from her husband: *Francie is comfortably resting at home, where we've got a hospice nurse to make sure she'll continue to be comfortable. She would love to hear from you all and she sends her love.*

Bart had disappeared too, but for different reasons.

"I'm done with the being sick stuff," he told Dahlia on the phone. "Gotta move on with *life!* You give me a call if you ever want to have coffee or something." (He was a chapter or three ahead of Dahlia in the book, see.)

She got a surprising email from Rabbi Douchebag: *Dad has been keeping me posted. I would like to talk to you if you think that would be okay.*

Dahlia had not seen Danny since her ordeal had begun. He had shown up in the hospital the one time, but Dahlia had been busy in her comatose ether. And *that* was the best he could do? Months of silence following years of silence and that was it? The dumb prick couldn't even make use of a nice contraction or two? Dahlia was gratified (and probably a tiny bit closer to sealing her doom) in her response: *Go fuck yourself, you piece of shit.* She was not about to make this easier for him. He should suffer, too.

It had taken her a long, long time to come to her complete and total hatred of Danny. She had, stupidly, spent years maintaining her platonic ideal. He loved her! They were buds! He was the coolest! — despite his refusal to comply with that ideal even a little.

As a junior in college, Danny had spent a semester in Israel, of all places. All his Jewish summer camping had successfully instilled no small amount of cultural pride and Zionistic leanings. But he boycotted Margalit the entire time he was there, at Hebrew University in Jerusalem, only about an hour on the train from Tel Aviv. His ongoing strategy of completely ignoring Margalit's existence caused angst for everyone.

"What is *wrong* with him?" Margalit took to wailing on the phone, demanding Dahlia's involvement. "Why won't he see me? What did I do to him that's so awful? He's a troubled bird, *motek*. Talk to him! He loves you so."

This was not the first time Dahlia had heard her mother or father make this assertion — "Danny loves you" — but she'd taken a moment to wonder: *He does?* Despite his not having acted at all in such a way in roughly a decade? She crept toward the awareness that it was a bullshit leftover mythology, this tripe about Danny being her beloved big brother. But she was still willing to believe — though only partially, and with growing hesitation. (Willing to believe, Gene. *Faith:* trusting in something of which you have absolutely no proof!) She was downright proud when her parents asserted this as fact: Danny adores his sister Dahlia. She was still absurdly excited whenever he deigned to take her calls or scribble her a note. "I farted on this!" he'd actually written on a piece of paper before putting it into an envelope and airmailing it to Dahlia from Turkey. He also sent home some snapshots of himself at the pyramids in Giza. *Guess what,* he'd written. *You're ugly.*

He had grown tall, athletic, outdoorsy, leaving in his wake an endless trail of besotted youth group girls. He was into hiking. He'd become a Dylan freak. Dahlia remained faithful to the belief that he knew all there was to know and might let her in on a secret or two if only she played things right, didn't act like such a — what was his word? — "spaz." Which she supposed she was, after all. Spastic, lame, a dork. Okay. If compliance with that diagnosis was what it took to encourage Danny's intermittent presence on the other end of the phone line, fine. She was cool with that.

"Yeah, but I'm dumb," she learned to add to the end of any voiced thought. This seemed to keep him on the phone longer, allowing her to pretend even harder that they were buddies. "I'm such an idiot," she took to advertising, apropos of nothing. "Ha ha ha ha, what a dumbshit thing to say."

She did eventually work up the courage to ask him, thinly, why he wouldn't be hanging with Margalit in Tel Aviv.

"You think I want to see that bitch?" he barked.

"I dunno," she said. How revelatory that it was, in fact, a "want" proposition.

"Fuck that bitch."

Not helping matters, Dahlia's tenth-grade year was a profoundly grisly one. First, on Halloween, River Phoenix had OD'd at the Viper Room. Then Grandma Alice had "slipped away" (Bruce's words) in December, just before her eighty-fifth birthday. Kurt Cobain shot himself in April, and Nixon died that same week. In June, O. J. Simpson (er, allegedly) hacked Nicole and Ron to pieces not three miles from where Dahlia was sleeping soundly, sliced-up arms elaborately bandaged so someone might notice, in her white trundle bed, on her Laura Ashley sheets.

And. And. Julia G. had died in the wee hours of a Thursday in May. Dahlia remembered this perfectly, because Thursdays were *90210* and *Melrose Place* nights and thus the anchor of her weekly existence, so when an assembly had been called for Thursday morning, her consciousness was shaped particularly by the fact of its being the blessed day of her most favorite television.

The tenth grade: Death.

River Phoenix had inspired a massive outpouring of grief. Carloads of grief-stricken adolescents cruised past the Viper Room on Sunset as though in funeral procession, some even stopping to place offerings of love and longing. Candles, photos, letters, flowers.

Grandma Alice, too, merited considerable upset, but on a much smaller scale.

"La La," Bruce said to her one morning, setting down a glass of fresh-squeezed OJ by her cereal bowl, wearing that crumply face she knew so well. "Grandma died last night. She wasn't in any pain, she just slipped away."

Immediately Dahlia had burst into tears, equal parts horror (just like that? Grandma Alice was dead? Just like that? She was over and done with? That was *it!? Really?*) and guilt (she had not visited often enough, had not knowingly kissed her grandma goodbye; but hey, this meant Danny would be coming home!). *Saying Goodbye to Grandma* had prepared her not at all for this awful sense of having lost out on something huge. The chance to say something, to do something, one last thing. Gone. They waited a day longer than custom allowed to bury her in order for Danny and Margalit to fly, separately, home from Israel. Dahlia wept quietly throughout the funeral, wanting so badly — and feeling utterly robbed of — the chance to tell her sweet old Grandma goodbye. Or that she loved her. Which, really, she had. She clung to a single composite memory of Grandma Alice singing her a song from *Guys and Dolls: I love you a bushel and a peck, a bushel and a peck and a hug around the neck.*

"Oh, please," Margalit said to Bruce. And then, to Dahlia: "How often did you go see your Grandma? Never! Pull yourself together. You're being ridiculous. For god's sake."

Danny, stone-faced and silent, threw a half-loaded shovelful of dirt into the grave and then strolled purposefully away to stand over by baseball great Hank Greenberg, who was interred nearby. Dahlia, looking closely, could see something approaching woe in Danny's face — fleetingly, and almost indistinguishable from the usual scowl — as he gazed at Greenberg's plaque.

Kurt Cobain was a shock. "How could he do this?" Mara had said. "What a fucking asshole. How could he *do* this? Why would he *do* this? Fucking motherfucking *fuck*."

And then Julia G. Whispered word of her demise had spread like wildfire that day. "Everyone's *dying*," Dahlia remembered saying, over and over again. "Why is everyone *dying?*" The Westwood School administration had invited some rightfully harsh criticism when, after the requisite memorial assembly, they had insisted school go on as usual. Advanced Placement exams were coming up. A lot was riding on grades for sophomores and juniors. It was vital to go on with the "business of life," the headmaster/CEO told them. And that meant giving those SATs and PSATs and APs the serious effort and attention they demanded. Julia would have wanted us all to go on to the Ivy League.

Then O.J. did his butcher bit on Bundy.

By the time school let out, it was like a joke, the death. Death, death, everywhere, and not a drop to drink! Dahlia even quit it

241

with the arm slicing for a while: There was so much external evidence of mortality and pain that she (for once) didn't feel the need to act it out upon herself. (By that logic, she might have done fantastically well, later on, to join the Peace Corps or dive right into relief work in the Sudan. Why hadn't she? Shit: the things you figure out too late.)

She had rocked driver's ed, passed with flying colors, and was gifted, for her birthday, with a baby blue 1986 Volvo station wagon ("Values!"), which she immediately hot-boxed and plastered with pro-choice bumper stickers. Bruce upped the limit on her credit card — "For gas *only,* La La" — and she had gone directly to Betsey Johnson and Fred Segal.

"What do you want to do this summer?" Bruce had nudged as July flew by. "How about a job?"

"I'll think about it," she had replied, assuming she could "think about it" all summer long. Then the Visa bill came, and Bruce hit the roof (Bruce-style, but still): "I'm *very* disappointed in you, La." The shame! The terrible shame. Bruce was so rarely disappointed in her. "I trusted you." He was stern, unrelenting, like a total stranger. He was not amused.

So Dahlia wound up in the mailroom at

his firm. The guy in charge, Eric, a thick-necked ex-linebacker with fat hands, a perfectly trimmed goatee, and a buzz cut, reminded her of Uri. It seemed she had a "type," then: big, sweaty underacheivers. But Eric was harmless. She flirted with him all summer.

"What's up, jailbait?" he'd greet her.

"Not much, perv," she'd reply, curling her lip, enjoying her power, power afforded simply by being the boss's daughter and by being sixteen. The girls with boyfriends at the Westwood School were Kantrowitz-twin-esque, which was to say twiggy, giggly, vapid, inane. *Westwood Ho,* Mara called them. With Eric, playacting, Dahlia felt almost like she was one of those girls. Thrilling.

The summer had dragged. Bruce paraded her around his office — "This is my daughter, Dahlia!" — with such pride and excitement, it was excruciating. Everyone smiled thinly at her, the entitled little brat, Daddy's girl, "working" here for the summer. Her "job" entailed getting coffee, running errands, Xeroxing, whatever. She and Eric walked around the block smoking cigarettes, listened to FM radio, and got high in the bowels of the big office building every afternoon.

"My wife is depressed," he had told her, his thick silver chain bracelet and cheesy single hoop earring catching the dim light. "She never wants to go out anymore. We used to have so much fun; now it's just bitch, moan, bitch, moan, bitch, bitch, bitch. It's like PMS, but *always*."

"That's . . . a bitch," Dahlia had said, laughing at her echo, wondering what kind of sad-sack woman would marry this guy, sweat beading on the rippled back of his fat neck, making a confidante of a sixteen-year-old.

School started again, a blur. Dahlia could not force herself to care. She could not force herself to do her homework, write papers, study for tests. Her grades were abysmal.

The cutting, after that brief reprieve, resumed and got worse. She imagined herself working up to the main event. She considered herself in training. She had telltale trails of faint lines up and down both inner wrists. She cut shallowly but often; the scars were slight and numerous. She fervently hoped and compulsively feared she'd be found out, exposed.

Let's just get it out in the open, enough pussy-footing around: She wanted to kill herself. She wanted to finally work up the courage to transcend the cuticle scissors bullshit. She wanted to wash down a bottle of Tylenol with a bottle of NyQuil and fall asleep and never wake up, a big fat fuck you to everyone she knew and everyone they knew. And right at the end, right before she'd pass out, before she'd have the chance to choke on her own vomit and die, she'd be one drunken, giggly bitch. She'd have herself a grand old time. Real mortality never crossed her mind in these fantasies. She was excited more than scared; excited for the immense redemption an ignoble end would surely entail, excited for the posthumous attention and tragic glory. She felt better already, just thinking about it. She'd wipe the slate clean.

She called Danny late one night, huddled in the corner of her bedroom, shaking and crying. Mary Chapin Carpenter on the stereo. The spring of her junior year, college brochures and Westwood School syllabi piled high on her desk.

"Danny," she had sniffled. He was living in New York City, fresh from college, teaching inner city junior high history.

"Hello?

"Danny?"

"What the fuck time is it?"

"Danny, I —"

"What?"

"I dunno." She hiccuped.

"Well then why the fuck are you calling me?"

She hiccuped again. "I dunno."

"What?" She could not respond. "Dahlia, what do you want?"

"I'm just really sad," she said, breaking into another jag. "Sad" came out like *saaaaaaaaaaaa-aaaaad.*

Silence.

Silence.

She went on. "And sometimes I really don't feel like being alive, you know?"

"I'm hanging up."

"No, I just want to talk."

"No, you know what? You do not *say* shit like that, you fucking dumb psycho. You need help."

You Need Help was the premier insult. It meant that any and all feelings were moot. If, at base, you were simply fucked up, that's all you were. Get help. And in the meantime, your human rights were in question. How had Danny managed to imbue those three small words — You, Need, Help — with such an awful, pejorative, insulting nuclear glow? And furthermore: Then why the hell *didn't he help her?*

Drinking green tea with Margalit in the lounge of a spa in West Hollywood, waiting for a shiatsu, Dahlia calmly wondered: "Do you remember when I used to cut myself?"

Margalit shuddered. "What in the world are you talking about?"

"I used to cut myself. In high school."

"Oh, for god's sake. What are you talking about? What is wrong with you?"

"Well, I have cancer, for one."

"Uch, Dahlia." Margalit shook her head as if to loosen the reality and toss it out. "Stop it."

Dahlia watched her mother pretend to read a tabloid.

"I used to cut myself, *Ima.* With razors. And cuticle scissors."

"You read that in a book somewhere."

Dahlia took a deep breath and let it out. "I *wanted to kill* myself, *Ima.*"

Margalit rolled her eyes. "So why didn't you?"

They must have known something was wrong. They *must.* Dahlia refused to believe they were all that careless, stupid, scared of the truth. They: her sweet father, her piece of shit brother, her selfish mother, the savvy administrators who'd stood sentry at the gilded gates of the Westwood School. Where were the grown-ups, for god's sake? Had she been walking the tightrope of life all by herself all along? The *entire time?*

"You honestly didn't realize anything was wrong with me?"

"You think you're the only kid whose parents split up? Ridiculous. Get a life, Dahlia." Margalit never did have a way with the colloquial. She could never quite swing the right one at the right time.

A rueful laugh — it sounded a little like one of Danny's joyless barks — escaped. "I used to cut myself, *Ima.* In high school. You weren't really around, if you recall."

"I was always *very* involved in your life. You try to make me out to be some kind of monster."

Dahlia held out her arms, hating herself for stooping to prove it. "Do you see these scars?"

Margalit barely glanced down. "Oh, for god's sake, Dahlia. Where?"

In fairness, everyone was having issues as high school drew to a merciful close. Her old pseudo-pal Saree Lansky had stopped ingesting food sometime that spring, but so long as she kept her grades up, neither her parents nor the Westwood School administration seemed to care. The same went for at least half a dozen visually identifiable others in Dahlia's grade. (It's a well-known fact, by the way, that white, affluent, suburban girls get "sick" with this particular wasting disease far more often than their poor, urban sisters of color. Think about it, Gene: Rich girls get sick and depressed more than struggling ones. The experts have weighed in on the reasons: The cushy whiteys have more time on their hands for inventing and actualizing and reveling in their own suffering; the pressures of an affluent background are that much greater; the life perspective afforded by Beamer convertibles and pool parties and early application to Yale can fall short when the shit hits the fan.)

Dahlia and Mara relished their school lunches, purchased from the gourmet-deli-style cafeteria and consumed with aplomb right in the middle of the quad, under the largest, fattest tree they could find. They ate for dear life while frail, dead-eyed girls with Tiffany diamond solitaires on bony chests — total Westwood Hos — floated by, making elaborate excuses for lack of appetite. Dahlia, for one, was very, very hungry by the springtime of senior year, when all the private-school automatons were anxiously awaiting their college admissions letters. Dahlia had applied to exactly three schools: a safety, a likely, and a reach. This was unheard of at the Westwood School, where two-hundred-an-hour college counselors routinely helped kids compile odds lists and celebrity recommendation letters and essays for ten, twelve, fifteen schools at a go. Dahlia was a freak, seemingly the only senior whose conversations encompassed any topic *but* college admissions. Who cared? She was an unlovable, overweight wretch and the same would apply at BU (safety), Sarah Lawrence (likely), or NYU (reach). Which, needless to say, did not inspire much confidence in her previously compiled lists of Reasons To Live.

Margalit carped constantly, from afar, about Dahlia's unstellar academic record. She made absurd threats about college. "We will not pay for her to attend a second-rate institution," she shouted at Bruce. "She's wasting her opportunities!" (What Is Her Battle Plan?)

"You'll be fine no matter where you go," Bruce reassured Dahlia, seemingly unconcerned about her pathetic grades, work ethic, ambition. "You're smart. I'm not worried about you." (But why did What Is Your Battle Plan resonate so much louder?)

Dahlia didn't really care what happened to her, one way or another. Sensing a theme? She couldn't care. She was tired. She looked toward the day when she might finally hit bottom and manage a real attempt at suicide: What a day that would be!

It was like her get-out-of-jail-free card. She hoarded it secretively, protectively, her golden ticket. Since she had yet to attempt it, it was still *out there,* a chip she could cash in whenever things got too tough, to continue the gaming metaphor. The thought bolstered her. Knowing she could one day off herself actually kept her from offing herself.

She and Mara drove all over L.A. late at night. "Night Disease," they called this: the mysterious condition wherein you just couldn't bring yourself to go to bed. *I refuse to let this day be over,* they'd say. *No fucking way is this the end of the day already.* Midnight, one, two. They drove around, went to late movies, diners, smoked packs upon packs of American Spirits. Mara's father was mysteriously dead and her mother was very busy with a strict regimen of aerobics and plastic surgery. Margalit was in Israel. Bruce Finger wouldn't think of imposing anything so restrictive as a curfew. "Have fun, girls!" he'd say if he happened to see them coming or going from the Brentwood house. ("Your father is just a ridiculous 'yes' man," went Margalit's characteristic phone tirade on the subject of their different parenting styles. "Yes, yes, yes, yes, yes! And that's why you're a spoiled brat." "Who *is* this?" Dahlia would respond. "Don't call here again! We're not interested!")

Dahlia and Mara were as close as ever in those days. Both treading water, adrift in their respective family oceans.

It was only in recent years that Dahlia had begun to get the sense she was a burden to Mara. An old friend to be tolerated, borne; Mara's wild, out-of-control old pal. In recent years, Mara was more and more polite and formal. Did she feel bad for Dahlia? Did she pity her? Mara, having successfully outgrown her own nihilism and apathy: stable, ambitious, well groomed. In medical school, sharing a Boston apartment with her clean-cut fiancé, Nick. A sparkly diamond on her left hand. Dahlia could hardly breathe, thinking about that life. She stopped just short of demanding to know: *Are you* happy? How could dear, sharp, dark Mara, her true, bitter friend to the true, bitter end, be *happy* with that kind of fence around her existence? What was next? Was she going to, like, have a baby and blog about it? What had happened to their connection? Where had funny, angsty Mara, with all her companionable venom for the status quo, disappeared to? Her true, bitter friend, to the true, bitter end. Dahlia dreaded with all her heart having to attend

Mara's wedding, the inevitable bridesmaid duties, and whatever mysterious, shadowy form of friendship would come after that. In whatever shadowy, ethereal form of existence Dahlia might inhabit by then, that is.

Back then, though, driving around — to Swingers on Beverly, to the Santa Monica pier for a joint, up Pacific Coast Highway and back, blasting Counting Crows even though they knew it was kind of dorky, chain smoking — they could never articulate where they were going, or why. Night Disease: the imperative that they just keep on going. Now Dahlia understood it perfectly. It was because the day needed something more. Whatever the day had contained somehow wasn't *enough*. They weren't ready to let go of it. Something more had to happen. Something *else* needed to occur. The day could not be over. They Would Not Submit. Not until they were ready.

And what would make them "ready"? Who the hell knew? Eventually, whether at 1:00 a.m. or 2:00 a.m. or 4:00 a.m., they'd had no choice: They went home; they went to sleep. They had fought the good fight, but ready or not, sleep is always, ultimately, stronger than malaise.

12. LIVE NOW

Now is the time to live right. None of us knows how much time we have left. Live the best life you can, now. Today is all that's promised any of us, illness or no. Live today!

Exactly. That was exactly what she had been doing. *Exactly* that. Never a thought for the next moment: how did she feel *right this second?* What did she want at this very moment? What does anyone (especially anyone young) do *but* Live Now? All that Now leaves a mark, though. Living takes its toll. Use up all your life *now* and then — poof! — it's gone. Following her feelings — big feelings, and often — up and down and around and around and near and far. Wasn't that rough, scary, vertiginous hell ride at the very root of all this wrongness, all this cell perversion?

Drugs Dahlia had sampled, from around fifteen, in order of preference (excluding the goddamn Temozolomide, which was no fun at all): pot, Ecstasy, Vicodin, cocaine, mushrooms, Ritalin, Wellbutrin, Zoloft. Each of which offered its own very special tutorial in *Living Now*. And hadn't all that *living now* led right up — nice and linear, when she looked back — to her life now? Which was, hang on, let's glance at our trusty literary timepiece — crap! chapter 12 out of 18 — almost over?

But enough of this wondering, this obsessive tracking: enough. Just one question, here it is, and then we'll bury her and move on: Was she depressed because she was dying or was she dying because she was depressed?

Or, to put it another way: Fuck you, Gene.

It's all beginning to sound like meaningless *Peanuts*-adult-blather. All your *wa-wa-wa-wa-wa*-ing. It was as if there were a different kind of blood-brain barrier at work in Dahlia, one that would allow nothing positive or useful to pass. Still, she continued carting around the pretty green book, continued eating the pretty green foods, continued smoking that pretty green herb, and got further and further away from any serious understanding of anything actually happening to her. She did the dead man's float, face up, of course, so she could look

at the metaphorical sky. New chemo protocol. Aggressive. Blood tests. Mondays:
CCNU, a pill. Tolerable. Next Monday: Vincristine, an IV injection. The following
week, Matulane. Then another Vincristine
injection. Then probably on and on. More
tests. Whatever. Dilantin. Lots and lots of
Dilantin. She could barely keep track. And
who cared, anyway? Cancer treatment is like
wedding planning or child rearing: No one
but you gives a fuck about the minutiae or
wants to know about the minutiae, or would
give a fuck even if they *did* want to take the
time to understand the minutiae. And, like
wedding planning and child rearing, it's all
eventually a giant, moot blur, of no conse-
quence to anyone else.

Basically, she ingested pills, had needles
stuck in her arm, got prodded, felt in
general not her best. Slept hard and often.
The cure is worse than the etcetera.

At Boston University ("A third-rate
school!" sniped Margalit. "All of your
advantages and you can't do anything with
yourself!") Dahlia had gained thirty pounds,
started ritualistically pulling out her eyebrows, and become a true insomniac.

Danny was, by this time, in rabbinical
school in Philadelphia, only a few hours
away from Boston on the train, preparing,

no bullshit, to become a Reconstructionist rabbi. Rabbi-to-be Dan worked at a private girls' school as "Student Clergy." Rabbi-to-be Dan was gaining a reputation for being quite the dedicated faculty member and mentor to the more troubled of the teenage girls in his charge. Dahlia called him and called him and called him, exceptionally proud of him (a *rabbi!?*) and excited to commune with him as an equal, finally: She was all grown up, spread out on her very own bed in her very own dorm room on the third floor of a crappy dorm tower, her stereo alive with Tracy Chapman and Ben Folds Five, her life unfolding now, finally, on her own terms. This was it, Dahlia felt certain: the beginning of her *life.* Her real, actual life. It was time they became friends, for real. She would not take no for an answer. She would make him into her friend if she had to kill him to do it. They were two Fingers afloat on the East Coast. She was in college now; what possible reason could he have for not wanting to hang out with her? She hated their mother, *too!* Furthermore, he was a rabbi-to-be, which surely portended great spiritual growth and potential. She resolved to tone down her "spazziness," for whatever that was worth.

"Want my new address?"

"Whatever."

"Got a pen?"

"Nope."

"Do you want to get a pen?"

"Nope."

"Do you want to call me later?"

"Uh, wait, wait: Nope!"

Spring semester of her sophomore year, she flirted with a girl. Alexis. She thought Dahlia was "hot," and told her so often. Who else but a burgeoning undergraduate lesbian would find Dahlia — unwashed, hairy, overweight, undergraduate Dahlia — "hot"? She would take it where she could get it, dammit.

Dahlia was fairly certain that her own female sexual organs were the only ones she wanted to touch, but they don't call it the "college try" for nothing. She and Alexis never got as far as a sexual relationship, though; it was simply a friendship that had crossed a line, and once crossed remained ruinously entangled until, of course, it ended badly. It was a doomed friendship, really, more than it could be called a romance, infused as it was with just the kind of competitive jealousy and undermining that characterized, so far as Dahlia could tell, just about *every* female relationship. Alexis — perhaps contrary to assumptions about undergraduate lesbians, who Dahlia, at least, imagined to be an overall kind, benevolent, non-judgmental lot — turned out to be neither kind, benevolent, nor non-judgmental. Alexis, with her soft, round body and red cat-eye glasses and penetrating stare and unyielding scorn for everyone and everything, managed to make Dahlia feel downright sunny by comparison.

The main appeal, truth be told, was that Alexis's father just so happened to be a big-shot Reconstructionist rabbi. He'd published four books about combining Jewish practice with other, non-traditional forms of spirituality that would inform and enrich Judaism. Very limited Internet research had revealed that he was a sometime-professor at Danny's rabbinical school. Dahlia loved this coincidence. It was a connection: her *own* relationship with someone in a position of power over Danny. The four of them would have coffee!

"My brother's in rabbinical school where your dad teaches," Dahlia had admitted a few weeks into their relationship. "Isn't that funny?"

Alexis was seriously defensive and pissy about many things: her father, Judaism, not having gotten into Cornell. (BU, she claimed, was for "dumbfucks.") The fact that her older sister (a Harvard alum) was slated to get married that summer. Mention of her father, and of his connection to Dahlia's brother, was unwelcome.

It was the beginning of the end. At nineteen you just followed the scent of whoever showed any interest and only later seriously wondered what the hell you'd been thinking. Live now.

One terrible night, weeks later, in the grip of the kind of sadness she had wanted so much to leave behind when she'd fled high school and home, Dahlia had had the stupid impulse to call Alexis.

"I just feel so alone," she whispered, wept. "I don't feel like I belong here. I don't know where I belong."

"That sucks," Alexis had sighed, impatient.

"Yeah," Dahlia sniffled. "Sometimes I, like — I dunno. Want to die."

At which Alexis had hung up the phone and called the campus police, who showed up at her dorm room, a pair of them. They sternly told her they needed to file a report with the campus health center.

"You're gonna need to attend two sessions with a campus therapist, miss," one of them said. He was meaty, thick; her type! She gave him a flirty half-smile, eyebrows raised, which he ignored. "Procedure. Sign this."

"You know," Alexis said when they talked the following week, both in the market for that quintessential undergraduate *closure,* which was seasoned accordingly by a quintessential, seething female undergraduate aggression, "I wasn't going to say anything, but honestly? You have some serious issues."

"*I* have serious issues? No offense, sweetie, but you're a closeted bitch." *No offense.*

"The thing about you is, you're the kind of person who'll never be happy."

"Fuck you."

"Lovely."

"You don't know me, you fucking cunt."

"I know as much as I need to."

"Look, I'm really sorry that you're a cunt, but please deal with it."

"Whatever."

Phones had been slammed. Later Alexis had written Dahlia a long, hyper, chickenscratch letter, and slipped it under her door. It implied that if Dahlia told anyone remotely connected to the Reconstructionist movement about Alexis's burgeoning lesbianism, Alexis would "fucking kill" her. Also: *Get help.*

There it was, *again:* You need help. You have problems. You're fucked up. It was déjà vu, this refrain; in all its permutations, on

261

an infernal time loop. Dahlia was confounded by it. If she really *did* need help, if she really *was* so very fucked, it would seem truly cruel to simply state so as a parting shot. An insult. The opposite of concern, really. No help whatsoever, if you stopped to think about it.

The campus-mandated therapist prescribed Wellbutrin. When that made Dahlia woozy, she switched to Zoloft. When Zoloft haunted her dreams with a terrifying lack of affect, a black hole of feeling, she'd quit altogether, sold her remaining pills to a guy on her hall who crushed and snorted them, to questionable effect. What did help, however, was pot. Lots and lots of pot. When she was high, she felt whole, and good, and real, and workable, and hopeful. Self-medication, Gene, in the service of self-healing.

She kept trying with Danny. She even went to BU Hillel once or twice, thinking she'd be a real Jew now, too, and make friends, and play insipid, endless rounds of Jewish Geography, the rules of which went something like: my friend's younger brother slept with your sister's friend but then they broke up and now she's dating this guy who was a year ahead of me in USY. Then she'd report back to Danny, telling him about this or that person, this or that person's sister's friend's new husband who was the guy that girl used to date. If this was what it took, though, okay. She'd learn the rules, play the game. She'd go to Hebrew U for her junior year. They'd have mutual friends!

Explanations abounded for Danny's reluctance to be remotely nice to anyone in his family at any time. Excuses were made. Prognoses offered.

"He's just a wounded bird," Margalit would sigh. "He's just an unhappy little bird."

Bruce presented a different line of thought: "Is he dating anyone?" Danny had never, to anyone's knowledge, despite his popularity with the adolescent summer campers, been in a relationship. Hmmm: So maybe Danny was just cranky. Maybe Danny just desperately needed to get laid.

To their collective surprise, Margalit and Bruce and Dahlia were all invited to the girls school graduation ceremony, at which Rabbi-to-Be Dan was awarded a special award by the senior class: The Robert and Melissa D. Krauss Award for Excellence in Mentoring. Shrill, excessively lip-glossed graduate Kadee Horowitz spoke movingly about Rabbi-to-Be Dan's unfailing belief in her. The speech later went up on the school's web page:

Even when I was failing three out of four classes and skipping a lot of school, Rabbi Dan still helped me believe that I could change the course of things, and with his support I worked with a tutor, pulled my grades up, applied early to Tufts, and got in! Rabbi Dan, I just want to tell you that you made a difference to me, and all because you cared. I will never forget what your support did for me, and I am so proud to award you with the etc.

Dahlia reread it obsessively — and was, indeed, a frequent, baked, insomnia-racked, late-night visitor to the school's website — riveted by this bizarr-o alterna-Danny Finger. Here he was "Rabbi Dan." Here he "cared." Here he saw a teenage girl in trouble and "made a difference" to her. There was an accompanying photo of Rabbi-to-Be Dan with his arm around little Kadee. And this was the same Danny? Her *brother,* Danny? Was this some sort of time-space-continuum muck-up? Some impenetrable sci-fi plot replete with evil twins? A parallel universe? What, in other words, the fuck? When all he ever had to offer her in those days was:

"You know, Dahlia, you're kind of intense."

"Sorry," she'd stutter, baffled, having

barely figured out how to duck "spaz," still reeling from the farting-on-her-face days, and not fully able to interpret this kinder, gentler abuse.

The facts were becoming very gradually clear, though, appearing like images in developer bath. Danny was closed to the people who mattered the most, and open to everyone else, not unlike the way store windows read "Closed" to those within while proclaiming "Open!" to everyone without. It was not what it appeared; it made no sense. He flashed *closed* to Dahlia, but announced his openness to every fucking stranger, every spastic, "intense," messed-up high school girl, every acquaintance and acquaintance's sister's boyfriend's mother. Why? She could not, for the life of her, figure it out.

And thus began the setting in of reality. Here she started — slowly and silently, at first — to realize: You know what? My brother is just kind of an asshole. Holding fast to those outdated, untenable assumptions ("Danny adores you!") wasn't possible in the face of reality. Danny was pretty much a bastard. No shit, Sherlock.

She cut down on the calling, the postcards, the one-sided friendship in which she'd invested herself since the home movie days had come to their unceremonious end.

She began to accept that her only brother was a stunted, shitty excuse for a human being, but because she knew just how popular Rabbi Dan was with the prom-court set, and because it was just plain funny, she would just sing Police lyrics whenever she saw him:

"Young teacher, the subject of schoolgirl fantasy." This didn't ruffle him as she hoped it would. It evoked no response at all, which was Dan's signature response. No emotion his characteristic emotion. Fucker.

"Do you know Rabbi Schrier's daughter is a lesbian?"

"I'm getting off the phone, Dahlia."

"Fine, get off the phone."

"You need help."

So help me!

Her jokes increased in offensive pitch. "Hey 'Rabbi'!" she'd yell to him. "How's that school handbook statutory rape amendment coming along?"

Sure she was angry. For years she'd been offering herself up to her beloved big bro, dutifully trying hard and then harder still, fully vested with the faith that if she only kept it up he'd *have* to be kind to her (and maybe even pick up where he'd left off years and years and years before in those cozy, pajama-clad, companionable early mornings, her sweet buddy), but the facts were plain as day, right in front of her eyes on the girls' school website, in Kadee Horowitz's own words, blaring into Dahlia's sleep-starved eyeballs late into the night: he wasn't an asshole to *everybody*. So long as you weren't related to him, he seemed, in fact, like a real mensch. Who apparently collected damaged girls like figurines. It wasn't that he was incapable; it was that he was an asshole. The injustice of this, the sad, sad realization, came like a blow to the head, rearranging everything.

She declined, after all, to spend her junior year in Israel, and instead joined a hippie collective, stopped using gendered pronouns, and went with her friend Lauren to Jamaica Plain, where they got shitfaced on rum with an old black woman who gave them cornrows with extensions all the way down their backs. She switched her major from Sociology to Women's Studies, and wrote a tour-de-force thesis on cultural/ historical perspectives of "mental illness" in "unconventional" women. "The Yellow Wallpaper," *Gaslight,* Frances Farmer. She'd arranged a screening of *Safe,* wherein Julianne Moore becomes mysteriously, horrifically, literally allergic to *everything* in her life and the modern world.

From Dahlia's (admittedly "intense" or, if you prefer, "spazzy") introduction:

For as long as wimmin have had the temerity to experience feelings of anger, sadness, frustration, and deep resentment, patriarchal society has denied them these feelings and, in fact, punished them heartily for feeling anything at all. It won her high honors. She was one of the only high honors designees in the history of the department, her advisor tersely informed her, with a GPA under 3.0.

She shared a filthy house with her filthy friends — one of those student houses that get passed down, year after year, to yet more filthy generations of filthy students. The furniture made you itch and no one ever cleaned. You inherited ancient cookware and got so stoned you didn't mind eating the instant mac 'n' cheese you'd made in it. Dahlia and her housemates sneered at the monthly Pimps-and-Hos theme parties their Greek-oriented classmates threw. They had "processing" meetings, during which they passive-aggressively sniped at each other for, alternately, leaving the toilet seat up, not locking the front door, waking everybody up at four a.m. with sex noise, and so on.

Everything in that house was "I feel." I

feel this. I feel that. I feel that your tone is disrespectful. I feel that when you leave the seat up, you're telling me you don't care about me. I feel that when you forget to turn the lights off, it's uncool. Finally: a place where feelings were unassailable, even if they were insufferable as well.

Night disease persisted. She could not seem to drag herself to bed. She'd sit at her desk, she'd mess around on her computer, she'd have yet another snack, she'd listen to music and read. Finally she'd persuade herself to brush her teeth and wash her face, but even after that she'd need another cup of tea, one more CD, a phone call to the West Coast, where her dad would invariably still be awake and glad to hear from her.

"Hey, Dad."

"La La!"

"Hey."

"What are you doing up? It's — oh my God, Dahlia, it's two-thirty in the morning!"

"Yeah."

"What are you doing?"

"Nothing."

She'd try to remember Margalit singing to her when she couldn't sleep as a tiny girl. Or had she imagined that? Had it been, in fact, a kibbutz babysitter or Uncle Moshe's wife Inbal or a complete fabrication? To the tune of "Taps," an old Hebrew song about the end of the day: *Rad ha-yom, shemesh dom, cochavim notzetzim bamarom; lilah bah l'menucha; shalom, shalom!* It's the end of the day, the sun has set, night has come, time to rest, peace, goodbye. Sometimes that worked. She'd hum herself to sleep, viscerally relieved when she woke up the next morning that she'd gotten to sleep at all.

Let go of the past; it's time to invest fully in this fleeting moment. Stop wasting your time worrying about bygone times or possible futures. No matter what happens in your current fight with cancer, our time on earth is limited.

Right, right. The here and now. The battery of drugs and tests. Her second round of chemo coming to an end. Her body ravaged, her energy depleted, dry heaves and flaky skin and mysterious twitches and itches and pangs and weakness upon weakness upon weakness. What next?

"We'll know more after another MRI in a few weeks," Dr. C said. "Think positive."

Another round of chemo? Experimental blah-de-blah? Targeted radiation? Hit me, she imagined saying at a card table led by an unsmiling dealer, full of ashen-faced

cowards with bad hands, all. Or should —
this was not exactly articulated — she be allowed to just deteriorate and die? But no
one said "die." "Deteriorate," however, was
obvious. She was wilting. At group, even
the stage-four Ovarians who'd make it
through a couple more weeks before going
into hospice *(if they were lucky)* gazed pityingly at poor, young, wilted Dahlia.

"I want to ask a favor," Bruce said to her
one sunny late afternoon. Soon, if she felt
well enough, they'd set out on a stroll, down
to the beach. He was at her house (his
house, really, of course), keeping her company. "Keeping her company" meant that
he basically lived *there* with her now. Margalit, on a three-week furlough in Tel Aviv,
could stay in his house when she returned.
It was musical houses: two houses, three
people. But somehow, when *this* particular
music stopped, there'd be one less person,
enough houses for everyone, and no problem.

"What." There was only one thing Bruce
could want.

"I know Danny's not your favorite person."

"Oh fuck, Dad. Please don't start."

"I know he's not your favorite person, La.
I know he's been very hurtful — to all of

271

us. But I want to ask a favor."

"I don't want to see him. And I don't see any reason I should. I hate that motherfucker. And he *is* a motherfucker, Dad."

"Just hear me out."

Dahlia drew her knees gingerly up to her chin. Her body felt less and less like a familiar, relatable object, a recognizable body. It felt, more and more, like an object-body, a thing having nothing at all to do with her. Foreign, inscrutable, impossible to inhabit, like an ancient, doomed civilization rife with tribal warfare. She hadn't seen or spoken to Danny (sorry: Dan) since his wedding to Nadia the year before. Nadia, the not-at-all-affectionately nicknamed *Velociraptor.*

"There are times in life, La La, when it's crucial to let go of anger."

She rolled her eyes. Anger wasn't something you could let go *of.* Anger held fast to *you,* not the other way around.

"Now, I know Danny has been horrible."

"Drop it."

"I'm worried about you, La, about *you.* Not Danny. Forget Danny. You're not wrong about him. I'm not blind."

So she was dying. Crappy timing, and tough shit. She refused. Let Danny suffer in the knowledge that it was too late to be nice now. Turned out that living "well" or "now" or whatever wasn't the best revenge after all. "Too late" was the best revenge.

"Can I tell you what I fear, La?" She blinked at him, twice. "I'm afraid that if you're stubborn about this, you won't be able to get better."

"Oh for fuck's *sake!* Nice. Way to make it all my fault! Jesus!"

"It's not your fault."

"Right."

"I just don't want you to have regrets."

But dead people don't have regrets.

It wasn't because she wanted to be a vindictive bitch. (Though maybe she did, a little; she liked the thought of Danny having to live out the rest of his pathetic life being perfectly nice to random strangers when he knew, deep down, what a total douchebag he was. Might extreme hypocrisy cause cancer, too?) It was because she understood — as she understood few things — that if she let Danny anywhere near her only to have him hurt, malign, ignore, steamroll, mock, or revile her even a fraction of the way he used to, that she would die without the last remaining shred of her heart intact. The end was in sight, and she was shoring up. Priorities. *I will die with the last remaining shred of myself intact and whole.* Say what you will, Gene, but life is precious. Live now.

"Will you see him, please? For me? We can have dinner."

"No."

"For me, La?"

"No."

"For me?"

Daddy Bruce. Such a good guy. But he just didn't get it. How could he? He didn't have cancer; he didn't understand what had to go on in order to ignite and stoke this kind of fire in the temple of the body. The opposite of love: Everyone knows it's not indifference.

The last straw with Danny had been Nadia, of course, his horrid Internet bride. But the *second*-to-last straw? He had fucked Kadee Horowitz. The year after her high school graduation, after she'd turned eighteen. Lo and behold, little Kadee had matriculated *(thank you, Rabbi Dan!)* at Tufts. And while Danny wouldn't dream of coming to Boston to visit *his sister Dahlia* (not once in the almost four years she'd been at BU), he suddenly had reason.

"I'm coming to Boston this weekend," he told her.

"Really? Cool! How come?" Because she couldn't help herself; leapt at him like a dog, practically pissed herself.

274

"I might need to stay with you. I might have another place to stay but I might not."

"Great!"

He had recoiled when he walked into her house. "This is disgusting."

Dahlia had looked around at the filthy living room, the dusty tapestry half hanging off a grimy window, the full ashtray on the coffee table. A guy with blond dreads was asleep in a moldering recliner. "Yeah. These guys are pigs. You don't even know."

"How can you live like this?"

She shrugged. She had the depressing sense that she had failed some sort of test, that she was being judged poorly.

He dumped his bag. "I might not be coming back tonight."

She asked no questions. Do not press Danny. Let Danny come to you. Let Danny think he originated the notion of acting like your friend.

"Danny's here! He came to visit," she had crowed to Margalit.

"I think he might be seeing someone," Margalit had whispered, via phone. She was in Haifa, where Gil was doing something mysterious and important and violent.

"Yeah, I think so too," Dahlia said.

"And I think he might be seeing someone *special,*" Margalit continued. How did she know? Was Danny talking to her about this stuff?

"Oh yeah? How do you know?"

"Danny told Aunt Orly."

"Really?" So Danny had been cultivating all sorts of new relationships. Maybe this was a good sign. Maybe Danny was opening up after all, like some kind of rare tropical orchid, painstakingly coaxed into trusting its environs.

"Can you keep a secret, *hamudi?*"

That fucking child molester. That stunted piece of shit. His former student!? The girl who'd been his charge from her earliest teens? Now she was a college freshman: and *that* was why he'd deigned to dump his overnight bag at Dahlia's filthy house? *That* was who he was "seeing"? His "mentee." Oh, the humanity. Who *was* this Danny person? That her brother turned out to be the kind of twenty-eight-year-old man who sleeps with teenaged girls was a staggering blow. Sleeps with! Not just ogles in *Barely Legal.*

But she *still* couldn't quite let go of him — the *imaginary* him, the Danny who was wise and mature, her shining big bro, rabbi-to-be, caretaker of lost teenage girls (all but one!). To kill off this mythological Danny would have meant setting her whole past ablaze. Tossing every hope she'd ever had that all was good onto the scrap heap. And where could she possibly go from there, her whole life in ashes?

Right before graduation, a real gem of a guy fell in love with her. Aaron, someone she'd seen around campus for years. He'd always seemed so quiet, nondescript, easy-going. Always had a smile in his eyes, always happy to see her. It was good: She'd needed a real, adult, sexual relationship that was gentle and sweet. She enjoyed his attention for about a month, the lovely way he kissed her, the piercing looks he gave her, the huge grin on his face whenever she walked into the room.

She'd been nowhere near a sexual relationship since Uri, and Aaron was perfect. Calmly, after their first time, she had admitted to him that she had done it once before and that it hadn't been okay at all. That it had been, well, the opposite of okay.

"Oh, sweetheart," he said, and stroked her hair.

This is a nice man, stroking my hair and telling me it'll be okay, she told herself, watching the scene unfold from miles and miles away. This is a nice man stroking my hair and telling me it'll be okay. Rinse, repeat. This is a nice man stroking my hair and telling me it'll be okay. This is a nice man stroking my hair and telling me it'll be okay.

But then, abruptly, she couldn't stand him. She could not fucking stand any of it. He was so *nice.* And kind. And *good* to her. He laughed at all her jokes, and thought she was, as he put it, "the most beautiful girl I've ever seen in my life." What kind of total idiot, she wondered, was this guy? What kind of loser would be so kind to someone like her: someone so obviously fucked up, problematic, issue-ridden? Would laugh at her stupid jokes? Would look at her and see anything but sheer ugliness? Would assert the dumbshit notion that everything would *be okay?* She dumped him in the most callous way imaginable. No explanation, no care — no returned phone calls, no email. When he showed up at the house, looking battered and tragic, she said something about not being "ready" for a relationship, which was the truth. She had just not been ready. Why hadn't she been nicer to Aaron? Such a sweetheart, he was. Her heart bled to think about how she'd treated him. She carried around the very real weight of regret; there had been no good reason to reject him. What had he wanted but to love and make her happy? And what kind of person rejects that?

Danny, she felt, should suffer in exactly this way.

"Dahlia." Margalit in on the act, back in town and skulking around the house in Venice. "*Abba* says you won't talk to Danny. Danny wants to talk to you. Why won't you please just talk to him?"

"Because he's a dick, and I don't feel very well, in case you haven't noticed."

"But he just wants to be your friend! Now is your chance."

"Too late."

"No." Margalit's eyes flashed. "No. It is never too late."

"Sometimes it is."

"Oh, *motek*. Why are you so angry?"

Ummm. "I'm not."

"Your anger worries me."

Dahlia's throat felt swollen, as if closing up. Or maybe it was just oral candidiasis from the last round of chemo.

"I'm not angry," she managed. "I mean, I am angry. There's nothing wrong with being angry. I have a lot to be angry about." It may have been oral candidaisis, but it seemed to be getting worse by the second. Plus, it was increasingly hard to find her way around a cogent argument.

"Oh, please. Right. You've had it *just aw-*

ful. You should know what real worry is."
No apparent irony whatsoever: Margalit's
particular irony.

"*Ima.*"

"No, no, this is important, *motek.* How
are you going to get better if you can't let
go of this anger?"

"If I'm not getting better, it's because of
my *brain tumor.*" Defensive, sure. It was a
challenge to regulate her breath. She tried
to inhale deeply. Margalit backed down,
watching with a pathetic mixture of skepti-
cism and concern.

"It's alright, Ma," Dahlia muttered, letting out the breath. "I'm only dying of
cancer."

13. LAUGH

Find a way to have some fun even while cancer has turned your life on its ear. What do you enjoy doing? What makes you giggle? There is evidence that deep, extended belly laughter can trigger the immune system and promote overall wellness. Try it: Ha!

Dahlia invited some people from the group over for a party. A pity party, she called it, but not out loud — lord, no — for fear of scaring her cancer friends away. Cancer scared her normal friends away (or would have, if she'd *had* any normal friends); she could not afford to scare her cancer friends away with normalcy. To make up for her covert pessimism, the cynical undercurrent, she played "I Will Survive" on repeat. She didn't want to poison her makeshift support system; they had all worked hard for their positivity, their good cheer, their respective bright sides. They deserved the happy endings they'd worked toward. Or at least the notion of the happy endings.

Dahlia herself was visibly worse, and the ladies were chipper and doting.

"Got anything else?" Arlene wondered after the fourth or fifth repetition, Gloria Gaynor gearing up for yet another round. But the insipid song felt good. Dahlia could barely remember, at the end of each cycle, having heard it before. She really was slipping. Slipping, slipping, slipping.

She'd found an old CandyLand in Bruce's basement.

"Let's replace all the candy stuff with, like, *surgery, chemo, biopsy, radiation, morphine drip,* you know, whatever," she said. She had been waiting to make this joke for days: "CancerLand!"

Blank stares all around. Bart had turned down her invitation ("I can't be around cancer anymore; I've reframed."), but having Ruth Ann and Carol and Arlene in her Venice haven was wonderful. She had missed, since forever, the benevolence of nice friends. They smiled and clucked approvingly at the warmth of the place, the pretty string-lights encircling the room, the fragrant candles Dahlia lit.

"Sweetheart, what a lovely home!" said Carol.

Bruce had picked up desserts from the raw vegan place in Santa Monica: dehydrated fig macaroons, spelt crackers with fresh guacamole, individual cups of banana-coconut pudding. A benign party, even with the cancer elephant twisting the night away, center stage.

It was an effort. It was the best she could do. And truly, having these three women in her bungalow seemed, for a fleeting moment, once she'd switched to some mellow Dylan (*New Morning* — and, indeed, it felt as though she was hearing it for the very first time; temporal lobe degeneration has its upside) and they'd all taken off their shoes and passed around her bong, so unexpected, so right and unforeseen, that Dahlia had the momentary thought: It's all good. Ruth Ann and Carol and Arlene, these kind ladies, were her friends now, and all because of this horrible thing they all shared. How cool, Dahlia thought, blissfully stoned, that when a door shuts God opens a window, or whatever. How on earth might she, were it not for cancer, have wound up sitting in a room with these ladies? These nice, giggly ladies?

Arlene smiled maternally, with total acceptance and bemusement, as if Dahlia weren't actually a doomed fuckup but rather a lively young woman with a hearty dose of passionate intensity. Ruth Ann confided in them all: *I think I'm actually okay with dying,* and began to laugh uncontrollably when she'd finished the statement. Carol listened, nodding, her eyes closed.

On deck for Dahlia: possibly radiosurgery, though Dr. C said that they generally didn't consider it for a tumor larger than 4 cm. Tests after the last round of chemo measured Dahlia's at 4.9 cm. An overachiever in terminal illness, if nowhere else: Her tumor had grown. But Bruce was resolute that radiosurgery was the way to go. Margalit, on the other hand, wanted to enlist the help of "healers" who would perform a laying-on-of-hands.

"That's fine," Bruce had said. "That is absolutely fine. We can do that. But we're not doing it *in lieu* of real treatment."

"*Mah zeh,* 'real treatment'? You are so ignorant. This *is* real treatment. An ancient, valuable treatment! As if 'real treatment' works any better. Jesus, *Bruti.* Always believing whatever they tell you. Such an idiot."

These three middle-aged women, who had much clearer-cut reasons for being sick — "Never had kids," Carol said; "Had kids too late," said Ruth Ann; "Smoked a pack a day from the time I was sixteen years old," Arlene confessed shamefacedly — sat on Dahlia's beloved, deep, plush sofa, their legs tucked under them, lapsing into a comfortable silence. And Dahlia had always thought "comfortable silence" was an oxymoron.

One pleasant evening in the company of three middle-aged women she never in a thousand years would've gotten to know if not for the disastrous failure of her body: worth it? She extinguished the thought almost as quickly as it emerged. No. It was not *okay.* Was not, would not be, had never been *okay.* No. She had only to reach up and palm her scalp, most of her hair gone in thick, ugly patches, her head naked and hard under an Hermès scarf from Margalit ("For you, *yaffa!*"), to find herself exhausted by just that gesture, feeling constantly on the verge of collapse. Impossible to adjust to her lack of hair. Dahlia needed her hair. She was not a chick who looked cute with no hair. Also, she was having balance problems. She. Was. Fucked.

"I've got *The Big Lebowski, Best in Show,* and the all-time best ever." She was referring to *Dirty Dancing,* but could not locate the words, even as she looked at them on the DVD. She held up the cover silently, to show them. She was under strict instructions from Gene to enjoy the hell out of herself. Guacamole, check. Pot, check. *Dirty Dancing,* check!

But Ruth Ann had to get home to her dogs, and Carol was tired. And Arlene took her cue from the other two, so by 10:00 p.m. Dahlia was alone in her apartment, their tea mugs still warm on her coffee table.

"Pity," she said aloud, ever so slowly rinsing out the mugs and making herself a fresh tea before putting the movie on anyway and getting back into position on the all-forgiving couch. "Pity, pity, pity." Bruce would be coming by soon, to check in and hang around, afraid to let her be alone. She knew she was deteriorating. Not allowed to be alone.

That was when she had her second, and worst, grand mal seizure.

The week after Dahlia had finished college and moved to New York City, all the daily papers (the *rags,* as the bodega guy on the corner called them) were in hysterics about a gruesome murder (sorry: "MASSACRE!") in Hell's Kitchen. A drug deal gone wrong, probably; they weren't saying. What they did say, however, was that eleven people had been "slain, execution-style" in a "dingy" railroad apartment on 48th Street and Tenth Avenue. Eleven people.

What they also noted, with editorial glee that increased as the days wore on and nothing worse had happened to usurp the story's horror, was that one of the victims, a dancer and sometime actress, had had a bit part in *Dirty Dancing.*

It was all Dahlia could think about. She watched the film again, freeze-framing at the exact moments (three of them, total) when this woman was onscreen. What did "execution-style" mean, exactly? And why was the word "slain" so much more brutal than simply "killed"?

Dahlia shivered at the thought of this innocuous backup dancer — here seen grinding with a partner during Baby's initial trip to the off-limits staff quarters, there seen cheering Baby and Johnny as they have The Time Of [Their] Lives in the just-try-and-sit-still finale — meeting her ignoble end in a dingy railroad apartment in Hell's Kitchen, execution-style. *Slain.* Gross. Fascinating.

There was little information to be found on how the "slain Dirty Dancer" had passed the almost fifteen years since her appearance in the film, but Dahlia's imagination more than compensated: there had been failed auditions, one after another; a dead parent or two; a brief stint with an escort

287

agency; the charming but abusive boyfriend; an escalating drug habit; the wistfully audited dance classes; the aging dancer's body. But onscreen, grinding with her anonymous partner, she'd had no clue what lay in wait for her. The girl appearing fleetingly in this movie was going to live another decade and a half before being *slain,* execution-style, in a railroad apartment in Hell's Kitchen. Was there anything more outrageous than that reality, now played out in its entirety?

After a protracted search, Dahlia had found a tiny apartment in the East Village for way more than she could possibly afford to pay in rent. She had no job, after all, and no idea (beyond "well, I just *will*") how to get one. She had no credit rating and zero savings. The landlord, unwilling to satisfy himself with Bruce's personal guarantee, threatened to give the lease to one of a half-dozen other slobberingly interested parties. The place was about four hundred square feet, with a single window facing an airshaft.

"This market is pretty hot," he'd said at the open house. So Bruce had — *Daddy! Thank you!* — simply paid the entire year's rent up front. Wrote a check just like that, and helped her move in a few days later. Then he accompanied her to Bed, Bath and

Beyond for a towel rack and curtains and a bath mat and all the other accoutrements necessary for outfitting the apartment of a single girl freshly arrived in the Big City. Then, after making sure her bank account was nicely padded ("Just a little extra, La La"), he left her there.

Margalit was in Africa, teaching Tanzanian children English for three months, a blessed reprieve from endless rounds of *What Is Your Battle Plan?* Dahlia guiltily, but not without some relief, imagined Margalit berating the Tanzanian kids about their battle plans. Better them than Dahlia. "I hope you don't think life is just a bed of roses," she'd be lecturing a group of hungry AIDS orphans. Dahlia wrote her a letter with the new return address clearly and carefully spelled out. In response she got a note:

I thought I was racist for a while, all the kids have short hair and the same uniforms and I couldn't tell them apart! But now I can. They're adorable. I love it. Maybe I'll move here.

"I'm so proud of you," Bruce told Dahlia on the phone.

Proud of her? For God's sake, why? For faking her way through a lazy liberal arts curriculum? For not yet having killed herself? For taking his money?

"Not everyone would be brave enough to

289

move to New York City at your age, alone."

"It's really not that big a deal, Dad." She hated herself for allowing things to be made so very easy for her. She hated herself, yes, but it was an old, well-worn equation: She hated herself less than she enjoyed not having to worry about it, less than she enjoyed the vast, plush safety net. The self-hatred was nothing that new jeans, a four-dollar latte, the promise of sushi for dinner and PJ Harvey at the Bowery Ballroom next week couldn't ease considerably.

"Sure it is, La. You're a brave girl. I'm proud of you."

She had no friends in the city; no one knew where she was or what she was doing at any given moment of the day. She walked and walked and walked some more, stopped for a smoothie, and shopped — there was always something she still needed for the apartment: Kleenex, wall hooks, a Phillips head — gearing up for whatever was coming next. She half-heartedly surfed job websites, looking for the "right" job.

She studiously avoided Hell's Kitchen: It was a ghostly part of town, writ large in her sense of the dangers of this definitive metropolis.

She was alone. No roommates or hallmates or community just outside her door.

No ready identity: *this* school, *that* major, *this* family. Maybe that's what Bruce meant. Proud of her, ha. She'd done exactly nothing to earn his pride, nothing on which he could realistically hang that pride, but this was always the way: It didn't matter what she did or didn't do. He was proud of her.

Still, by the start of that October, when she didn't have a job and didn't seem remotely closer to finding one, Bruce began to gently press her. There was the problem of what she would do.

"Any leads?" he'd ask.

"Yeah," she'd reply, though the job websites consistently offered the same boring shit she ignored.

Temping was something she might do, something nicely noncommittal, something that made sense while she formulated a Battle Plan (maybe graduate school? Or perhaps an artistic talent would make itself known? Design? Performance Art?). So she found a temp office and registered herself. Skills: typing, proofreading, phones. Availability: high.

Her first job was answering phones in a small midtown office, working for a man with an almost indecipherable Brooklyn accent whose company did something around executive recruitment. Dahlia couldn't be bothered to figure it out. Eight hours a day, she picked up the phone and queried callers with the firm's name. *Donaldson Associates? Donaldson Associates? Donaldson Associates?* She sat in the gray room — Styrofoam ceiling tiles, fluorescents, cubicle partitions, carpets, desks (black desk chairs, though; reprieve from the gray) — trying not to get caught emailing. She recalled with discomfort all the time she'd spent running around Bruce's office as a little girl: asking for sheets of paper on which to doodle, being fucking adorable and carefree to what must have been the discreet ire of the secretaries and paralegals. How she must have *looked* to those office drones: the boss's daughter, that lucky little fucking carefree brat.

It wasn't until this much later, until she herself had wasted hours upon days upon weeks upon months temping, that she understood just how awful she must have seemed to those secretaries, those office drones, counting the hours until they could go home and look at their new aluminum siding or whatever. How much they must have hated her. (Hence, cancer.)

She kept trying with Danny, who was almost finished with rabbinical school, still the go-to guy for every Jewish teenage girl in town. She had resolved to put Kadee Horowitz out of her mind. What was family for, after all? She took deep breaths and called him, acting nothing but sunny and lovable.

"Dude," she said to him. "I live like an hour away from you. Let's hang out."

"Dude," he said, unkindly as ever. "Dude? Dude! Who the fuck *are* you? *'Dude.'* " With that signature laugh, the barking dog. As though her idiocy was so amusing he could barely take in air.

She let it go. "I live like three blocks away from this ridiculous hummus place. What are you doing this weekend? Come visit." She wanted them museum-strolling, having a beer on the patio of the Spanish place on Avenue C, talking about *life,* about real shit. She yearned (hence, cancer) for his friendship, wanted it as openly as anything she had ever wanted in her life, wanted just a tiny bit of what he obviously had to give everyone else. Here she was: single girl freshly arrived in the Big Shitty. She had no idea what to do with her life. She had no friends. She had no love interest. What she needed first and foremost was a visit from her beloved big brother, her supportive and kind and funny big brother. All single girls freshly arrived in the Big Shitty had at least *one* ally, didn't they? The gay best friend? The pseudo-competitive girlfriend? The mock-abusive boss? Dahlia didn't feel like hanging out with her old college acquaintances, those fellow underachievers who knew her as surly, dykey Dahlia Finger. She wanted new friends, a new life. She was lonely.

"Yah, *dude,* I'll . . . uh . . . think about it."

Then he hung up on her, which she had always allowed as a matter of course: a marker of their unspoken connection. What had she ever asked in the way of a simple "goodbye" from her big bro, to whom she was, after all, so very, very *close?* They didn't need any conventional, universal "goodbye." It wasn't rudeness, she told herself, it was just proof positive of their enormous bond. No doubt Holden and Phoebe had gone on to have precisely this kind of one-sided, dismissive relationship. Right?

But No: Something bigger than her longing and denial took over, a wave of long-delayed disgust and fury. Dare we call it self-preservation? A brief opening, the light of her own self-worth shining through a crack? She dialed him again.

"You know," she said, "I don't know what I ever did to you, but you really need to stop being such a total fucking asshole to me, okay?" Silence. Exhilaration.

Very slowly, after another beat, he said, "Whatever." A word like plastic wrap: meant to suffocate and silence.

"Fuck you, you fucking child molester," she replied calmly.

He tossed out a requisite "You need help" before Dahlia could hang up. The pristine insult, the biggest weapon in his considerable arsenal. If she *did* need help, *that statement wouldn't help her.* He belied the apparent concern of *saying* "You need help" by actually offering none whatsoever. Hypocritical. Useless. Bastard. Fucker. A line drawn. They didn't speak again for months.

"He just needs a girlfriend, I bet," said Bruce.

"He's just a lost little birdie," said Margalit. Upon return to Tel Aviv from Tanzania, she'd begun one-on-one study with a young pseudo-celebrity Kabbalist who, she claimed, had told her that she'd lived many lives and was finally, in this one, getting the hang of the notion that she didn't owe anybody anything.

"He sounds like a total asshole," said Annemarie, whom Dahlia met in bartending school, because, meanwhile, screw temping; she needed a *trade.* "My crazy sister threw a mug of burning hot coffee at my dad last year."

"Well, that's just plain crazy."

"Yup."

Bruce had reluctantly put up the six-hundred-dollar tuition for the course — "You really want to tend *bar,* La?" — which ran for two weeks on the third floor of a loft building in Chelsea. The giant room doubled, under cover of night, as an event space. Every day they tried to guess at what had taken place there the previous evening, eyeballing the evidence: bits of tinsel, stray rose petals, streamers, a whiff of dry ice, or, once, the decapitated head of a deflated blow-up doll nestled behind an industrial-sized trash can.

"Bar mitzvah," said Annemarie.

"No way, man. That's only Saturdays," Dahlia told her.

"Not in this town, are you kidding me? Do you know how much cheaper event space is on a weeknight?"

"Wedding," Dahlia would guess. "They tried to do it 'their way,' because they're really cool and they refused to have the same wedding everyone else has, so it was all funky and subverted and whatever, but still lame."

"Right," Annemarie giggled. "And they're

both settling, because they're freaked out that no one better will come along, so they just did it. Two years, tops."

"No," Dahlia said. "They'll have a kid and move to Park Slope and distract themselves from the emptiness by stocking up on unpainted wooden toys and faux-vintage baby T-shirts and shit."

"You're right," Annemarie agreed. "Fucking bleak."

Annemarie, nineteen, adorable, had jaunty, short brown hair and the kind of sharp, angular bone structure to carry it off. She wasn't even legal drinking age, but one could serve liquor in New York even if one wasn't yet allowed to partake. She was a painter, studying at Cooper Union and skipping around lower Manhattan as though she owned it. She seemed to know everyone and everything. She took Dahlia to speakeasies and private parties in apartments the size of Bruce's house. She had a thing for musicians and was always meeting one or another at show after-parties where Ben Harper or John Zorn would be gliding through the room like Christ incarnate. She had been given a West Village floor-thru to "house-sit" for six months, its owner an ex-lover "spending more time in Brazil these days."

For two weeks they mixed fake drinks at the long bar in the empty event space, using colored water, plastic ice cubes, and a Kinko's-bound booklet of drink recipes they were supposed to memorize. They played weird mnemonic drink games. At the end of two weeks, Annemarie got 100% on the bartending final; Dahlia, having studied not at all, barely passed.

Nevertheless, officially certified to tend bar, Dahlia scored a job at a cavernous, Asian-themed club in the Meatpacking District, which was, then, just becoming the bridge-and-tunnel mecca of the decade. She had no clue how to make most of the mixed drinks she'd spent two weeks failing to memorize (maybe not for lack of trying, after all, hmmm? *Maybe* because she was, just then, unknowingly host to a diseased brain! Huzzah!). She tried to fake it. She made bullshit drinks, instinctively mixed whatever she felt like, and winked at patrons (especially the starfucker gym rats, with their muscle tees and hair gel) when they took their first sips and demanded, "What the fuck is this?" She lasted exactly three nights.

Annemarie helped Dahlia land another job at a bar owned by a friend of hers, a cozy wine-and-beer joint on Thompson

Street, where she could dispense beer and wine with ease. She was nicely suited to this job. She could sleep all day, then hang out all night behind the oak bar amid dozens of votives and a consistently excellent soundtrack, over which she herself had control. She perfected her bartendress outfit: asymmetrical and always black, a shoulder exposed, or cleavage; never both at once. Tied-back hair, glossy lips, and large hoop earrings. She scored great tips from both men and women: via wordless it's-us-against-them commiseration with the women and wordless you're-so-beneath-me-but-you're-cute flirtation with the men.

And she actually liked her life for a while. The energy she saved feeling defeated by Danny and her family in general she channeled into painting her apartment a restful shade of purple. She got the number for a private, referrals-only pot delivery service from Annemarie, and was surprised when a guy she recognized from high school showed up at her apartment door.

"Hey," she said. "You're Jacob Shatz. Westwood."

"Yeah," he said. "Deborah, right?"

"Dahlia!" she said.

"Dahlia! That's right! What is *up*, Dahlia?"

In her hand were two twenties, in his a

red plastic egg exactly half-full of weed. They traded.

"Not much," she said.

"Wow," he said. "You're all grown up." By this he meant: Wow, you're no longer that miserable ugly beast you were when we were fifteen. He gazed at her intently, the kind of stoner who falls in love easily, and repeated her name like he had stored it away for just this occasion. "Dahlia Finger."

"How do you know Annemarie?" she asked. He sipped lemonade from a glass she'd handed him while he perused the pictures and postcards on her fridge.

"She dated a friend of mine for a while. You been living here long?"

"A year–ish," she said. "What about you?"

"Williamsburg." He paused before adding: "Since back before it had any fucking soy milk."

They sat down on her bed and she watched him expertly dismember a cigar to roll a blunt. He was taking a real estate licensing course, he said, but didn't feel like it was necessarily what he wanted to do. He'd had to drop out of Wesleyan after his parents got divorced freshman year and his dad had absconded with all the money to punish his mom for an affair. He'd been in Brooklyn ever since.

"I'm so sorry," Dahlia said.

"What are you gonna do?" He handed her the blunt. "Not like I wanted to, like, go to law school or anything, anyway."

Two hours later — "Shit, I got like fourteen more deliveries to make" — they were the best of friends. It was familiar and new at once; it was comfortable and exciting together. She wasn't attracted to him in the least — he was short and skinny, sporting a ridiculous jewfro, with lambchops to boot. But he was funny ("With a name like Shatz, obviously your kid's gonna grow up to be a drug dealer. C'mon."). And he was immediately, clearly infatuated with her, which was reason enough. She needed that: someone in her life who thought the sun shone out of her ass. Someone other than her sadsack, far-off dad, that is.

"We gotsta hang," he said when he left. "Here's my number, yo. Use it." He was a hip-hop white boy, a Jewish reggae aficionado. (Standard greeting: "How you doin'?" or "What up wit'chu?")

He took up virtual residency on Dahlia's couch, got her high, and pretended they were just great friends. She entertained the notion of sleeping with him, imagined it, decided it would be okay but nothing she needed, nothing she needed to prove. But

301

she figured she might want to one day, so why not keep the option open? He gazed into her eyes and shook his head, told her she had no idea how beautiful she was.

"I'm so not," she'd demur, needing to hear it more.

"Yes, you are," he'd repeat.

"Shut the fuck up," she'd say, loving it.

In high school, Jacob Shatz had been socially accepted, a full human. Hanging out with him now felt like personal restitution for the loser she'd been. She was still compensating for an under-developed ego, and she had a lot of catching up to do.

"You're the perfect woman," he'd joked. "The self-esteem of a fattie in the body of a pinup." She spent whole afternoons lying around with him, laughing, hanging. Nice afternoons.

"You're gonna find the girl who loves the Beastie Boys, and you're gonna find the girl who loves Leonard Cohen," Jake would marvel, going through her CDs. "But you ain't *never* gonna find the girl who loves the Beasties *and* Leonard Cohen."

Rabbi Dan broke six months of silence with two relatively large pieces of news: One, he was going to be in New York the following week, and two, it was because he had "met someone" and this "someone" lived on the Upper West Side. He parlayed both pieces of information tersely, in an email.

If you would like to have coffee, I would be open to that, he said.

Dahlia was wary. But hey: Maybe Danny really *had* just needed a lady friend. Maybe this lady friend was lovely. Maybe this lady friend and Dahlia would be buddies. Maybe there would be some simulacrum of a kind of happy family after all. She agreed to coffee with Danny and his lady friend, who'd met, long distance, via a website for Jewish singles. Be open, Dahlia told herself. This is good news.

Though she and Dan had, of course, had their problems before — solidified when Dan had slept with little Kadee, and ossified when Dahlia had finally realized *you know what? fuck you* — the entrée of Nadia (aka the Velociraptor) had been the last straw. The final nail in the coffin, if you will.

Nadia had earned her nickname ("quick thief," from the Latin) not only via the accelerated nature of the aforementioned Internet courtship and the openly gleeful manner in which she had insinuated herself into Dan's trust-funded existence, but also because she looked not unlike the paleontological creature: bony, hard, an evil glint in her eye, out for whatever she could get and more and still more after that, a hungry rampaging skeletal baby dragon, big covetous glassy eyes over a beak of a nose dominating the lower half of her face, the poor posture of the much-much-too-thin (perennially hunched over as if to say: *Look! Look how skinny I am! I'm so so so so very THIN! I Take Up Almost No Space!*), her head reliably tilted forward, leading the rest of her body as though on the hunt.

She had emigrated to the United States with her parents at seven. Her father owned a jewelry store in Atlanta and her mother gossiped with all the other Russian ladies and made it her mission in life to humiliate her only child, who starved herself ostensibly in revolt. Nadia had the nicest jewelry of anyone in the neighborhood, however. Sizable diamond studs (wholesale!) for her sweet sixteen. They shone like headlights above her hunched, eternally ravenous frame. Why, Dahlia wondered, no nose job? She had, apparently, suffered from severe anorexia as a grade-grubbing, perfectionistic adolescent, and had grown up to become — of all things — a social worker specializing in eating disorders, self-esteem issues, and "healthy lifestyle choices." An inappropriate calling for a woman who remained incapable of sitting down to eat a full meal, a woman who delighted in matching shoes and handbags, and whose stated "lifelong dream" (couldn't she have meant this *at all* sarcastically?), fulfilled when Dan had come to visit her in New York, Dahlia's turf, a few months into their lightning courtship, was to stay at a certain downtown boutique hotel.

("You don't know what it's like to be an immigrant," had been Margalit's strident response to Dahlia's attempted commiseration.)

Nadia was never without a perfect French manicure, someone having impressed upon her at a formative age that French manicures were the classic calling card of the American upper class. On the summer Thursday Dahlia met her (with Danny, at a Starbucks on 72nd Street), Nadia had sported, as well, a French *pedicure,* on display through the open toes of green leather high-heeled sandals. None of which boded well. But Rabbi Douchebag finally had an honest-to-goodness girlfriend, and was finally (it could be assumed) getting laid, by someone of appropriate age, no less. All cause for celebration and hope. Because, Dahlia reasoned, it might just add up to the long-awaited moment when he might act at last like a shadow of a brother, friend, and/or decent human being.

"So, Dan tells me you might be going to graduate school?" Nadia had asked in her diabetic-coma-inducing voice — Paris Hilton on helium, but dumber-sounding — over air-conditioned cappuccinos.

"Not really," Dahlia had said. "I don't know." Her brother, she had noticed, was busy ripping his cuticles off with his teeth; his fingernails down to the quick. He frowned, vacant.

"So, what are you going to do?" Why was she acting like the executive assistant to the special education specialist?

"Develop a serious drug habit, I guess." Dahlia was bored and irritated. The setting, the conversation, the way Nadia kept glancing over at Dan for approval, to make sure he saw just how hard she was trying to "connect" with his lunatic sister. A little later, a priceless moment, the ultimate clarifier: Nadia, in conspiratorial tones, confided that she disapproved of her own little brother's new girlfriend because said girlfriend was "just, *honestly?* Like, not that *pretty.*"

Dahlia understood that Dan was nothing like her, that he was, if you asked her, a shallow loser (rabbinical school notwithstanding). But even still: How could it really be possible that he had chosen this insufferable, vapid manicure whore? Was there really so little of interest in the guy? No remaining vestige at all of the sweet, smart small child he'd been, lying in Dahlia's bed with her when she couldn't sleep and singing her an invented, cherished, and never-to-be-replicated song about M&M's of every color ever conceived and some entirely imagined?

Indeed, there was not. And Dahlia knew this, had known it for years and years, but it took his coupling with Nadia to officially drive the point home: Danny (sorry: *Dan*) was useless, a vacuum where his heart and soul might've been, no chance he would ever redeem himself and be a human being again, a brother, a son, a friend. Dahlia had been ridiculously dumb to hope otherwise. The extent of her budding contempt for Rabbi Dan was matched only by the love she'd once had for her brother Danny.

"Your girlfriend is a twat," she'd said at the end of twenty-five minutes of excruciating small talk, as though Nadia wasn't right there with them. "Sorry," Dahlia had added as an afterthought.

"You see?" Dan had said, nodding, the order of the universe confirmed. The Velociraptor had nodded back at him, her mouth set and that fake veneer of girlish charm vanished. "Great to see you, Dahlia," he'd said.

Dahlia had gone home and fed Danny's email address to a mail-order-bride website, so that for months he'd be on the receiving end of endless missives: *Halo. My name is Svetlana. I want meet kind nice man. I like USA mens and europe's also canada's. I am study englisch in school. I am 25, and have blonde hair. My nice body, to! I am look for nice man's for friendships. Maybe to visit one day. Please say halo to my email with hope we talk soon.*

She'd assumed all along that he was being an asshole because he was *in pain himself:* lonely, lost. But now, look. He'd found a real, live, adult girlfriend. He'd become a *rabbi,* of all things! He'd made himself over sometime in the last decade as *Dan,* mono-syllabic spiritual guidance counselor ex-traordinaire. *Dan* — with all that prefabri-cated fucking *chumminess* — was what his teenage acolytes called him, as though he was just the swellest ever. And he seemed, to the casual observer, like a regular, warm, functional human being. Never once along the way had he paused to address the central fact of having been an enormous prick to his family and only sister, for no apparent reason. And Dahlia and Danny had a great deal in common, really: She and Danny were both damaged, lacking, hurt. But in order to survive, Danny had chewed off the limb of his own attachment, while Dahlia had allowed hers to gangrene.

Danny and Nadia had apparently carried out a sort of pseudo-intervention soon thereafter — they sat Bruce down, Margalit on speakerphone ("What? I can't hear you!" she'd said from somewhere in Costa Rica, continuing her spate of do-good tourism, building houses for developmentally disabled, malarial orphans), and the Velociraptor had carefully laid out, in her best junior-college therapy-speak, with the *DSM-IV* open on her scrawny lap, Dahlia's primary, central, irrevocable diagnosis. The *original* disease. Dahlia was, it was made clear (with the help of the *DSM-IV*), a Borderline Personality.

"She needs help," Nadia had concluded, smiling beatifically at Bruce, who hadn't known quite what to say.

(Mara, upon hearing about the ambush, had kindly freaked: "That's *exactly* what dumb unqualified therapists say about anyone they personally *don't like*. Oh my god, we had a full-on seminar on this during my psychiatry rotation. It's a serious thing. D! Jesus. She can't just say shit like that. You are not a borderline personality."

"Maybe I am."

"Yeah, but you're not.")

A pattern of unstable and intense interpersonal relationships characterized by alternating between extremes of idealization and devaluation (check), frantic efforts to avoid real or imagined abandonment (check), recurrent suicidal behavior, gestures, or threats, or self-mutilating behavior (check), chronic feelings of emptiness, inappropriate and intense rage, and/or difficulty controlling anger. Check.

14. REFRAME

While you're reading these words, *you are alive.* This is it: your life. All living beings cease to live eventually. Can you choose to live with that knowledge and still be happy?

Bruce found her after the second seizure, stopping by her house as promised. She woke up in the hospital for the second time, in the land of the living.

"The tumor has not responded in the way we'd hoped," said Dr. C. "And the seizure was obviously not a good thing."

Dahlia had requested a private meeting, it having finally dawned on her that, cancer or no, she was an adult, and that her parents' flanking her was not a requirement. She was embarrassed that it had taken so long to arrive at that awareness. The things that made you grow up, finally.

She waited for Dr. C to continue.

"Radiosurgery is not a viable option; the

311

tumor has simply grown too large. We do need to increase your antiseizure meds." She nodded. Her neck was stiff and range of motion limited; she'd been slurring her words ever so slightly ever since the seizure. "Mm-hmm."

"To be honest," he said. Had he not yet been honest? "There's not a whole lot more we can do, here."

"So . . . ," she said.

"So . . . ," he repeated.

"That's it?"

He raised his eyebrows in response, held her weak gaze.

Effortless tears (that biological function, at least, still intact) leapt from her eyes, furious tears, shameful for belying any sort of surprise or disappointment or upset. Treatment had not worked. This was no joke. She had a brain tumor. There was no way around it (as it were). The end of the book was nearing, sentence by sentence, word by word. She was a fool if even one tiny part of her had wanted to believe, from the beginning, that it might turn out differently.

She admitted to the mounting neurological symptoms that heralded the beginning of the end: the questionable balance, the narrowing peripheral vision, increasing memory trouble, auditory slips, the occasional language muck-ups, the slurring. Twice in the week preceding the second seizure she had been unable to locate her father's name; once she'd walked slowly down to the end of her block to look at the sign and remind herself of her street name. Saying the word "slur" caused her, necessarily, to slur. Humiliating.

"These are all symptomatic of irregularity in the temporal lobe, and if you look here" — he waved at her MRI images — "you can see quite clearly that the cancer has spread." The tumor encased in shadow.

The real beginning of the end. Well, the *new* beginning of the end, anyway: The old beginning of the end had been, as discussed, conception. What a relief to be alone in here, admitting to these symptoms and feeling sorry for herself in private. How precious little she'd grappled with this on her own, outside the context of family and daily life, away from expectation and relation. Her life. Hers, alone.

"How much longer?" The million-dollar(s round-the-clock hospice care would cost) question.

"It really depends," he said. "If you're finding that alternative treatments are doing some good, there's no telling what kind of quality of life we're looking at. But from the

313

looks of it, it's probably time to start making plans for the worst case scenario."

What was the worst case scenario? That she'd become a vegetable and live forever? Or that she'd die before that could happen? Or that she'd get better and have to do some more godforsaken living, find some fucking health insurance of her own? What was the *best* case scenario?

His eyes deepened. He held up his right hand in what looked like a peace sign. *Two months,* he mouthed.

"In the meantime," he went on, "there are a few clinical trials you could consider. There's no telling what might happen. We have to keep fighting." Here the peace sign morphed into a weak fist. "We've had some success with Tamoxifen."

"Breast cancer stuff?" In Group she'd become familiar with vocabulary no regular almost-twenty-nine-year-old needed.

"Yes. Well, no. In low doses it's effective for breast cancer. For your kind of tumor, we would use up to ten times the dose. About a dozen large pills a day. It could stop tumor growth for a matter of months, but there are potentially very disruptive side effects."

"Is it worth it?"

Again he softened and shrugged, held his

palms up, and swayed as if in mindless prayer.

"Regardless," he said, "I want to start you on Phenobarbital and Decadron, which will help control some of these neurological symptoms you're already experiencing."

The tumor was refusing to do the polite thing, which was go away. It was unresponsive. It would not play nice. Why hadn't it responded? (Tumor! Goddamn it. Listen here!)

She was dying. It was time to say it. Say it. Say it.

"Let's stop at the pharmacy." Bruce clutched her new prescriptions as he drove her home, afraid to let go for even a second lest the disease sense a momentary lapse in vigilance. Disease could sense when you weren't on the case; disease would rush in, no doubt.

"I want to be home," she told him.

"You want to go home?" he asked, about to turn the car around. "I can do the pharmacy myself, no problem."

"No," Dahlia said. "I want to be at home. I don't want to be at your house. I don't want to be at the hospital." She didn't fill out the statement: *to die.* She stared at him until he got it. He winced. "Okay?" she asked. Back when her life had been a taken-

315

for-granted entity, which would go on and on and on forever, Dahlia had imagined herself one day giving birth at home, having a baby "naturally," the way it had always been done, primal and messy and personal and painful. Pain held meaning. One was born at home and died at home. Anesthetize something and meaning was lost. "Okay?" she asked.

"Okay," he said.

The clinical trials for which Dahlia would have been eligible weren't starting until January, and Dr. C didn't want to wait that long. She had to decide whether or not to try Tamoxifen. In the meantime, she'd take the Phenobarbital to prevent any future seizures and help her sleep, and the Decadron, steroids, to lessen swelling in her brain.

Margalit broke down when they got home. "Oh," was all she could say. "Oh," she said, crying. It was real now: the real end.

"*Ima,*" Dahlia said. "*Ima,* it's okay." She held her mother in her arms, feeling something approaching pity; watching the dying was way less fun than doing the dying itself. Who knew?

The neurological inevitabilities were freaky, at best. All her memories would bleed and fade and shrink and float, untethered to a coherent timeline or to her specific experience. She would lose track, she would become helpless even to narrate her own demise. She would sleep more and more and more until finally she'd sleep for good.

Which struck her as odd, in light of the years-long battle with insomnia: in high school, in college, in New York. Whenever she had been capable of getting herself to fall peacefully asleep at all, Dahlia always had recurring death dreams, usually in which she got shot at by vaguely menacing entities (gangsters, crooks, rapists, mean-looking adolescent boys in backwards baseball caps), showered in a hail of bullets. While riding in a car or trying in vain to run away or pleading for her life. And the interesting thing was the way the moment got stretched out — that moment after shots had been fired at her, that infinitesimal moment, stretched out and expanded before any bullet hit her. She'd think, in those dreams: *Oh, okay. So this is it, then.* It being "just" a dream, she'd simply hang there in that suspended moment. Unharmed even if she had, theoretically, been hit. No death, no pain, no fear. Only the lingering moment, the *oh, okay, so this is it, then,* like a residue on her pillow, hard to shake even as she wiped crust from her eyes, stretched vigorously, threw off the covers. An anecdotal truth: One never actually died in one's own dreams. One died without dying.

Her East Village M.O. had been to stay up through the wee hours, sleep into the late afternoon, and tend bar late into the night. She was floundering. Maybe grad school (this, after all, was the handy refrain that kept Bruce's seemingly limitless cash flowing). It was always *maybe grad school,* even as the application deadlines came and went. They had purposeful conversations about it. One such conversation had included, on one of Bruce's visits, a list of things she hoped to do to improve her life, written down on a yellow legal pad. Dahlia "needed to figure out what she wanted to do." She would nod purposefully, but then Dahlia would do approximately nothing, invoke the failsafe *maybe grad school* so Bruce would leave her alone, leave her to her bartending job and her pot and her friends who didn't have jobs, send a check if she needed it, which she invariably did.

And all the while Danny — Rabbi Dan, that is — was working as an assistant rabbi at a congregation in Murray Hill, engaged to and sharing a brand-new condo with the Velociraptor on 83rd and Broadway. Bruce had paid, 80 percent down, in cash; there was just the microscopic mortgage in place (again with the "values"!). From what she could find on the synagogue's website, late at night, hoping in vain to avoid the anonymous assassins of her dreams, Rabbi Dan *("Dan the Man!")* was chiefly responsible for shepherding the temple's youth group and running the Hebrew School. Fantastic: another generation of faithful Jewbots, trailing in formation behind their beloved, boundary-violating, ego-challenged rabbi/buddy. She browsed snapshots of camping trips, dances: Which one of these thrilled pubescent lovelies might Rabbi Dan secretly be groping in the dark?

Margalit was back in Israel, deeply involved with the kabbalist "movement" (this is what she called it; Dahlia had to work hard not to picture a group of seekers taking an arduous communal shit) near Eilat. She "followed" Yarom, who, in his official capacity, served as mystic, Kabbalah scholar, and psychologist all wrapped up into one. In his unofficial capacity, he served as Margalit's new boyfriend.

Dahlia skimmed the emails:

We all chose the family's [sic] *we're born into, Yarom says. We choose before we're born, when we're between lives, and it's because we need to work something out with these people in our family before we can move on. I want us to figure our things out,* motek. *Okay?*

Margalit had swept through town one spring, Yarom in tow, to spend some quality time with Dahlia. They'd had drinks at a bar on the Lower East Side, one Dahlia had picked in a misguided attempt to somehow impress her mother; it was across the street from an abandoned Romanian synagogue, dark as hell, noisy as possible. She knew the bartender.

"Your mother wants very much to fix your relationship," Yarom had yelled over the bass. Margalit smiled bashfully at Dahlia, and — what the hell? — was she really batting her eyelashes?

"Then she should fucking take some steps to fix our relationship," Dahlia had shouted back. "Like maybe tell me that herself."

"Dahlia, Dahlia, Dahlia," Margalit said. "If we refuse to heal our relationships, we will only be tormented by them twice over next time around."

A chance Dahlia was willing to take. She had, with the patience of a saint, waited out the evening and gone home with the bartender.

Dahlia had emerged, at the mark of her mid-twenties, into a kind of beauty no one could have predicted. If you'd told a sixteen-year-old Dahlia Finger that she would one day be valued and appreciated on the basis of her looks, she would have laughed. (Then she would have dragged a blunt pink razor across her inner arm and wept bitterly for the awful, awful, bovine train wreck she knew herself to be.)

But by her mid-twenties her face had hollowed out some; flesh melted away from her collarbone. Her breasts were full, her legs were long, and men and women alike looked at her like she mattered, like she was something worth looking at. It was a heady feeling, this being looked at, this *mattering,* and she walked around the city high on it. High on any number of things, but not least the fact that she was, finally, at long last, a visual presence to be reckoned with. *Well, well,* her boss at the bar would comment whenever she wore red lipstick, *if it isn't our Black Dahlia.* She'd figured out how empire waists and jersey knit and halter tops showcased her boobs and shoulders, respectively; how bangles and arm cuffs made her arms look long and fluid; how her hair, long and lovingly conditioned, dried naturally in thick waves, swung effortlessly down her back. She'd picked up from Annemarie a priceless tip about the benefits of senna tea. She dabbled in yoga. She gave free drinks to an acupuncturist who'd occasionally adjust Dahlia's chi in return. She'd blossomed, and was, if ever so briefly, without having to try too hard, lovely. Her sweet spot, according to Annemarie, tonguing the lip of a Brooklyn Lager. "Every woman has a sweet spot in her lifetime; the moment when everything is working for her. Then it all goes back to shit."

"So enjoy it, right?"

"Hell yeah."

Dahlia was, not infrequently, taken *by* Israelis *for* Israeli, like during those long ago visits. *"Ma Shlomcha?"* someone would ask her at the bar. Exhilarating.

Or people would cock their heads at her: "Where are you from?"

"Huh?" she would feign ignorance.

"Italian? Greek? Spanish?"

"Nope," she'd say. Israeli wasn't quite accurate, and she refused to say Jewish — it was a fucking religion, a belief system; not an ethnic prison.

"Middle Eastern?"

"American."

"No, no," they might continue, getting impatient now. "But where are you *from?*"

"California."

"No, but where are your *parents* from?"

"Chicago," she'd reply, sanguine, and it

was true: Bruce had been born in Chicago.

It would have been simpler to cop to being Jewish — it wasn't like anyone in some shithole Smith Street bar or party or taxi would hold being Jewish against her; not like she'd suffer Ivy League quotas or irregular passport categorizing — but something about it rubbed her the wrong way. The notion that one could spot a Jew the way one could spot, say, an Asian.

Those were the days when Urban Outfitters was selling multicolored *keffiyahs* as scarves, and nothing gave her more joy than to one-up a smug white liberal with a simple: *My mother is Iraqi.* This shut them right up, without fail; knee-jerk lefty politics harbored no soundbite to counter it.

"Israeli policy amounts to Arab apartheid," some smug cocksucker would proclaim, palming a glass of wine at a party, and Dahlia would pounce, gleeful: My mother is Arab, and her family was chased out of Iraq and forced to flee as refugees to Israel, the only place in the world that would take them. This threw those lefty hipster anti-Zionists for quite a loop! (It was sort of like having cancer: a trump, the ne plus ultra of *shut the fuck up,* unassailable!) They would stammer, hem, haw. Jon Stewart and Steven Colbert had not prepared them for this. Dahlia had especially loved to do it in conversation with, say, a pretty, loudmouthed, indie-rock chick in a lime green *keffiyah* who'd skimmed The Week in Review and wanted to show off. It made her feel potent, like she would live forever, like she would have the last word. The *last* last word.

Assumptions bothered her, is the point, Gene. Make an assumption about her, go ahead, she'd dare you. And then she'd do whatever the hell she had to do in order to duck it. Because fuck you.

Jacob came by the bar almost every night; she plied him with free beer and enjoyed the reliable audience for her sexy bartendress act.

"When are you gonna realize you're in love with me?" he'd ask good-naturedly, walking her home, across Bleecker at 4:00 a.m. She'd laugh it off just as good-naturedly. She was not now, nor would she ever be, in love with him. But it was nice to have him for a friend and bolster, and they each got something out of the bargain. Could he borrow $600? Sure he could. She had a vast safety net; what did she care? Could he pay her back in weed? Yeah; why not? Could he borrow another $600? Okay.

Even now, curling up in bed for one of

many, many, many naps (so many naps that being awake was now like the nap and the nap was like the being awake), Bruce and Margalit in hushed, urgent dialogue somewhere just beyond earshot, her nightstand awash with medication and more medication, Dahlia slept in Jacob's ancient XL Lemonheads T-shirt; Evan Dando's forehead forever angst-cratered, the cotton worn silky.

Looking back, it was easy to cast this period in a rosy, fetching glow: her sweet spot, indeed. Screw law school, man. She got the word *"emet"* tattooed near her left shoulder blade; *emet,* truth, and, incidentally, the recipe for animating a golem. She was a pretty decent bartender. She was energetic, she could talk to people and/or distance herself behind the bar with considerable ease. She could offer smiles or winks or nothing at all, depending on her mood, and no more was expected of her than that she perform a few rote tasks and otherwise just *exist.* Which, it turned out, she could do! She loved New York. She met people and more people; made friends and friends, a swath of buddies, a wide horizon of friendly acquaintances, stretched out over the city, the only place there was.

Jacob introduced her to his favorite clients

— the Wonder Twins, he called them: Kat and Stephanie, not actually twins, but wondrous indeed — and Dahlia was swept up. She'd take any opportunity whatsoever to cast other people in the hopeful role of chosen family. Kat and Stephanie, both painters, had met at Yale, where they'd received MFAs. They lived in a loft in Clinton Hill so spectacular Dahlia was speechless the first time she walked in. A former toothpaste factory. A long wall of windows, exposed beams, twenty-foot ceilings. The place was furnished like a Zen-retreat-cum-brothel-cum-art-studio. Organic lemongrass soap at the granite-surrounded kitchen sink, gorgeous kilim demarcating different living areas of the open space, giant floor pillows around a vast, square, hand made wooden coffee table. Kat's canvases lined the whole wall opposite the windows; giant, abstract renderings of bodies in very subtly different configurations. The changes from one to the next were miniscule, almost undetectable, but in series one could see the figures move. Like giant-scale, blurry, lumpy animation.

"How the fuck . . . ?" Dahlia had demanded of Jacob. Could two burgeoning artists live like that?

"I know," he said, shaking his head, smirking. "I know."

In due time she would figure out exactly how two post-MFA painters could possibly live the way Kat and Stephanie lived, but for now they feasted on Mexican food, they got high, they went to openings, lolled around in the loft. They were her first real friends in a long time — they were as interested in her as she was in them — and she was in love. Yet more of Dahlia's easy love, misplaced. Mara seemed like such a conventional dork by comparison. Dahlia had to stifle yawns when she talked to Mara: the recounted anecdotes about her responsible, reasonable life. Her serious studies and her lame Internet dates and the bridesmaid dress she had had to wear to some wedding or other. Kat and Steph, in contrast, were brash, careless, fucked-up girls with enormous, entertaining contempt for anyone and everyone less so.

"We're massage therapists," Steph had said to explain the loft, the copious free time for painting and yoga and cavorting and lying around giggling, baked all afternoon long. The truth, slowly revealed, was that Kat's father — a Mayflower descendant and CEO of a company that did something esoteric and toxic and lucrative — had purchased the loft. And the interest on Kat's trust fund, almost forty grand a year, made for some excellent spending money. Steph had grown up in Wisconsin, the daughter of a doctor and "a nothing." Both had an intoxicating tendency to behave as though everything difficult about life was an illusion. So *they* had Daddies, too! Still, it was over the top even to Dahlia: the artisanal cheeses and weekend getaways to Amsterdam. Something was off, but what did Dahlia care?

On her own, Dahlia got stoned and rode the subway, her favorite thing to do in those days, her iPod blaring playlists assembled expressly for the purpose. She marveled at the people around her, at her unlimited opportunity for staring, the way everyone seemed just like her and nothing whatsoever like her. The lovelorn, the pretending-to-reads, the child abusers, the truly checked out, the sinister. A surprising number of small children furtively licking subway poles (Christ almighty, Gene, are those kids okay?). She felt deliciously plugged in. It was all a harmless game. She read *US Weekly*, tapped her feet, and giggled out loud.

Once, she had forgotten her headphones, and spent the ride on the F train from 2nd Avenue to Jay Street listening to a couple fighting pitifully, the man practically shrieking, the woman higher pitched still, whining, but both strangely calm throughout, as though they were badly play-acting a script:

"I ain't never had no *chance* with you, Victoria."

"Baby, that ain't *true* —"

"Yo, don't talk to me. Don't even *talk* to me. I will get *off* this train at the next stop if you say one more thing to me."

"Baby ——"

"Nuh-uh, Victoria, I don't want to hear *nothing*. This what I'm *talking* about, Victoria. Exactly what I'm *talking* about."

"Baby, that ain't *true*. Baby, c'*mon*."

"Nuh-*uh*, Victoria. Don't say nothing *else* to me. *Nothing* else."

But the worst, another time, was the excruciating wail of a baby whose teenaged mother was ignoring it. Those screaming for dear life screams, screaming hoarse, screaming raw screaming screams, screaming and screaming and screaming. She could hear them for days afterward; that pitiful sound had etched itself into her brain, a nails-on-chalkboard echo. Her sweet spot, indeed.

Margalit had called, out of the blue, to share big news.

"Oh my god, *haruti!* Guess *what?* Danny and Nadia are getting married!"

Dahlia had, with some effort, all but managed to forget Danny existed. Bruce was under strict orders never to mention him. Margalit was usually too busy workshopping her personality with Yarom to mention much of anything else at all. Dahlia never, ever, for any reason whatsoever, ventured north of 14th Street or, for that matter, near anything remotely Jewish. She had removed herself from that whole sideshow, and she had surrounded herself with other things: friends, weed, good times, better times.

Dahlia at Danny and Nadia's wedding, plain and simple, equaled cancer. Of course, she didn't *have* to be at the wedding. She could have opted out, a conscientious objector. But there was some unseen hand guiding her. She could no more miss that wedding than she could avoid tweezing an ingrown hair or ripping off a scab. Which is to say not at all. *We would love to have you there. If you're going to be supportive,* Danny had said in an email.

Dahlia had responded with: *a) go fuck yourself, you fucking child molester, b) dad is paying for your idiot wedding, so I'll be there to avail myself of the open bar, and c) your intended is a retard with split ends.*

She took Jacob as her date, and spent a week beforehand regaling him with her fantasy toasts. They wanted to see Border-line Personality Disorder? She'd show 'em some Borderline Personality Disorder!

"Ahem!" *Clink, clink, clink* [butter knife on champagne glass]. "Hello, everyone! We're here tonight to celebrate the marriage of Danny and Nadia! Danny and Nadia. Nadia and Danny. Yes indeedy. Danny is my big brother. What does that mean, 'big brother'? George Orwell meant one thing by it; people with honest-to-goodness siblings who are there for them as friends and to help light the treacherous way through life mean another thing entirely. I guess I mean something closer to Orwell. Danny was a total shitbag to me growing up. Once he gave me a concussion with the remote when I wouldn't relinquish it during a Dodgers game. He tried to light my cat on fire. He abandoned me at sleepaway camp. Ah, childhood folly. Things got much, *much* worse as I entered my post-adolescence and he tormented our sad-sack parents and left me an only child. But you don't want to hear about any of that tonight! That's all in the past, Danny! We're all really happy for you. Grandpa Saul's really relieved that you don't like to take it up the ass. But let's talk about Nadia! Seven years on J-date, and look what Danny finally landed! I've seen a big change in my brother since you showed up, toots. The leather slides, for one. And the fancy hotels. He still has no discernible depth or sense of humor, but you can't make a mountain out of a molehill. You really hit the jackpot, sweetcheeks! Please don't let that little tryst with his high-school student weigh on your mind, *at all.* Really: She was eighteen, and a *total* babe. It's a nonissue. You got him now! Way to go. And just under the wire! What are you, like twenty-nine-and-a-half-half-half-half? Man, look at those bridesmaids of yours! They're salivating all over their orange spray-tans! Don't worry, girlies, somewhere online there's a sexually arrested trust-fund baby for you, too! *It will happen,* I promise, so long as you keep waxing your cooters like good girls! Let's all raise our glasses. To Danny and Nadia: Really and truly wishing you a long, long, long, long, looooooong — seemingly endless! — life with each other. L'chayim!"

Jacob had laughed. "Man, you really hate them, don't you?"

"No, why do you say that?"

"Maybe we shouldn't get high for this."

"My *ass* we shouldn't get high for this."

The wedding, at the goddamn *Plaza,* was like a greatest-hits wedding expo: Nadia wore a beaded, strapless A-line and enormous white veil. Her hair was in an elaborate updo replete with curl-ironed tendrils ("tendrils," said poor Julia G.). She carried red roses and walked down the aisle to Pachelbel's *Canon.* The thirteen bridesmaids (of which Dahlia was not one; she had patently refused) wore peach (*not* a good look with the spray tans) and screamed *whooooo-hooooo* like Girls Gone Wild during the first dance (to — what else? — Etta James's "At Last").

Dahlia and Jacob were seated near the edge of the dance floor, to the left of the band. The Kantrowitz twins and their respective husbands, along with two Israeli cousins, Rafi and Eitan, Dahlia hadn't seen since she was ten, comprised the rest of their table.

"I feel like I'm in a cliché," Jake had said. "Like, I'm actually *inside* a cliché. It's pretty amazing. Maybe we should've done X."

Dahlia had spent a good chunk of the reception outside sucking on cigarettes with Rafi and Eitan, whose respective wives, Talia and Neshama, were politely ripping the party to shreds. ("It's nice, the tablecloths, but too many flowers looks trashy." "Her hair should have been up nicer." "Is this an American thing, this small portions?" "Her family, they are . . . different, no?")

Nadia's younger brother, an effeminate, hyper, light-flyweight UCLA sophomore, had offered the first toast.

"My sister is one of the *most smartest* people I know," he had said. "And for her to find this amazing man makes me the happiest little brother in the world. Dan is like the brother I never had. He is so kind, and caring, and generous, and amazing. They make an amazing couple."

This was more than Dahlia could take. She stepped up to take the mic. She'd had too much champagne, admittedly.

"Welcome to this wedding, y'all! Do you believe this shit? Who are you people?" She couldn't continue. She looked woozily around at the familiar and unfamiliar faces. All of them were unfamiliar, she decided, and added "Fuck it," before shoving the mic back at the bandleader.

After this debacle — "She ruined my wedding!" Nadia had wept, dabbing at her epically made-up eyes with a cloth napkin: "My *wedding!*" — things were a wee bit strained.

"Are you seeing anyone, La?"

"No, Dad, Jake's just a friend."

"I mean a therapist, La."

"Oh, for fuck's sake. It was funny! They're fucking idiots, Dad! Come *on!* You know as well as I do that they're retards."

"La, this is not funny anymore. You need help."

"I don't need help. I'm just not an idiot."

"La, were you on drugs?"

"Dad."

"Dahlia, I'm worried about you."

"Dad, please."

"You've been in New York for almost four years, Dahlia. What are you doing?"

She had glared at the ceiling.

"I think you need to see someone. I'm worried about you. You come to me when you're ready to act like an adult."

She was being cut off. Unbelievable! She never thought she'd see the day. How could she simultaneously have a personality disorder *and* be responsible for fixing it herself? Assholes.

But regardless, oh, *shit.* What now?

Reframing, dear reader, means, simply, letting go.

"Come live with us," said Steph. "You can help out and it'll be awesome!"

"Yeah, Dahl. You're coming to live with us. We need a third wheel, anyway."

Her only brother lived sixty blocks to the north, her father was a banal phone call away, and her mother still walked the earth, somewhere or other, adventuring and exploring, loving life. But Dahlia existed in a world that contained solely herself, in which she was entirely unconnected to anyone and everyone, from which she stood alone and apart. She had been moving toward this disconnect all her life, and she felt, finally, that she had achieved it. Which was something, all right. No investment, no hope, no expectation. She didn't belong to her life and her life didn't belong to her. Now what?

15. Be Grateful

You've been blessed with life. Cultivating gratitude is an essential part of wellness. When we overlook what we've been given, we inhibit wellness. Every moment is a whole and perfect experience: Be thankful.

Returning from a slow, slow walk with Bruce — where had they walked? They had walked somewhere — Dahlia found Daniel and Nadia in her precious bungalow. There they were, huddled with Margalit on the couch and looking generally terrified.

"What are they doing here?" Dahlia wanted to know, heart slamming, words painstaking. Her house! Her retreat! Her private bastion of okayness! Contaminated. Invaded.

No one said anything. Danny and Nadia and Bruce and Margalit looked at each other. No one looked at Dahlia. There were balloons from the group, a basket of candy from the cousins, a teddy bear holding a jar of purple-foiled chocolate kisses from Aunt Orly. Offerings.

"What *the fuck* are they doing here?" Dahlia asked again, trying in vain not to slur, feeling her grasp slipping, not wanting to forget her own immediate rage. She turned to Bruce, pleadingly. "Dad."

"They want to be here." Bruce said. "They flew in, La. We're still a family."

Dahlia let out a small, bitter laugh and turned toward Dan. "I don't want you here. I fucking hate you." It was very, very important that she hold on to that reality. It took concerted effort to keep it in focus, but she was willing to go the extra mile. *I hate,* she reminded herself. *Hate Hate Hate Hate Hate.*

"We don't appreciate being talked to like that," Nadia volunteered.

"Well the royal *we* doesn't give a flying fuck, you . . . ugly bitch." It wasn't easy to summon the appropriate anger; her vocabulary — those words of well-worn indignation — felt compromised. *Was* compromised. "Get *out.*" Silence. She would never have gotten away with that kind of direct hostility before cancer. Chalk up something else for the bright side: A brain tumor overrode purported borderline personality disorder. A hierarchy of illness, in effect.

Nadia was a nervous-smiler, the genuine article. A small, infuriating smirk stretching her microdermabrased little chin. Dahlia watched it, frozen there, dumb as an ice sculpture in the tropics

Here they were, like an intervention. What new diagnosis would be leveled now? What internal, inherent wrongness was poor Dahlia harboring now? She widened her stance like a boxer. God, she must have looked ridiculous.

"Dahlia," Dan said. "It's the time to let go of old stuff. This is not helping anyone. Now's the time for us to let go of old stuff."

(Where had she heard that before: *let go?*)

"Oh? What are you, like, Zen master? It's helping *me.* Fucking asshole. That feels great! I think I'll skip the Tamoxifen, Dad. How about we tie Rabbi Dan to a chair and I'll beat the shit out of him for a half-hour a day instead. That just might do the trick."

Grief is the price we pay for love, it seems, and we're all on some mysterious payment plan. The bigger the love, the bigger the grief. She had wanted a different family. She had loved that nonexistent ideal. It did not exist, but she had loved her belief in it. She had held on to the belief as long as she possibly could.

Margalit giggled, a nervous-giggler

through and through, the genuine article.

Dahlia wanted these people out, whoever they were. Out.

"Okay." Danny got up, spoke in low tones to Bruce. "Okay. I think we'll be going now."

But Nadia wasn't moving. "You know," she said to Dahlia, condescension as thick as her slightly off-shade foundation, "I'm a therapist —"

"You're a fucking community college night school social worker, you dumb, dumb, dumb cunt." Yes, there it was, the right rage and the right words in the right order — she had it! They would have to pry her rage from her cold, dead hands.

"And I just want to say that they've done a lot of research and found that a good attitude really makes all the difference where illness is concerned."

"Free advice, wow! Thank you! Thank you *so much!*"

Nadia shook her head at Margalit, that awful smile intact. "Her bad attitude is really unhealthy."

"You think my *attitude* is unhealthy, you ugly bitch? You think my *attitude* is going to kill me? You want anger? You want *angry?*"

She was gasping for breath. She was shrieking. She was wild-eyed and dizzy. She was screaming herself hoarse. But you know what?

She felt better.

"Motek," said Margalit. "You need all your energy for fighting this disease now. Please save your energy for that."

"Get out! Get out! Get out!"

It took a soy chocolate ice cream/Phenobarbital/Ativan milkshake — lovingly, silently prepared for her by her sweet Daddy Bruce — to get her back to zero.

An ugly scene. She didn't care. If not now, when? How could something that felt so good be bad for her? Who cared if it was bad for her? What, if anything, was *good* for her? Sending her brother letters and mix tapes and clinging to him desperately in the wake of her parents' virtual and literal disappearance? Gearing up over months for quality time with her crazy mother? Taking advantage of her ineffectual dad's willingness to burn cash? Moving through the world alone, untethered, invisible? Getting stoned every day, all day? The GRE!?

This level of hatred was its own brand of exhilaration, the most complete, simple *feeling* she could achieve. Fine, her antics around that ridiculous wedding had been sort of borderline. Admittedly. But — Gene! — two things: One, wasn't keeping it all *in* supposedly really unhealthy? And two, weren't only the good supposed to die young? Answers, Gene. Please.

A bad period had followed the wedding. The worst, really. (Well, or the pre-worst.) She had cut ties. She had decided to jettison whatever crumbs of family she might still claim as her own. Margalit had started in again about the battle plan (or lack thereof). Bruce had gently but firmly let her know that his checks were contingent upon her getting "help," and she had decided that he could go fuck himself alongside the pathetic rest of them. She had thought, distinctly, *fuck them all.*

She had moved in with Kat and Steph, who were giddy and enthused, unaccountably happy to have Dahlia around. "We love you, babe," they told her, apropos of not much. "Now our family is complete!" Dahlia was taken aback by their overtures of welcoming, of "love," but she had no better offers, no option but to believe them: Chosen family was where it was at.

"I love you guys, too," she told Kat and Steph.

"Move in with *me*," said Jacob.

"You live in a squat in Bushwick."

"Home is where the heart is, cherry blossom."

So she had bid farewell to the East Village Daddy-pad, sold most of her stuff, and moved into the loft. She contributed a measly six hundred dollars a month, wondering for the hundredth time what the hell the deal was with Kat, Steph, the half-finished canvases, the copious drug supply, and the extraordinarily fabulous space.

"Well," said Steph. "We're massage therapists."

"I know," Dahlia had nodded. She was beginning to be embarrassed about tending bar, wary of the way she'd be perceived, sooner or later, by some imaginary, menacing conglomerate of high school classmate, Kantrowitz twin, Mara, and everyone she'd seen at that goddamn wedding: A loser. A failure. A ne'er-do-well. She thought, alternately, *maybe I'll go to grad school* and *maybe I'll become a massage therapist* and *maybe I'll smoke a bowl* and *maybe I'll kill myself.* She got a "save the date" card for her ten-year Westwood School reunion, set for the following year. (How many suicides might be prevented by the simple termination of alumnae mailing lists? Twenty-five percent? Get on that, Gene. Save some real goddamn lives.)

Kat worked hard on her canvases, putting off the advances of galleries who wanted to show her, always swearing that she was "not totally ready." Steph had a studio in Williamsburg, but she worked only infrequently. Her paintings contained black shapes that invoked graffiti-type words, fragments. They were energetic and modern, but even Dahlia could see that they were wholly unoriginal. No point. Nothing to say.

"We're the *best* kind of massage therapists," Kat had giggled.

"We give the best massages *ever!*" Steph added.

"I bet," Dahlia said, clueless. For all her bottom-reaching and rage and self-destruction and purported psychiatric wrongness, she really was kind of naïve.

Kat's sweet, paunchy older brother came over one night with a friend in tow. Had it been *Will* or *Bill?* She could not recall. Will/Bill the North Brooklyn hipster with the handlebar mustache, who had, for some godforsaken reason, wanted to watch Dahlia's home movies. Maybe she'd been talking, the way she got to talking, when she was stoned or drunk or both, about what a shitty family she had.

"Man, you were cute," he told her. An irony thing for him, this home-movie watching? Or did he somehow know it was her PIN? Because it's a well-known fact that every woman has a secret code, a password which, when entered correctly, garners complete and total (if temporary) access. Dahlia's PIN: admiration for the spectacle of the Finger family in all its glory.

"What a cutie." His hand in her hair at the back of her neck, eyes on the child she'd been, lips grazing the edge of her earlobe. And so yes, of course she was going to sleep with him. Hardwired.

They threw massive drug-themed parties on the roof deck. One night it was blow. Another was Ecstasy. At one, they 'shroomed. Once, going "retro," they tried an alcohol-only party, which was widely acknowledged as an outright failure, over just past midnight.

Dahlia had met Clark on the roof on Fourth of July. Hotter than, as Steph put it, "fuck." He'd stood near her with a beer in one hand, rumpled blue linen shirt unbuttoned halfway down his broad, hairless chest, sleeves rolled up around veiny forearms. They'd said "hey" and Dahlia had casually drifted to the other end of the roof, feeling him watch her. He was older — much: mid fifties, at least — and Dahlia sought out Kat to find out who he was.

"Clark," Kat said.

"Who is he?"

"He's . . . Clark! Clark Anselm. The musician! He's a fucking genius."

"Who *is* he? How do you know him?"

"From the welfare office," Kat said mournfully. "What do you think, D? He's a client of Jake's. He's totally one of the best rhythm guitarists ever. He's played with like everyone."

They had flirtatiously avoided each other, a thrilling pas de deux, all night. Clark stayed until the very end of the party and finally cornered her.

"Hard to get," he said with twinkly eyes. She had shrugged, and pulled out the two lacquered chopsticks (Margalit had gone to China the year before) which held her hair in a messy pile atop her head. Close up it was clear that he was even older than she'd assumed. They were both covered in sweat. He gave her his card — just his name, in black, and a number.

Such good fun. He was born in 1949, a measly year after her father and the state of Israel. He had lived a long, storied life, according to wild rumor: snorted heroin with Basquiat in the doorway of an abandoned building on Avenue C, built a cabin in Northern California from the ground up with his own two hands, squatted with his best friends in the East Village before buying his once-fetid DUMBO loft-cum-recording-studio in 1988, for a pittance. His ex-wife was an experimental poet who'd gotten a MacArthur and left him. His two daughters, now indifferent teenagers, lived with their mother on an organic dairy farm in Vermont, making cheese and butter. He'd played rhythm guitar and bass for a long roster of luminaries (listed gleefully by Kat), lately doing, he told her, "a lot of studio work." And the true marker of greatness, sealer of the deal: He dropped names approximately never.

They took up residence in a series of dark, wood-paneled downtown bars with cloth napkins and maître d's who called him by name, drinking martinis until 4:00 a.m. He gave her lingering kisses and twenties and put her in cabs. Quite the gentleman.

She would wake up the next morning feeling fortified and wise, unafraid to continue onward, sure she was just doing the messy living required of her, Clark having provided a sort of benediction to make it all okay. She was *artistic,* not merely fucked up. She was fetching and funny and charming, reflected in his eyes. They had long, rambling, pseudo-intellectual conversations.

"I feel about religion like I do about Dylan shows," he'd start: Unlikely comparisons were a prerequisite for their preferred brand of banter.

"How's that?"

"You're skeptical that it can be as good as you want it to be, as good as it's supposed to be. You're almost afraid to hope that it will be, because it's just too much expectation."

"Uh-huh."

"But you go and you try to keep your expectations low and your mind open, and you're not gonna be disappointed if it sucks, if he's mumbling, if you can't tell what song he's playing for a good while, if he just shuffles onstage, plays, shuffles back off again, whatever."

"Right." Dahlia had yet to attend a Dylan show.

"Because whatever: it's Dylan. He's unassailable. He rocks, even if the show sucks. I believe in him. I love him. He's Dylan. Period."

"Mmm-hmmm."

"But it turns out he's amazing, of course, and from the opening bars of his first song you're like, 'Okay, this is awesome.' "

"Right."

"But all around you are these high fucking frat boys and elderly hippies and drunken assholes talking too loudly to their

348

drunken asshole girlfriends about this or that bit of Dylan trivia, and you start getting annoyed because you're missing out on enjoying Dylan *himself* up there. You get to feeling like if you could just fucking kill everyone around you you'd be in this blissful state of communing with Dylan and having this amazing experience."

"Huh."

"So you're just irritated and fucking pissed at everyone who's ruining your personal moment with Dylan, this incredible moment. And, of course, wanting to kill all those assholes makes *you* an asshole, too. That's how I feel about religion."

"So you'd just rather go home alone and listen to Dylan on the stereo? That's the only way to really enjoy it?"

"Sort of, yeah. Like why bother trying to have this public, communal experience of Dylan when the only real experience you can have is by yourself, alone, in your own head?"

"So Dylan's like God and all the annoying people fucking up his show for you are religious people?"

"Exactly. They all have the wrong idea, see? It's abject worship, and for the wrong reasons. One guy is going 'Whooooooo!' and making devil horns because all he knows is that Dylan is, like, *famous* and *rad* and whatever. And another guy is trying to impress his friend by predicting what song is coming next. And someone else is just waiting to hear a song he knows, so he can recite the lyrics. And another guy is busy fucking *writing down* the goddamned *set list.* So no one is really having an organic moment, in their own head, with this music and this performer and their own *sense* of it all. They're incapable of actually having a moment, so they write it all down and muck the moment up completely while you're just trying to *be* there."

"Hm."

"Yeah. And then you want to, like, eradicate everyone who doesn't get it the way *you* do, you know?"

"Yeah."

"It's fun kissing you."

"Yeah?"

"Yeah." He drew her toward him and really kissed her. She may have actually blushed.

"I've wanted to do that for a long time."

"Yeah?"

"I want to take you home and do filthy things to you."

"Do you?"

"Yeah."

She took a final swig of her Bourbon-and-ginger and nodded. "So let's go."

He fumbled joyously with his wallet, threw a couple fifties down, and hustled Dahlia directly out of the booth. Endearing how keyed up he seemed to get. A man's specifics mattered very little; old/young, tall/short, fat/thin, smart/dumb, successful/loser, rich/poor — they all just wanted, with that adorable desperation, to put their dick somewhere warm and alive.

She had never been with anyone as old. Clark's body was unlike any she had ever experienced: loose, in its way, and disarmingly soft in places, his pubic hair gone gray, erection gentle. She felt oddly protective of him, offering herself up tenderly, feeling as outlandishly succulent and unexpected as a perfect, locally grown, organic peach in winter. With somebody this much older she experienced her body — truly — as an object of beauty; its relative youth so extraordinary, so precious, that there was no room for bedroom irony. None of her usual tricks: the sucked-in stomach, the arms placed just so to keep her breasts from rolling toward her armpits, lights off. None of her well-worn jokes and apologies for this or that perceived flaw or jiggle (her left breast slightly larger than her right, the faint stretch marks on both hips, her total inability to change positions with any athletic grace whatsoever, etc.).

They got stoned, ate cheese and grapes, and listened to Dylan.

Dahlia, one rainy late afternoon, a half-dozen candles burning in Clark's nonworking fireplace, realized what it was about Dylan. They were alternating between *Desire* and *Love and Theft.*

"I know what it is!" she said after "Mississippi."

"What is it?" Clark asked, purring, content, baked.

"Dylan songs never end before you're *ready* for them to end."

"Hmmm, yeah."

"They go on until you're absolutely okay with them ending. They never leave you short. They never stop too soon."

"Right."

"They carry you through and deposit you safely on the other side."

"The other side of what?"

She shrugged; pretended not to know what she herself meant.

It wasn't a traditional relationship; sometimes they'd go weeks without seeing each other. Clark would occasionally drink her under the table at Bar and Books on Hudson, where even today they allow you to smoke inside, Bloomberg (and cancer) be damned. He would call her out of the blue, wonder what she'd been up to, how she was, suggest they meet up. Then they would close the place down, exchanging their banter, both well aware that she would of course go home with him.

It did occur to Dahlia during this period that she had exchanged one father figure for another, but that was silly psychobabble, rudimentary baloney, Nadia-level analysis.

When she finally figured out — so, so late, Clark laughing himself halfway to a cracked rib in bed next to her — what Kat and Steph *really* did to support themselves with "massage," she was flabbergasted. Yet another of those late-coming (no pun!) realizations. Dahlia unable, for all eternity, to figure out the obvious realities unfolding around her. No shit, Sherlock.

"Come on," he had said. "You knew."

"No," she had said. "I really didn't." She was agape. Kat and Steph were *prostitutes?*

A whole universe of things allegedly readily apparent, which she did not, could not, would not see. Was this what separated her from everyone else? Was this why everything hit her so much harder? Everything. Every *thing.* Even the stuff she knew as well as her own name, which was slipping away now anyway, bit by bit. It was not unlike being stoned, day in and day out. Always the last to know about everything important, always surprised and betrayed by what it seemed everyone else already knew without having to be told, always flummoxed by the workaday paradigms that comprise life on earth. So what, pray tell, was she supposed to be grateful *for?*

16. Have Faith

There is no need to worry about how things happen, or why. Accept that all is as it should be, and you will be at peace. It doesn't much matter what shape your belief system takes; the important thing is to believe *something*.

Gene, really. *What?* Things will unfold as they should and she needs to be at peace with whatever? But that's so passive! She might *die!* Now she's supposed to be *okay* with that? Fucking A, Gene. She's either a fighter or she's accepting and passive. How can she be both?

Here's an idea: a book about what happens when a young woman can't (or won't) adequately follow your advice for survival. A Dahlia, the antihero. Title: "It's All in Your Head"? Whatever. Just donate her portion of the proceeds to PETA or Planned Parenthood. Understood? And make sure to contact Oprah's people!

Dahlia prepared for death the way stewardesses pantomime emergency protocol: bored, distracted, disconnected, a mask of seriousness and duty over a deep valley of uncertainty and — buried way, way, way down — fear.

She moved like an old woman, sluggish and frustrated, her memory inconsistent at best and totally fucked at worst. Bruce was there with her all the time now, fixing her endless Phenobarbital/Avitan soy milkshakes and gently reminding her what time it was, where they were, where they were going. She was present only in each exact moment: every second was its own complete world, contained as if in a droplet of water. And the next moment was its own droplet, quivering and self-contained, and then it was on to the next. The moments kept coming, each its own, drip, drip, dripping away. By the time Dahlia might have begun to get upset, she was on to another fully encompassing moment.

There was talk of hiring a full-time nurse. Just as Dr. C had promised, comprehension, naming, verbal memory, language function, transference from short- to long-term memory, and spatial memory were all on a precipitous decline. She was sleeping more, too (thanks only in part to the milkshakes), which was also consistent with Dr. C's prognosis: As the cancer progressed, she'd just sleep and sleep and sleep and, finally, not wake.

She befriended a series of Post-it pads, decided now was as good a time as any to remind herself of the bare facts. She felt herself always about to lose track of *something*.

Dahlia, she wrote. It was useful to work it out of a pen, though she was still perfectly capable of speaking. *Fuck this,* she wrote. *Lampshade,* she put on the lamp. *Ground Zero,* she put on the couch, but that one didn't stick so well. It slid down and under. Maybe someone would find it when they moved her stuff out of the house, someday. Soon? She wrote down *headache,* and stuck it to her forehead. *Hi, Dad,* and stuck it to his chest when he came near.

Bruce looked worried. So, so worried. His forehead a mountain range, his eyes tragic. *Don't worry,* she wrote, just to see those awful ridges above his eyes momentarily disappear. *Poor Daddy Bruce,* she wrote. "Don't worry," she told him, a door opening, a sliver of a memory of the time when she wanted, absurdly, to spare him the gory details of his own failed marriage, wanted nothing but to cheer him the hell up, this sad man.

"Okay," he smile-cried.

She wondered if she'd be alive in a week, a month, six, a year. She wrote down future dates and looked at them, contemplating. Until the second hand clicked ahead and she was in a whole new moment, all but forgetting what she was worried about in the first place. What was this date in her hand? It was like a hangover; the worst hangover ever, magnified by a factor of ten. Of a hundred.

The house was overwhelmed with stickies. Once upon a time, off to Israel to visit her vanished mother, excited as hell, she had tried to brush up her pathetic Hebrew with stickies, stickies everywhere. On the coffee table: *shulchan.* Over the sink: *ka'ara.* On the doors: *delet.* Everything covered in yellow. It was like walking into a house that was in the process of becoming a different house, like some kind of construction site; everything Dahlia knew intimately and had taken for granted was in the process of becoming something else, translating itself into an *other.* She had wandered through the rooms bewildered, trying to work out the sounds of the transliterated words for everything familiar, but her Hebrew had remained pathetic.

She thought about Julia G. and couldn't remember "Grielsheimer" for the life of her.

"What was her last name?" Dahlia asked her father.

"Why aren't you asking *me?*" said Margalit, who seemed now to be there all the time too, hovering, frantic. "Why do you hate me so much? What did I ever do to you? Well, I'm sorry, Bruti, but she acts like I'm not even here! Why does she act like I'm not here? What am I supposed to do? I'm her *Ima!*"

"Whose last name, La?"

"Julia's!"

"I don't know Julia, La."

"But what was her name?"

"Julia's name?"

It was a pain in the ass to try and think at all, about anything. She was not supposed to be smoking pot anymore. They had taken away her stash. Or hidden it. Her stash, stashed!

Andy, 48 and a lapsed Catholic, returned to the Church of his upbringing when he was diagnosed with metastasized esophageal cancer and found immeasurable comfort there. Belief in a higher power can help you come to terms with an unthinkable diagnosis.

To be high was to be forgetful, which meant, in turn, feeling great. Being unable to focus for any extended period of time on any thought process was actually quite a lot like meditation. She had done yoga with the Wonder Twins. She'd never been entirely able to sit still; never capable of quieting her mind the way you were supposed to. But it turned out that the whole thing about how you weren't supposed to hold on to any one thought — just let them go and go and go — seemed rather well-matched with temporal lobe degeneration. She was a killer yogi now, yes indeed. Who needed silent retreats, a guru? Suck it, yogis: Brain tumors rocked non-attachment like nothing else.

Reincarnation, existentialism, fatalism: She should probably figure out where she stood. For real, now; not like getting high and watching a *Groundhog Day* and *Defending Your Life* double feature and musing aloud that "gosh, between Harold Ramis and Albert Brooks, this afterlife racket seems to make some pretty great fucking sense, don't you guys think?" and getting the blankest of blank stares in return from whoever had been next to her on whichever couch that was.

She supposed it would be like it had been before she was born, and this was a not-at-all-bad thought. Before her birth: exhaustive possibility and hope abounding. Everything still ahead. A whole new world just out of sight, around a bend, unfathomable and okay until proven otherwise. Or not. Who knew?

Any belief system, Gene? Any which one?

Certainly not Christian Science, which had never made sense in the first place: Why couldn't you pray really, really hard *and* take a pill? Scientology, though: There was some sense talk! *Every* disease is psychosomatic. Everything that happens in your body (constipation, depression, insomnia, cancer) a product of your mind and your emotions. Christianity, blah.

Every single human life shares birth and death and eleventh-hour theological dabbling.

Traditionally, Judaism said some great stuff about reincarnation, but Dahlia's lazy-ass, watered-down brand of "cultural" Jewish identity (there had of course been that yearly, pun-heavy Christmas Eve round of parties for Jewish singles in New York) had offered her nothing of the sort. Besides, what of value could there be in a tradition that had ordained Rabbi Dickhead? Those kabbalists were certainly intriguing, but their accounting practices were, to be kind, a bit off. On a good day. At some point during this period — which Dahlia had heard referenced now and again with the improbably lovely word "hospice" — Margalit had tied a red-string bracelet around Dahlia's wrist. It had been blessed by Yarom himself, and rubbed up against the tombs of the matriarchs.

"This is the string to keep you safe," Margalit said. "It has to be tied on you by someone who loves you deeply and perfectly. And who loves you more than your *Ima?*" She valiantly fought back tears. "No one loves you as much as I do, *motek*. No one."

The closest Dahlia had ever gotten to an experience of God: her stoned subway rides. It couldn't be rush hour, and it had to be either the F, the A/C, or the 2/3. And like a veil had been lifted from the surface of life, she could see with absolute clarity that *everyone* was the same! Everyone was her; she was all of them! Each and every rider, a special and unique being, tiny parts integral to the whole. Some ugly, some attractive; some smart, some stupid; some nice, some terrible. And they all needed each other to exist; they were just cells of one single being. It was all so very clear.

And there was all this fantastic, scary female rage in New York City, too, this palpable rivalry between women. Increasingly violent stares, up, down, up again. Snide intimidation, jealousy, a challenge everywhere you looked. It was the women who dared stare at each other that way — always and only the women who narrowed their eyes at each other and dared. Their simple, boring, interchangeable men: Who cared? Not like in L.A., where everybody looked everybody else up and down, yes, but only to gauge the simplest answer: Does this person have more money than I do? A quick once-over, cataloguing of subtle class markers (Thin? Properly accessorized?) and nothing else mattered. Oh, no. In New York: Who *were* you? What did you *do?* Where were you *going?* Were you wearing something idiosyncratic? Did you look like you didn't give a flying fuck? Women stared each other down. I am better than you. Smarter than you. Cooler than you. And the ultimate: I give less of a shit than you what anyone thinks of me. How, how, how could anyone fail to love a city such as this? A city in which the goal was to give the smallest possible shit what anyone else thought?

With her twenty-eighth birthday looming, though, Dahlia had begun to feel officially old. She had been in New York for almost six years, and what did she have to show for all that time? A handful of temp jobs, a long stretch of bartending (and bartending well, though the alumni magazine didn't care), solid pot connections, some amusing friends and acquaintances, and now, because she had not spoken to her father in going on a year, mounting credit card debt. Forget even the most half-assed suggestions of grad school; the possibility of a redemptive future seemed, daily, to recede.

Her thing with Clark ended when he had OD'd — took twice the recommended dosage of Viagra and flipped out soon thereafter, started seeing everything turn blue.

"Something's wrong," he'd said. "Oh, shit."

"What?" Dahlia had asked. "What's wrong?"

"Everything's blue! Oh, shit, everything's blue!"

She didn't need this. She wanted to be taken in hand by this man and shown her own inherent hotness, loved like the rarest and most gorgeous of flowers, cupped like a butterfly when it was over, bathed generally in all manner of naturalistic metaphorical worship. She was his trophy, goddamn it, *he* was supposed to take care of *her,* and there he was, hugging his knees in the corner, jamming his palms into his eye sockets to try to erase the blue. "Everything's blue!

Everything's blue!" he kept repeating, freaked beyond all reason by the lapse of perfection in his body. The Viagra, he'd casually volunteered in the first place, was just "for fun."

Dahlia had calmly gone online (where had we been, as a species, before the advent of instantaneous e-diagnoses?) and found that "everything's blue!" was in fact the number one side effect of Viagra overdose.

"You'll be fine," she told Clark, helping him into a car service to Long Island City Hospital. "This sure is fun, though!"

"Oh my god," he said. "Oh my god, oh my god." She couldn't help but laugh at him, especially now, in retrospect: what a baby.

And after the emergency room — "Your Dad's gonna be fine, don't you worry!" said the front desk nurse — she had soothed him to bed, made him tea, and reflected bitterly on the fact that she was taking care of him. She was taking care of a person whom she had wanted to take care of her. And then it — whatever their thing had been — was irrevocably over, in its place a gaping, lonely hole. Lots of time to consider her lack of a life. And the debt. She hadn't even barely managed to pay the minimum on her credit card in who knew how long.

"Why don't you make deliveries with me?" Jacob asked her. Why not, indeed? Weren't you supposed to make your avocation your vocation? What color was Dahlia's parachute? Jacob had barely spoken to her while she'd been sleeping with Clark, and was now back, full force, her friend once again, hoping now she'd sleep with *him.* Too, too depressing. Anyway, she could continue bartending if she wanted to bust her ass.

She'd gotten a long letter from her father, which expressed yet more concern for Dahlia's well-being. *We're all worried about you. We love you.* Whatever. They had failed her and failed her and failed her, and now they were going to tell her what was wrong with her? Now they thought they could get away with *concern* for her?

She was in a fog, literal and figurative. She did the easiest thing: she let Kat and Steph school her, a crash course, in the art of full release massage. At two hundred dollars a go, it was just too easy. It was nothing, they said. Money for nothing.

"It's the easiest cash you've ever made in your life, and they *adore you.* Like little puppy dogs. Right, Steph-a-licious?"

"Dahlia, yeah. And it's not like you're going to jump right into nipple clamps and enemas. Jesus. How many guys have you

366

jerked off for free?"

Dahlia, never one for working harder than she needed to, was perversely fascinated with the prospect of getting paid handsomely for such a rote, mechanical act. Sleeping with someone, she told herself, would be different. She thought, in succession: *Who cares? What the hell?* And *Whatever.* The cash was bananas. The massage part was pretty simple — perfunctory, repetitive strokes across each shoulder and down both sides of the spine, intuitive touch she had no problem getting the hang of. Kat demonstrated on Steph, and then vice versa. Dahlia practiced on each of them, using pricey lavender lotion. The release part she would have to hone in action.

"Pretty simple," said Steph. This was Dahlia's kind of vocational training, too: It took forty-five minutes, consisted of a lot of "like, you know," and, for graduation, they smoked a bowl and watched *Crumb.*

Kat and Steph let her have some of their client runoff (so to speak). They had moved into pricier territory, mostly, entailing costumes and midday hotel rendezvous in the city. The few times Dahlia did it (a dozen, tops; but she couldn't really remember, exactly), the men were clean-cut and stank of privilege: an i-banker, a couple of

367

lawyers. They were hygienic, polite, and, with one exception, wearing wedding bands. The i-banker asked if she'd blow him for an extra hundred, which she politely declined. An extra two hundred? Still, no thanks. To put something in your mouth is to sort of let that thing become part of you. She may have been fried and lost, but wasn't quite there.

Needless to say, she was smoking a lot of pot. *And* making full use of Kat's Vicodin prescription (courtesy of a doctor client). She was watching a lot of television. She was a step past numb.

Kat, meanwhile, had gotten a gallery, finally, and had a huge, important, career-making show coming up.

"Not to be a bitch," Steph said to Dahlia one night, alone, "but honestly? Her paintings are not even that good."

But Kat's paintings *were* that good: stately, radical, arresting. Steph wasn't half the artist. Girls are such threatened bitches. At base, yes: all of them. So much nicer to be friends with men.

Strangely enough, the notion had popped into Dahlia's head that fall, unbidden: She should go to High Holiday services! She should find one of those myriad free services, honey to the bee of the single, unaffiliated, urban Jew, and go! Years of arduously avoiding anything remotely Jewish (that minefield encompassing various and sundry family sorrows), and suddenly she wanted to go to Yom Kippur services.

Steph, as it turned out, was half-Jewish, and Dahlia had tried to sell her on the idea: Let's go! High for the Holidays! Who shall live and who shall die? Who by fire and who by water? Who in length of years and who before?

"No, thanks," said Steph.

"Please? Come on, it'll be cool."

"Still no."

So Dahlia had gone alone, to a large synagogue in Park Slope, wanting her own experience, curious about the process of reclaiming this whole aspect of her identity, long abandoned though it may have been. Unfortunately, she had merely seen Danny everywhere — not Danny himself, just Danny *in* everyone, everywhere: the young, well-groomed parents with their adorable, colorful progeny, everyone with one eye on little Hayden/Madison/Maxwell in the Bugaboo and the other eye scanning the room to see if anyone was *watching* them watch little Hayden/Madison/Maxwell in the Bugaboo, and oh my god, Danny and Nadia are probably going to have children, of course they're going to have children, and Dahlia didn't *want* them to make a whole new person, a whole new person to avoid in this piece of shit family, and how could she avoid a *baby?* — and she'd been filled, predictably, with a foul hatred even *she* understood to be the antithesis of why she'd come.

Shuffling around her house under Bruce's watch, Dahlia scribbled *it should have been you* Post-its, mentally addressed to Danny. She'd crumple them up and trash them, thinking of their existence as its own kind of mail delivery system. (The Ether!) *It should have been you,* over and over again, sent directly via existence to the very root of the problem: Dahlia was dying and she was still, still, still fucking furious at her lame excuse for a brother. She did not know how or why, but it was his fault, all of it. She was sure of that, at least, even as everything else turned shifty and soggy and foggy and, finally, disappeared.

Then one day Dahlia fell down and could not get back up again. Bruce struggled to lift her, but she was nearly dead weight, more than half-unconscious, and Bruce pulled a muscle in his back, and overall it was such a harrowing scene that they resolved, finally, to hire full-time help.

Enter the male hospice nurse, Marco, with his compact torso and strong arms and short legs and black ponytail held in a chartreuse scrunchie! A man of few words: meaty, *so* Dahlia's type. And much preferable to the chipper running commentary of her parents, who went on and on with ridiculous, can-do cheer:

"How's my girl?"

"Good morning, *yaffa!* It's a beautiful day outside!"

"What are you watching?"

"How are you feeling today?"

"I'm going to call the doctor; let's ask what he thinks."

"You're looking *great!*"

She was "remarkably" coherent, according to Marco the male nurse; though the "attitude problem" was "worrisome."

She had visitors from the group. Arlene came twice, offering best wishes from everyone else. Bart sent flowers. Yellow ones.

Mara came, too, all the way from Boston, home for Thanksgiving to visit her parents. Dahlia made no effort to appear well, to seem better than she was. For some reason, Mara's presence felt like a betrayal of some sort, and Dahlia was immediately pissed, though she couldn't articulate why. Dahlia both rejoiced to see her walk through the door and then quietly, purposefully shut down, refusing to play hostess, refusing even to hold up her end of the conversation. She begged exhaustion and pretended to take a nap soon after Mara arrived.

"Oh my god," she could hear Mara saying to Bruce, sobbing outside the front door, on the night-blooming-jasmine-beset path. "Oh my god. I had no idea. She sounded like it was just — Oh my god."

Danny's wedding had seemed to set off a chain reaction, a line of dominoes: Suddenly everyone was doing it. She'd gotten an ornate engraved invitation from the runty Kantrowitz twin — the one with the face like a rat-terrier. How on earth had they found her? She was hiding out with the Wonder Twins. She had left no forwarding address. She hadn't been back to L.A. since the Danny/Nadia debacle.

"Nick proposed!" Mara crowed over the phone shortly thereafter. Dahlia, stupefied, stifled a yawn. Was this supposed to make her happy? Unhappy?? Excited? Was she, in the end, supposed to care one way or another how/when Mara and her boyfriend (or anyone, for that matter) legalized their relationship? Jesus, people, who cares? Get married, don't get married, but why is it anyone else's fucking business? Marriage seemed, to Dahlia's way of thinking, pretty quotidian. Not exactly a rarity or singular or, given the way those clients' wedding bands had glinted in her dimly lit peripheral vision, necessarily meaningful. And yet she was supposed to respond to news of an engagement with "Omigod, that's *amazing*, I'm *so* happy for you!"? She was supposed to go through some procession of events and rituals connected to this meaningless thing? *Why?* (Shit, no, have we learned nothing? Asking why *was* why.)

Dahlia sat at a succession of bars with Mara and four fellow bridesmaids-to-be, drinking and drinking and drinking but unable for some strange reason to get the least bit drunk. How was it possible to consume those quantities of alcohol and skip right over the getting drunk directly to the hangover? Had all that liquor simply hightailed it straight to the source, the burgeoning tumor, feeding it poison? Probably. The girls had sat around cooing at the engagement ring, passing around penis-shaped lollipops, and having increasingly giggly conversations, shocking themselves and each other with sexual secrets.

"I like it when Alan puts his finger in my butt!" said one, immediately snarfing her drink in exhilaration and embarrassment.

Clearly, these girls had, with the greatest respect and dedication, fully absorbed *Sex and the City* and were now taking it upon themselves to somehow embody it; ever so stylish and quite of the moment, trading deepest, darkest secrets about relationships and shopping. Amazing, what the power of cinematic suggestion could effect in the lives of real, breathing, (somewhat) sentient human beings.

Dahlia felt unmoored. Her tether let loose and flung aloft (or was that the way you were *supposed* to live?). Life was barreling forward with or without her: Mara engaged and in medical school, Margalit (when last Dahlia had heard) settling into a duplex in North Hollywood after leaving Yarom to his many admirers, Bruce following Danny's lead and joining JDate, awful Danny married to some awful, random wench. No one else was obsessed with old wounds, with ancient hurt, with what was *real* and what was *right*. Everyone else just continued on, one foot in front of the other, A-okay. Not Dahlia. For Dahlia the past always outpaced the present, relentless.

She had been living in a state of anxiety, waiting for the nails-on-chalkboard announcement that Danny and Nadia were expecting a child. It would happen any minute now, she was sure. Dahlia's biggest, secret fear was that they would have a little girl and name her after Grandma Alice. To the untrained eye, that'd be a lovely sort of reclamation of life, but Dahlia knew better. Dahlia knew that, once fucked, things remained fucked, got even more fucked, would never be right again. (But *hey,* it occurs to her now, fleetingly, all at once and then no more, *here's what's good about dying:* She won't have to be around for it.) She couldn't bear the thought of Danny and Nadia procreating. She prayed for their infertility. She had the sense, even then, that it was not okay for life to continue until old wrongs had been righted. Which is to say it was not okay for life to continue at all.

She could name none of this. She just smoked a joint with Kat and/or Steph and watched *Raising Arizona.* They went out for decadent, wine-warmed dinners at small, gorgeous bistros. They listened to good music, sprawled out on their floor pillows, watching the sky turn dusky beyond the wall of windows. Sometimes — and this is how you'll know they really meant it — they put on latter-day Luna and danced around unselfconsciously. They invited people over for dinner and made rice in the rice cooker. She was what passed for happy, even if it was a checked-out, self-medicated happy. Even if it wasn't *really* happy.

Kat's paintings had started to sell like mad. Collectors were constantly coming by to see her stuff. And Steph was barely managing to conceal her jealousy and resentment. She was passive-aggressive and obnoxious:

"It's cool that you can avoid making a choice between real abstract and real representation," for example. Or "I guess that's why your work is so popular; it's, like, super accessible." She roped Dahlia into shit-talk ("Kat's paintings are pretty repetitive, don't you think? She really only does one thing.") and then used it against her ("Dahlia wonders if you can paint anything *else*").

Their threesome was slowly rotting.

On top of which, Kat and Steph were beginning to piss Dahlia off, in little ways. Steph was always extravagantly farting and giggling, and waiting for a response from whoever was in the room.

"Nice," Dahlia would say, obliging. Or: "Heh." It got old.

And Kat, self-absorbed Kat, had this irritating, sarcastic habit of "gifting" Dahlia with shit she didn't want. Like: "Hey, I got you a present! This very special moisturizer, just for you," and it was clearly some generic brand giveaway or half-used sample.

Then there was Dahlia's nasty little habit of sowing seeds of betrayal with Kat and/or Steph's boyfriends. It was just so easy: Those who grew up ugly and later became somewhat attractive will surely understand — your own ability to hold the attention of anybody you want, the sheer novelty of it, trumps moral decency *every time.*

That competitive jealousy popped up relentlessly between them, like carnival head-whackers. Dahlia flirted shamelessly with whoever Kat or Steph happened to have an eye on. Triangle dynamics already threatened their little family: Dahlia knew that the primary friendship was Kat and Steph's, that she herself was only an interloper, a third wheel. Maybe this knowledge was enough to fuck things up. At any rate, she was annoyed to be the eternal extra, annoyed with the knowledge that Kat and Steph were *Kat and Steph,* the Wonder Twins, while Dahlia was just Dahlia. They spoke in "we," while Dahlia was forever, when she felt worthy of identification at all, an inescapable "I."

Her ultimate tool of sabotage had been a particularly unsavory love interest of Steph's. Twin-Bed Ted, they called him; Steph had been horrified, spending the night for the first time at his place, to find that he had, indeed, a twin bed!

"Worse than a futon on the floor," Kat had giggled.

"But he's kinda cute," Steph reasoned. "Whatever."

He was not kinda cute. Tattooed forearms ("Fuck-You tattoos," he called them: ink you got where everyone could always see it, thus putting an end to the hope you might Go to Law School After All). He was the kind of guy who had to shave the back of his neck. Swarthy, self-hating Dahlia could not have found Twin-bed Ted less attractive. So why did she launch a full-scale seduction? Because she could? Because she could! Men wanted her. She could not get over it.

Besides: Was she supposed to adhere to some random amalgamation of *boundaries* here? Living it up with two nicely subsidized prostitutes? Please. There were no rules. She had made a few thousand dollars in her brief foray into the massage industry (a handful of happy endings!), and persisted in using her ever-expanding array of almost-maxed-out plastic to buy beautiful food and concert tickets and cocktails and lattes and gorgeous boots and slip dresses and asymmetrical haircuts and music and drugs (Mara's "What-would-Carrie-Bradshawdo?" buddies would, in theory, be *so* impressed), a functional orphan. She could do as she saw fit. She belonged to nobody. There had to be an upside.

She and Twin-Bed Ted shared a few in-jokes late at night in the kitchen and traded exactly four text messages ("what are you doing?" "not cleaning the rice cooker" "what, then?" "bored"). The way he followed Dahlia everywhere with his baggy, Billie Joe Armstrong eyes was as clear a statement of purpose as ever there was one, and Steph was not amused.

Then it was on to Archie, a bike messenger and speed freak whose mother was a congresswoman from Oregon. Kat had met him at a Jonathan Richman show.

And then, of course, after a long, drawn-out period during which Kat and Steph performed an intricate, extensive, insular dance — leaving Dahlia out of plans and commiserating about all the "mean" things she had supposedly said to Steph about Kat's paintings — they actually kicked her out.

"You should find somewhere else to live," one or the other of them told her, arms folded, leaning against the countertop in the kitchen, and Dahlia supposed that, yup, she probably should. She'd known it all along, of course, the unarguable "we" of them versus the eternal "I" of her. She'd tested it, and been proven right. Still, she had to work hard to keep from crying. Another family, gone.

17. Forgive and Forget

Free yourself from the negativity you have stored up over the course of your life. Wrongs done, old hurts, ill will, hatred, sadness, and disappointment in others: Say farewell to all of it.

On Craigslist, Dahlia had found a temporary, furnished sublet in Fort Greene. It belonged to a writer named Audrey Rubens who was going to Vietnam, Cambodia, and Thailand with her boyfriend for five months. Audrey's first novel had come out the year before; copies lined the bottom shelf in the entry hall. Dahlia read the beginning, but couldn't manage to get into it. It was a highly experimental metanarrative based on a semirecent news story about a man who'd been exonerated of a heinous sexual crime after twenty years in prison. Audrey had done some sort of shape-shifting thing wherein the man was, in each chapter, an entirely different being: a 300-pound shutin, an elderly Jewish lady, the skinny twelve-year-old boy who'd been the crime's victim. Cool, but unreadable.

Audrey's apartment was lovely, in any event, even if it was a fifth-floor walkup, and even if the hallways always reeked of industrial chemicals. Dahlia's airways stung with toxic cleaning solutions whenever she climbed those five flights (Wait for it: Cancer). But she felt temporarily okay in her temporary abode. On the apartment walls there were quantities of family snapshots that put to shame even Dahlia's feverish memory cobbling of yore, and that made her feel quite at home.

She went to visit Mara in Boston, seeking comfort from her recently imploded friendships. Back to the source. She still had friends! Well, a friend, at any rate. Mara was in her residency (dermatology; the best specialty for "women who want families," as she'd said with a grin), and shacked up in a gorgeous apartment with Nick, who was, Dahlia had to admit, very, very nice. Mara and Nick set up the foldout couch with touching teamwork.

They had arranged an outing in Dahlia's honor — dinner on Newbury Street with a few of Mara's sensible, shiny, similarly-affianced med school friends, then trivia night at their favorite local pub. It was all very wholesome and fun. All except for Dahlia, that is, who got utterly shitfaced on wine at dinner, then beer at the pub, then did a line with the bartender in the back before briefly making out with him.

"Scott Baio!" she'd screamed, out of turn, when the trivia emcee very somberly posed a tie-breaker query to the rival team: *Who starred as the title character in the sitcom* Charles in Charge? A collective groan had been directed at her; she had ruined the game!

"New question!" said the emcee. "New question. And whoever's responsible for the drunk spoilsport, please shut her up."

"I'm going to take her home," Dahlia could hear Mara explaining to Nick. There was exhaustion in her voice, and worry, and resentment. On their way to the car, she had not made eye contact.

"This isn't cute anymore, Dahl."

"Cute?" Dahlia had chirped. *"Cute?"* Then she had vomited into the gutter.

Dahlia was obsessed with Audrey's family, looking in on them in all those framed photos: There were two handsome, doting older brothers, one of them a pilot! There were gorgeous black-and-white grandparents, so in love; and look at them later, too, with their beautiful grandchildren, grinning, and then *great*-grandchildren. Astonishingly good fortune, these people. There were the three Rubens children mugging for the camera in an impossibly green and expansive backyard. There were the trim parents, traveling the world in their sixties, Audrey's father with his arm around the shapely waist of her benevolent-looking mother, sunset on a cruise ship.

Audrey had excellent taste in music and books, too, and the place was spotlessly clean. Dahlia made believe she *was* Audrey, thus lessening the pain of having broken up with pretty much everyone she knew. She left her cell phone off for days on end and cooked herself food in Audrey's kitchen from recipes Audrey had bookmarked and watched Audrey's DVDs and read Audrey's books and listened to Audrey's music.

She had abandoned most of her belongings at the loft and tried to pretend she was on vacation (Quoth *What About Bob,* an apparent favorite of Audrey's: "A vacation from my problems!"). She bathed infrequently. She charged groceries and toothpaste. She refused to talk to anyone. Even Jacob, who owed her money, but had found himself a real, live girlfriend and thus had less time for propping Dahlia up or, for that matter, calling her back.

"Jake, can I have some money, please?"

"Things are tight right now, sweetheart."

"You owe me like eighteen hundred dollars."

"I know. And I would give it to you if I had it."

"Can you borrow it from your girlfriend? I wouldn't ask if I didn't really need it."

"I'll see what I can do. Can I pay you back in weed?"

"Maybe a little."

Clark called a couple of times, inviting her over for Ecstasy, unpasteurized cheese, and *Oh Mercy,* but she could not deal. She looked around for a waitressing job, felt pathetic, gave up, went for long walks to the Brooklyn Promenade, and made believe she'd taken a vow of silence. Her best moment in months had come in the midst of one said walk: through Brooklyn Heights, looking up suddenly at a tiny, charming, dead-end street called Love Lane, the sign of which read, simply, "Love La." So desperately lonely was she that, seeing this sign, she had taken it as a personal message from God.

She stayed up until dawn, watching infomercials about state of the art mattresses,

mattresses so profoundly wonderful you could get the equivalent of twelve hours of sleep in half the time.

One night, Dahlia had dreamt that she was actually herself, in her own body, in her own life, just as it was, and woke up in a terrible sweat, the rankness of her identity clinging to her like a toxic wet suit.

"You have a bunch of mail here," Steph said in a voicemail. "Like, a kind of huge pile. It's, like, a lot of shit. And you left a lot of other stuff, too. Can you please come get it?"

Bills and collection agency notices, probably. And, when she finally did go over there to get it all — she still had her key — she found her formal invitation (letterpressed!) to the Westwood School Class of 1996 Ten Year Reunion. To be held at the Biltmore in downtown L.A. Classy. (You've heard the expression "like a hole in the head"?)

Audrey's neighbors had parties. Dahlia would hear them laughing late into the night and invariably feel indignant that she hadn't been invited. She'd never met them, but still.

She obviously wasn't going to see any clients. It was too odious, without the backdrop of Kat and Steph and the good life at the loft, to do it — *that thing* — even once more. The idea crossed her mind briefly before she could banish it.

She got a job waiting tables at a café on DeKalb, then quit it a week later.

She registered with her old temp agency, but refused jobs when they came up. "Eight a.m.?" she'd ask. "I actually don't, uh, think I can do it tomorrow. . . ."

She was not Audrey. In a few months Audrey would come home and resume her wonderful life and Dahlia would do . . . what, exactly?

She wasted hours online, reading self-aggrandizing blogs and stalking acquaintances. What had happened to Saree Lansky after high school? Cornell Law. Whoopde-fuckingdo. Nothing spectacular; nothing to warrant special mention in the alumni newsletter. (Not like, say, *death*.)

The Velociraptor had a website advertising her therapeutic services, with an image of a woman riding a horse, bareback, on the beach: *Helping you achieve your most fulfilling, healthy lifestyle since 1998,* it said. The website itself was kind of an emetic. And how was *that* contributing to anyone's healthy lifestyle?

Alexis, her college ex-friend, had done a stint in the Peace Corps and was currently a graduate student in philosophy at Berkeley.

Her sweet, brief boyfriend Aaron was a sports medicine expert! With a chubby, heavily made-up wife! And a wedding website! They had registered for, among other things: an ice cream maker, puce-colored towels, and service for fourteen.

There was nothing whatsoever on Annemarie. Or the Israeli cousins whose names she remembered. She couldn't recall Dorel's last name, though Googling just "Dorel" led to an endless ream of *Doral*s: a city in Florida, a line of commercial boats, golf equipment, conference centers, cigarettes, a dental plan, and mortgage bankers.

Look at all these lives. There really was no such thing as death. There was death itself, yes. But no real end to actual people. There were only shopping malls and movie complexes and food courts! There was only college and then a tidy, respectable career (say, law) and then a tidy respectable wedding to a tidy respectable partner, and then a honeymoon, and then a child who'd be feted and photographed as if it were the first child born, anywhere, to anybody, ever. There was no death. There was only this promised life with its expected pit stops, and no good reason it could not, or would not, be so. She felt shameful, Googling at 4:00 a.m., boundaries effaced. Not unlike how it felt to jerk off a stranger for money.

She thought about suicide again, her old standby. Her chip to cash in. She had prudently saved it, all this time. She weighed it: an option.

You'll be surprised by how easy it is, when you set your mind to it. Just think about everyone who's hurt you and repeat these words: I Forgive You. Letting go is the best feeling ever; I promise you that. Try it.

Not getting it, Gene. Why don't you get it? Letting go is the hardest thing ever. Harder than: turning off the television, accepting horrendous people as your own flesh and blood, falling asleep at night. Impossible, all. There was no letting go. *She* wasn't holding it; *it* was holding her.

In a pot-addled dream, Julia G. confonted her: "Why are you trying to live some weird version of someone else's life? Do relief work. Go away. Live in India. Take a boat to a Greek isle and fuck a fisherman. Leave. Be happy."

"Fuck off, you dork. What do you know about anything? All you know is SAT prep and Ivy League hopes. You probably would've gone to law school."

"But I didn't." She was an older version

of herself; the woman she might have grown into. Heels, professional attire, attractive. A capable, comforting sort of glow: fetching, warm.

"Because you didn't live long enough to."

(Dreaming and dying are so much the same: it's all in your head, only yours, all by yourself.)

"Go to Israel. Why not just take off? If you've got this life anyway, why not? Go to the Negev, meet me there!"

" 'Me'?"

"Just go, go! You don't have to worry about money, it's there when you really need it! You're free!"

"Whatever."

"Seriously. And then if you still want to die, you can always kill yourself later. You can kill yourself *anytime.* Go away and enjoy!" Julia G. was on her side. Julia G. was supportive of anything Dahlia needed to do to make her life livable, to be happy. It was a good dream. She was smoking way, way, way too much pot.

She surrendered and called her father with a week to go before Audrey's return.

"Hello, La," Bruce said carefully.

"Hi, Dad," she said, exhausted.

"How have you been?" She could hear a pitiful tremble in his voice: eager to talk.

"Okay," she said, not at all attempting to disguise her misery.

"Do you want to come home?"

"Yes?" she said, admitting it, tearing up. "Yes."

"Okay," he said. "Come home."

"I want to come home," she said, repeating, meaning it. It was her "Goodbye to All That" moment, inevitable and at least a little familiar to many single girls in the big shitty.

So she did go home, even though they say you can't. She stayed with Bruce for a couple of months until they found the house in Venice.

She had left a note for Audrey: *Awesome apartment. Thanks for everything. Sorry about the fridge door.* (She had let it swing open on its hinge, stoned, contemplating potential snacks, and it hadn't closed properly thereafter.) *Enjoy your life; I did!*

But Gene. Lest we lose our place in the Book, it was time for hospice care, the best one could do: not hasten death and not attempt to prevent it, either. Beep-beep, beep-beep went the machines, machines brought into the Venice house alongside a hospital bed with remote control, adjustable height.

"This is barbaric," said Margalit of hospice care. "She needs to be at a hospital.

391

How can we just let her stay here? Who does this?" Hospice care was no battle plan, no battle plan at all.

Oh, but Dahlia was grateful, in her way, to be at home. Whatever that meant, "home." Hospitals: yuck. Death, illness, loss, terror, fluorescents. Hospitals were the true houses of worship, you can keep your churches, et al. In hospitals people worshipped life — the agreed-upon divinity. In hospitals people worshipped life with the wild-eyed, fanatical desperation of true believers. To die in a hospital would be to die in a pejorative sense: the ultimate failure.

Home, though: home. It was a word she could still manage, "home," the linguistic building block of a simple *mmm* sound, a child's first word. Even if it wasn't quite "home" anymore, no longer her private bastion of okayness. It was overtaken, inch by inch, with flowers and cards and balloons and people. The cards were hopelessly meek, inappropriate: "Dear Dahlia" and then "Love, [Whoever]," with Hallmark's prepackaged condolences preprinted in between. The flowers were funereal and would begin dying immediately, cheap complimentary florist vases growing mossy and filling the house with the stench of plant decay.

Where did this crap come from? From Danny's congregants, from Bruce's office, from the cousins. From the Kantrowitzes. From mysterious friends of Margalit's. A bouquet from the Group, signed by Rick from "all of us."

Audrey Rubens had used Dahlia's forwarding address (at Bruce's house) to send a manila envelope full of junk mail — *I didn't know if any of this was important, so I'm just sending it all. You might want to let the post office know about your new address! Hope all is well! Best, Audrey* — which remained on a table near the door, where it had been stashed months before. Oh, and her GRE results had arrived at some point, too. They'd gotten lost in the shuffle, but eventually Bruce had spotted and torn into them. What do you know? Sure as she lived and breathed: flying colors. 790 verbal, 680 quantitative, 5.5 analytical. Bruce affixed the scores to the refrigerator.

"I'm so proud of you, La! Congratulations!"

She had, diseased brain notwithstanding, aced a standardized test. She would have options, after all. She could do anything she wanted. Maybe grad school.

Danny and Nadia made a silent, sheepish final appearance, horribly awkward and uncomfortable even as things were so obviously all moot. Dahlia was just lying there, excused from discourse. No fun to harangue a borderline comatose enemy. Words beget more words; silence begets silence.

Newsflash, there is really no such thing as forgiveness. Forgiveness just means the cessation of any import attached to any thing/one. That's actually what it means to "forgive": forget. Ever notice how, when people say "bad memory" as in an unpleasant experience, and "bad memory" as in a poor *recall* of experience, they're actually often saying the same thing?

"Assholes," Dahlia managed when at last they left.

Marco smiled, handed her a cup with a straw. "They did seem shitty." He gave her shoulder a squeeze, and within a quarter-hour Dahlia had only the vaguest recollection of Danny and Nadia sitting there, all tense smiles and silence. Default forgiveness; de facto forgetting. It was so, so simple. Who knew it would be so simple? She simply lost the memory, or the memory lost her. Like the ideal refugee, in exile, leaving home, never looking back, starting all over again in a foreign place. There was no such thing as forgiveness, there was just fleeing. Forgetting.

Really the near-dead are floating in an ether ("ether" as previously defined: "a very rarefied and highly elastic substance formerly believed to permeate all space, including the interstices between the particles of matter, and to be the medium whose vibrations constituted light and other electromagnetic radiation"), remember?

There was some sand between her toes on the beach in Tel Aviv, her uncle laughing loudly at a dirty joke someone told in Hebrew, Dahlia understanding somehow what the joke was about based on the charades of its teller, tomatoes for breakfast, the dull pain in her pants when she'd sat unthinkingly down the day after Uri, the whole-house-vibration of Danny's door slamming shut, air mail letters from her mother. The way it felt to get high and put on headphones and disappear, dragging a Daisy Gillette razor across her arm, the Ben Folds Five song that had constantly been on the radio while she drove around L.A. on winter break in the fall of her sophomore year of college. Jacob's searching, lovelorn gaze, the infantile expression on the face of every man she'd ever watched hovering over her, beneath her, inside her. The bad karma of sitting down to eat in a restaurant but then deciding to leave instead — the way the staff/host/whatever would act so fucking wounded, as though you'd made them a bogus promise and knifed them in the fucking *heart* or whatever, instead of just not really wanting to eat anything after all. The fake smile on the Velociraptor's face — dead eyes giving her away — when they shook hands for the first time. Margalit weeping at Danny's wedding, specious and distant. All that dumb shit. What it meant to be a person thus affected by such things. Affected forever; even now, barely conscious, in the good old ether.

Once, another one of those UCLA sorority girl babysitters had had an idea for a game: "It's the coolest thing," the girl had said. Dahlia was home alone; Danny, too old for babysitters, had gone off to be somewhere, anywhere, else. "You stand against the wall" — she had arranged Dahlia up against the wall — "and I take this dish towel" — she had brandished a dish towel — "and hold it up against your neck and you black out and see crazy cool visions. I do it all the time; it's trippy."

"Okay," Dahlia had said.

"Okay," the girl said. "Cool. Here," and she had leaned into Dahlia, her fists on either side of Dahlia's neck, holding tight to the dish towel so that it cut off Dahlia's air.

Dahlia had struggled for breath, pinned, and wanted to cancel the game, please, after all, but the babysitter had grinned and pulled the towel tighter, until Dahlia had given up, let go, and, bizarrely, giggled once before blacking out.

When she came to she had no idea where she'd been, or for how long. She felt alert and tense, spring-loaded but blurry, like her brain had stayed too long in a Jacuzzi.

"That was . . ." said the babysitter, shaken. "Are you okay?"

"Yeah."

"You were jerking around."

"Really?"

"Are you okay?"

"Yeah."

They had settled in for *The Golden Girls,* and the sitter had been uncharacteristically kind and accommodating for the rest of the night, constantly glancing back and forth between Dahlia and the TV, and letting Dahlia eat an entire pint of coffee Häagen-Dazs right before bed.

So: this travesty almost intercepted by an earlier one. What later travesty, pray tell, might *this* now be intercepting?

She was just a collection of likes and dislikes, like every other human being, just a jumble of experiences and reactions and prejudices and insecurities and biases, stubborn and incorrect, stupid and tormented. Feelings and feelings and more feelings. Where would they go? All these feelings were just frayed ribbons in the wind, nothing tied up, nothing resolved. What might things have been like if she'd lived longer? Five years? Ten? Fifty? What gifts might time bestow? How might things evolve, turn out? Different, for sure. Somehow, yes: different. Time, after all, was just a camera pulling back to reveal the big picture. But Dahlia's time was just about up, so this was the big picture. Almost.

She had this horrible sense — fundamental, obviously, and ethereal — that her disappearance would be a sort of relief to them. Bruce, because all this suffering was over. Margalit, because all this suffering was now hers to bear noisily, and hers alone. Grandpa Saul would not register at all; he was probably at that very moment drinking a hearty roast beef puree with a contented, toothless smile.

And what about Dan? No, this would not be a relief to Dan. This would be the opposite of relief to Dan. Dan-the-man would stand inert at Dahlia's grave, a block of nothing, a human headstone. If only he'd care enough to piss all over her! To shout and scream! To hurl fistfuls of dirt onto her pine casket, weep unbecomingly, unable to hold polite conversations later, at *shiva.* If only there were that much passion in him, that much care. Which is all she'd ever wanted from him in the first fucking place. But there wasn't. There hadn't been, ever. She was an idiot. Still: He would be tormented for years to come, if only by his own lack of affect. She was sure of it. He would suffer. He would hole it up inside himself and it would fester; he would live with the awareness that, whenever his mother or his father so much as looked in his direction, they would be thinking, clear as morning, *it should have been you.* Yes, he would suffer, in his way. Maybe eventually he'd get cancer, too. For this thought she almost loved him again.

Anyway, what was his name again, this brother of hers? She could conjure his face with some effort, but it kept melting into a younger version of itself, and then younger still, kept returning to some infernal lowest common denominator of being, so she couldn't properly love *or* hate him any further, regardless.

And at this late date it wasn't so much that she hated or loved him as it was that she simply wanted that little girl back: the one who trusted and loved, the one who was trusted and loved. She wanted the intactness back, and the family, and the womb, and the womb before the womb, and her mother, but not her actual mother. She wanted to be young again, very young, small, smaller still. And beyond that she wanted those things encased and encased and encased, like Russian dolls, or like whatever lame metaphor people used before there *were* Russian dolls, if they used any metaphors at all back then; furthermore, she wanted the whole thing packed in egg crates and stashed safely away somewhere warm.

But forgive whom, and for what?

Bruce had brought her back to L.A. and bought her a house.

And it was a new beginning. She adored her house. How nice it felt to orchestrate the sort of regestating she knew she needed. A fresh start, a new beginning. She would have been okay, truly. She would have! She really would have. After she was done being the opposite of okay, she would have been okay.

She was going to go to sleep at night, content to be alone in her dreams, glad to experience, for herself, whatever comprised those dreams.

She was going to start over. She was going to meditate and gestate and think and stroll and shop and smile, and be calm and composed and self-reliant and happy — especially that: happy, by herself, for herself, dependent on no one — and she was going to reapproach life in general. She was going to find her old poster chart of Hebrew fruits and vegetables, get it beautifully reframed, and hang it.

She was going to take the GRE!

And possibly it was time to dial back on the pot a little, right? Yeah, it probably was. Time. To dial back on the weed. A little. Indeed. Soon.

Square one. Time turned in on itself while she strolled the beach, got high (but she really was going to cut back), and curled up in the deep embrace of her new couch. She meditated, watching movies. She sighed, she stretched. She dusted and hummed. She thought: *I will paint the front door blue.* One of these days she really was going to paint the door blue.

18. Be Well

You now have all the tools you'll need for your new beginning. That's what cancer is, after all: a chance at a new beginning. The choice is yours. From now on you have the power to live, so live well.

For the next two weeks, the house in Venice, its door a smug, washed-out brown, was a hushed control room with Dahlia at its center, an immobile, unconscious commander-in-chief. Hanging out in the ether: brutally, deeply aware.

So she did not fight hard enough. She did not laugh hard enough or forgive well enough or reframe properly or, at the end of the day (the real end, you understand, of the *entire* "day"), heal herself. No happy ending for the girl who performed the occasional Happy Ending; oh the irony.

There are so many stories, Gene, about people who read your Book, fought back against the big C, and "won." About how grateful they were: They'd been given six months and instead just went on vacation with the wife and are expecting grandkid number whatever any day now. More power to them. Dahlia would certainly be lying, tendency toward suicidal bravado aside, if she said she wouldn't rather be alive than dead. At least she *thought,* with her extremely limited, still-breathing perspective, that she'd rather be alive. Maybe death would be like winning the fucking lottery — maybe she'd be the ultimate winner here. Maybe *you* were supposed to die twenty years ago, Gene; maybe death for you meant 75 virgins (heaven for you; hell for them) in a field of clover. Maybe, in cheating death for so long and making a hefty living off telling others how to do the same, you're basically the big-picture loser. Who knows?

So you'll say: A *vile, self-absorbed, depressing, lazy, messy, spoiled, fucked-up, probably mentally ill loser dies. So what?*

Well, that's disappointing, Gene. Because come now: It doesn't matter how vile or messy or lazy or spoiled or fucked-up she was. Life is still Life. And either that's meaningful all the time or it's meaningful none of the time, schmuck; no qualifying. No picking, no choosing. It either matters or it doesn't. Life has value or life does not have value: one or the other. Your eye still dry at the undoing of Dahlia? You disapprove of the way she lived her life? You look askance at her methodology for dealing with terminal illness? You sneer at her attitude? Then you don't really care about human life after all, do you? This one pitiful life, hereby relayed: simply a litmus test, dear boy.

The Book was lying around now, abandoned on the kitchen table amid piles of crap, Dahlia no longer capable of checking in to see how she wasn't. Bruce had flipped through and been unimpressed; his daughter was dying, and on some level he knew there wasn't anything to be done. Jews, Gene, bury their sacred texts when they're unusable or can't possibly be repaired: A broken book is just a useless vessel of faith, very much like the human body itself. If Dahlia had been able, perhaps she might have suggested, from deep inside the ether, that she be buried with the Book. Two unusable vessels, specks of matter intertwined for always.

Her life could simply be seen as a series of things she had failed to get over. And now it was over. And who's left here, to rail and rage and scream and kick and fight and cry at the loss of Dahlia? Who will be irrational and destroyed? Who'll think of her, late at night and early in the morning, in their happiest and worst moments? Who will think of her? And think of her? And think of her more? Who might send her silent, connective love from deep within the recess of a single, solitary existence? Say, whenever Cyndi Lauper came on the radio? She didn't want sorrow; she wanted Grief. Sorrow is perfunctory; *grief* is the real deal. Whose life destroyed, whose sense of security in life itself gone? Whose chance at any complete happiness ruined forever and ever?

She wasn't breathing well. She'd been having a lot of apnea. Someone — a nurse, or Bruce, when he could keep it together — counted seconds when that happened. How long was it before she took another breath? The longest gap was about 20 seconds. Then she stopped breathing again, and no one counted. Clearly this was not the usual apnea. She took another breath, finally. There was no struggle evident on her face (in the *ether,* however, as we have seen, it was a different story altogether). The breath was only a breath, there was no gasping, no effort.

"I'm not touching you, I'm not touching you!" Her brother, his prepubescent hands held aloft an inch from Dahlia's face, sang to her in spectral form. Please *do* touch me, she holographically screamed. *Please!* Do.

A (brief) lifetime of colloquials rang true: So lonely I could die. So hungry I could die. So tired I could die. So mad I could die. So sad I could die. So happy I could die. Feeling all those things so intensely equaled, yes, theoretical death. And indeed: When you're as full of feeling, good and bad, as you've ever been — think orgasms, think the funeral scene in *Steel Magnolias,* think rape, think stubbed toes and root canals and kittens and childbirth and kidney stones — that's when you're closest to understanding.

She used to sign emails this way when she was being bitchy and pseudopolite: "Be well." As in: *Fuck you.* As in: *I will have nothing to do with your being, so good luck with it; you're on your own.* That was the meanest thing she could think to say to someone: Be well. You're on your own. You're all alone! I will have nothing to do with you! I am not touching you! It was a last straw, the moment when she removed herself from dealing with some asshole or other. But it turned out there was really nothing mean about it; she understood now. Everybody *was* alone, and they would, every last one of them, all, ultimately, be well. Every one of them, though certainly they're inept and selfish and sad, like her. But they didn't know any better. And truly, because she could hardly remember anything at all now anyhow, she wished them all well. *Be well,* she thought in a way that was not really thinking at all. Thinking having nothing whatever to do with thinking. *Be well!* she nonthought. *Be well.*

Want the secret? Here it is: Dahlia was the very last to die. First went her dreams, followed in quick succession by her hopes. Idealization and longing went next, and then nostalgia for a made-up time when everything had been lovely and right. Only then did she herself go. And by that time: whatever. Or, in Dahlia parlance — Hey! Back off! It's her funeral! — *fuck it.*

Bruce was there with her, holding her hand. She was drugged to the gills (mandated drugs now, though they served the same purpose as recreational drugs: to ease her out of brutal consciousness, buffering an unmerciful reality, unlocking some copacetic, alternate perspective). Bruce spoke softly to her. What was he saying? Yet more of what Charlie Brown and the gang might hear: *wah wah wah wah wah.*

"La La," he said, holding her hand, his

whispers and sobs like branches held out to her to save her from drowning, reaching for her. La. "I love you, La."

Oh fuck. Fuck. *Fuck!* (Why all the profanity? Because she's *dying,* you dipshit prude. The most carnal knowledge, here it was.)

And hey: Would there be a light? Would there be a warm white light? Please, fuck, no, let there not be anything so expected as that: what would be the point, after all this noise, of something everyone could predict? Would it be torture not to tell anyone what she saw, what she felt, what it was? If it was warm and good? Or if it wasn't? What if it was terrible? Worst of all, if it was nothing? *Nothing!?* This awareness, this voice, these memories, these banal and typical and boring and singular memories, the being she herself understood completely and — honestly, really, at base — loved anyway: where would it all go? All these memories — things she couldn't get over, and didn't, and wouldn't, now — did an unconcerned circle dance, an Israeli folk dance, the slow, sweet kind. Gray, shifty, vague, ultimately consisting of nothing more than love and grief, and not one solid enough to grasp, cling to, hold fast.

She was carefully placing stickers on a homemade calendar to mark off the days until her mother returned from a mysterious trip, laughing gamely along with her own humiliation after Danny casually slapped her face for butchering the punch line of a middle-school joke. There was no one else who knew what these things felt like, these emotional fingerprints, no one but Dahlia: Paging through her life now like it was a porn rag she'd found much too young, seeing it all there, the basest thing there was, something *the matter* with this girl. But there was relief, too, in knowing it, in seeing it, in not looking away. It was base, it was bad, it was not nice. But there it was; and this was it. Post-orgasmic calm, wet glasses on a bar, the shake, shake, shake of a cocktail-in-progress, the screech of a subway train, coming to a stop. A toothbrush dragging Wintermint across her teeth. Danny snuggled with her, telling her a story, their cheeks flushed from a bath, a pacifier in her mouth, falling asleep. Margalit giving her a teeny-tiny kiss on the tip of her toddler nose. They all rushed by; not a one that didn't slip right through her grasp as she grasped and grasped at one after another after another. How would she — *her:* Dahlia! — survive? She needed time to figure it all out; time to make sense of the stuff that had happened. And worse, the stuff that hadn't happened. Especially that stuff. Because wait! There was so much more. Kibbutz Dalia, the sun on her neck, an avocado green and hard in her hand, rolling a joint, the blinking light on Bruce's prehistoric video camera, Clark's laconic smile, Mara with a Big Gulp nestled between her thighs in the passenger seat, wind in her hair, a Tuesday afternoon on the Brooklyn Bridge, smoking a cigarette and smiling into the air. She needed something good, something pure and whole to go out on, to hold on to, to take with her. Wasn't that the benefit of dying unsurprised? A minute to accept it, acknowledge it, greet it on her own terms? Perhaps not.

It was exceedingly simple: just a matter of release. Like the one inspired moment, years before, when Dahlia had given away her favorite book. Her *then* favorite book; it doesn't matter which. Some girl on her freshman hall had asked how it was, and Dahlia had responded, with enthusiasm, that it was fantastic. There had been a pause, and in that tiny moment, right before the girl could say, "Oh, cool, okay, I'll check it out sometime," Dahlia had understood that she was done with the book, had read it and enjoyed it and was done with it, that its place on her shelf was purely celebratory and vain, and that it would, sooner or later, be lost to her anyway, one way or another. "Here," she'd said to the girl, holding out the book with attempted nonchalance. "Take it." Would the girl actually read it? Or appreciate it, for that matter? Probably neither, but who cared? Dahlia had held in her hand something important to her, something meaningful, and, just like that, wham, had let it go. She had regretted it immediately, but then it was too late: the book was gone.

"La La," an echo. "La." Oh. So this was it, then. Okay. Where was her mother — or *a* mother, any mother, *someone else's* mother — to sing her to bed? She felt a panic rise and subside, like the nodding of resisted sleep. She wasn't ready. There was hesitation, like at the end of a phone call in which important things had been left unsaid. She wasn't ready. It occurred to her that lots and lots of people had died before this, though: like, everyone. Still, the panic rose and subsided, rose again before subsiding again, a kind of pull, steadily, firmly towing her out, sort of a song in itself. Confident, unhurried. Two steps forward, pause, one step back, and no looking down at her feet, now. It rose again, then subsided, then

rose again, then paused; she wasn't ready.
She wasn't ready. She wasn't ready.

ACKNOWLEDGMENTS

Elaine Albert, Carl Albert, Binnie Kirshenbaum, Jonny Segura, Maris Kreizman, Wylie O'Sullivan, Simon Lipskar, Martha Levin, Dominick Anfuso, Jill Siegel, Edith Lewis, Barak Marshall, Elanit Weisbaum, Robin Kirman, Nellie Hermann, Abigail Judge, Zac Kushner, Heather Magidsohn, Jen Mazer, Lauren Grodstein, David Gates, Jayne Anne Phillips, Joel Farkas, Stuart Ende, Gavi Roisman, Klatzker/Miller, Dana Frankfort, Paige Olson, Vermont Studio Center, Brooklyn Writers Space, Tahl Raz and Co., the Schwarzschilds, Grandma Helen, Papa Irwin, Susan Schaefer Albert, Bill Schaefer, and particularly, primarily, especially the sublime Ed Schwarzschild, whom I love, love, love —

— *Thank you.*

ABOUT THE AUTHOR

Elisa Albert is the author of the short story collection *How This Night Is Different,* which was named one of the best books of 2006 by *Kirkus Reviews.* She grew up in Los Angeles and received her MFA in fiction from Columbia University. Her writing has appeared in *Nextbook, Washington Square, Pindeldyboz,* and the anthologies *Body Outlaws* (Seal Press, 2004), *The Modern Jewish Girl's Guide to Guilt* (Dutton, 2005), and *How to Spell Chanukah* (Algonquin, 2007).

Albert is an adjunct assistant professor of creative writing at Columbia and editor-at-large of jewcy.com. She divides her time between Brooklyn and upstate New York.

The employees of Thorndike Press hope you have enjoyed this Large Print book. All our Thorndike and Wheeler Large Print titles are designed for easy reading, and all our books are made to last. Other Thorndike Press Large Print books are available at your library, through selected bookstores, or directly from us.

For information about titles, please call:
(800) 223-1244

or visit our Web site at:
http://gale.cengage.com/thorndike

To share your comments, please write:
Publisher
Thorndike Press
295 Kennedy Memorial Drive
Waterville, ME 04901